**PRAISE FOR THE NOVELS
OF *NEW YORK TIMES* BESTSELLING AUTHOR
JULIET BLACKWELL**

**THE HAUNTED HOME
RENOVATION MYSTERIES**

Home for the Haunting

"Just when I think Juliet Blackwell can't get any better, she ratchets it up a notch . . . an intense, riveting story."
—Lesa's Book Critiques

"Juliet Blackwell continues to craft enjoyable and fun novels with a woo-woo aspect that is surprisingly minimal."
—Kings River Life Magazine

"Fun . . . this story, with the usual characters as well as some new faces, is fascinating and keeps readers thinking that there is more than meets the eye."
—RT Book Reviews

Murder on the House

"A winning combination of cozy mystery, architectural history, and DIY with a ghost story thrown in . . . This well-written mystery has many different layers, offering something for everyone to enjoy."
—The Mystery Reader

"Juliet Blackwell successfully blends house renovation and gh⸻⸻⸻⸻⸻⸻mal mystery."
⸻Book Critiques

continued . . .

Dead Bolt

"Juliet Blackwell's writing is like that of a master painter, placing a perfect splash of detail, drama, color, and whimsy in all the right places!"
— Victoria Laurie, *New York Times* bestselling author of the Psychic Eye and Ghost Hunter Mysteries

"Cleverly plotted with a terrific sense of the history of the greater Bay Area, Blackwell's series has plenty of ghosts and supernatural happenings to keep readers entertained and off-balance." — *Library Journal*

"Smooth, seductive. . . . Fans will want to see a lot more of the endearing Mel." — *Publishers Weekly*

If Walls Could Talk

"A riveting tale with a twisting plot, likable characters, and an ending that will make you shudder [at] how easily something small can get totally out of hand. [It] leaves you wondering what you just saw out of the corner of your eye . . . a good, solid read."
— The Romance Readers Connection

"Melanie Turner may well be one of the most exciting, smart, and funny heroines currently in any book series. . . . There's enough excitement to keep you reading until late in the night." — Fresh Fiction

THE WITCHCRAFT MYSTERIES

A Vision in Velvet

"Another gripping and delightful story, sheer entertainment with all the ingredients: murder, danger, high stakes, love." — Mysteries and My Musings

"Blackwell blends vintage clothing, humor, an interesting corner of San Francisco life, a touch of romance, some powerful magic, and a history of witchcraft and women. *A Vision in Velvet* is just the latest captivating story in a bewitching series."   —Lesa's Book Critiques

Hexes and Hemlines

"*Hexes and Hemlines* carries you along with an unconventional cast where nothing is out-of-bounds. Extraordinarily entertaining."   —*Suspense Magazine*

"This is a fun and totally engrossing series that hooks you instantly and makes you want more. . . . I love the mix of vintage clothes, magic, and a lingering possibility of romance combined with mystery."   —Fang-tastic Books

A Cast-Off Coven

"If you like your mysteries with a side of spell-casting and demon-vanquishing, you'll enjoy the second title in Blackwell's Witchcraft Mysteries."   —*Romantic Times*

"This awesome paranormal mystery stars a terrific heroine."   —Genre Go Round Reviews

Secondhand Spirits

"Juliet Blackwell provides a terrific urban fantasy with the opening of the Witchcraft Mystery series."   —Genre Go Round Reviews

"It's a fun story, with romance possibilities with a couple hunky men, terrific vintage clothing, and the enchanting Oscar. But there is so much more to this book. It has serious depth."   —*The Herald News* (MA)

KEEPER OF THE CASTLE

CASTLE

A Haunted Home Renovation Mystery

Juliet Blackwell

AN OBSIDIAN MYSTERY

OBSIDIAN
Published by the Penguin Group
Penguin Group (USA) LLC, 375 Hudson Street,
New York, New York 10014

USA | Canada | UK | Ireland | Australia | New Zealand | India | South Africa | China
penguin.com
A Penguin Random House Company

First published by Obsidian, an imprint of New American Library,
a division of Penguin Group (USA) LLC

First Printing, December 2014

Copyright © Julie Goodson-Lawes, 2014

OBSIDIAN and logo are trademarks of Penguin Group (USA) LLC.

ISBN 978-0-451-46580-1

Printed in the United States of America
10 9 8 7 6 5 4 3 2 1

To Anna Cabrera,
Hermana del corazón
You inspire, just by being you.

Acknowledgments

Many thanks to my wonderful editor, Kerry Donovan—and a warm *welcome to earth* to little Maeve! Thank you to Jim McCarthy, agent extraordinaire. And to the whole Penguin crew who work so hard to make my books a reality—thank you for everything.

Special thanks to Mary Grae for her fascination with chandeliers made of bones, which inspired part of this story line. And to John Sperling, who—whether he knows it or not—always seems to influence my depiction of incredibly wealthy men.

To my writer posse: Sophie Littlefield, Rachael Herron, Nicole Peeler, Victoria Laurie, Gigi Pandian, Mysti Berry, Adrienne Miller, Cecilia Gray, Lisa Hughey, and LGC Smith. And a special thanks to the wondrous women of Xuni who make my life so much easier: Maddee James and Jen Forbus, you two make me look good! You *rock*. And to Lesa Holstine, may your love of books always be contagious.

My sister Carolyn always provides me with calm, steady writing support just when I'm about ready to blow. Thank you for all the brainstorming, rewriting, and general muse-worthy actions that never fail to help me get my manuscripts to the finish line.

Thanks to my father, Robert, who allows me to follow him around and write down the things he says for Mel's dad, Bill. And to my sister Susan, for her unflagging support and cheerleading. And Mom—I miss you, ever and always.

Finally, thanks are due, as always, to my son, Sergio, for making me happy and proud to be his mom every single day. And *merci* to Eric, for putting up with the crazy of book deadlines and creative crises—I know it's not easy to put up with an author, but you do it with a certain *je ne sais quoi*.

Chapter One

Communicating with the netherworld can be a game changer.

For instance, I never used to believe in bad omens. But ever since I started encountering ghosts on my construction sites, I'd become more open-minded.

And it was clear that the Wakefield project was cursed.

It had been plagued with ill portents from the get-go: Two well-respected general contractors had walked off the job; sign-waving protesters blocked the tall iron gates to the property; there had been a series of suspicious building mishaps; and the big, burly, and typically fearless construction workers—those who remained on the job, anyway—refused to linger at the site after sundown. I wouldn't have been surprised to note a line of crows perched nearby, or a ring around the moon, or some other sign of disaster ahead.

Luckily, this wasn't my jobsite.

"Coffee?" offered Graham.

"I thought you'd never ask."

I had driven to Marin County, north of San Francisco, bright and early today only because a very attractive man had asked for my help. Tall and broad-shouldered, with the cut physique of a man who worked with his muscles, Graham Donovan had a way of making me forget that, when it came to romance, I was a battle-scarred cynic.

Adding to his many charms, the green-building-consultant-to-the-stars also happened to be in possession of a thermos of piping-hot, dark French roast.

Besides . . . I was just plain curious: Why would someone dismantle an ancient Scottish monastery, ship it overseas stone by stone, and try to reconstruct it as a retreat center in California?

Graham poured coffee into a small tin cup and handed it to me. Graceful tendrils of steam rose in the damp early-morning air, the rich aroma mingling with the pungent scents of eucalyptus and dried grasses. The day was just dawning, and we stood alone on the hill. My mutt, named Dog, loped around, sniffing the ground and wagging his shaggy brown tail.

"I'll say this much for your client: He chose an amazing site," I said. "It's almost . . . magical."

A gently sloping meadow surrounded by lush forest opened onto a view of the faraway Pacific Ocean. Behind us was a gorgeous old Victorian manse; below us was the jobsite, where stones lay in piles or stacked to form partially built walls, as though a fourteenth-century Gothic ruin had materialized right here, just north of the Golden Gate Bridge.

"That's the to-be-assembled pile," said Graham, gesturing to a massive mound. Bright blue chalk marks—which I knew corresponded to a coded schema intricate enough to drive a Rubik's Cube expert nuts—stood out from the dirt, lichen, and moss clinging to the rough-hewn stones. Carved pieces were scattered among the rectangular blocks: Some were components of columns and vaults, others crude gargoyles and decorative plaques.

"Okeydokey," I said, sipping my coffee. "Would those be the suspicious ghost-encrusted stones, then?"

"I get the sense you're not taking this seriously," said Graham.

"They look perfectly innocent to me. Frankly, I'd worry more about spiders than ghosts."

"Some tough ghost buster *you* are, scared of a few tiny little spiders."

"First off, I have never claimed to be a *tough* ghost buster. Not even an official ghost buster, really. And I'm not scared of spiders per se. But you know how this sort of thing goes: A couple teensy arachnids hitch a ride to America, and next thing you know, they end up devastating California's citrus groves."

Graham smiled. "I've always admired your sunny outlook."

"I'm a native; I think about such things," I said. "Look what happened with William Randolph Hearst: He imported zebras to roam the grounds of his 'Castle' decades ago, and his rancher neighbors are *still* dealing with them."

"What have they got against zebras?"

"Turns out zebras are rather foul-tempered. Or maybe they're just grumpy about being displaced from their natural habitat. My point is, I'm not sure bazillionaires should be allowed to just import whatever they want, willy-nilly. It's asking for trouble."

"Which brings us back to ghosts. It's gotten so bad the men won't go into the building once the sun goes down."

"Ancient stones like these, in a setting like this. Throw

in a little fog and a moonless night . . . Could be people's imaginations are running away with them."

"Could be. But I think there's more to it. You know I don't say this easily, Mel, but I've seen a few odd goings-on, myself."

"You really think your client imported a ghost along with these stones?"

"Maybe. Is that possible?"

"I'm not sure. I would have thought a ghost would have remained with the land. But, frankly, I probably know more about spiders than the intricacies of ghost immigration. I'll have to look into it. Does your client have a particular affinity with Scotland? 'Ellis Elrich' doesn't sound Scottish."

"I'm not sure," said Graham. "You could ask him tonight. We're invited to his 'sherry hour.'"

"I'm not a big fan of sherry."

"It's just what he calls it. There will be other drinks available."

"Then why call it sherry hour?"

A slow smile spread across Graham's face, and he reached out to pull on a corkscrew curl that had freed itself of my serviceable ponytail.

"I do love your curious mind," he said.

"Curious in the sense that I always look for answers? Or in the sense that I'm strange?"

"Why limit ourselves to only one interpretation?"

I couldn't help but return his smile. After a few years of bitter sniping about men in general, and my romantic prospects in particular, I had been mellowing. Graham was helping me to regain my sense of humor.

"Anyway," I said, getting back on track. "I don't really feel like going to sherry hour. The man's not my client, after all."

"Perhaps we could change that."

"Yeah, about that: The whole project sounds like nothing but trouble to me."

"Mel, look at the big picture: Elrich is willing to spend a lot of money on this project. How often does a job of this scope and complexity come along that will implement cutting-edge green building techniques?"

"Not often," I conceded. And it was true that Turner Construction needed work. The high-end historic-home-renovation business in the San Francisco Bay Area had taken a nosedive in the past few months, and while I had so far managed to keep my workers gainfully employed finishing up some residential projects, the principals of Turner Construction—my dad, our friend and office manager, Stan, and I—had been forced to skip a few paychecks.

We were in dire need of a new client. An *important* client. The deeper the pockets, the better. But still . . . I'd already faced enough ill omens for one lifetime. I had been hoping to find a nice, quiet, non-ghost-laden building somewhere to renovate.

"And you're the only builder I know with ghost experience," Graham continued.

"I wouldn't be so sure. The builders who ran screaming from this jobsite experienced some ghosts. They just didn't want to admit it."

While we were talking, workmen had started trickling onto the jobsite, arriving in beat-up Jeeps, muddy Toyotas, and full-sized Ford pickups, a few with grinning dogs in the passenger's seat. Many were Latino, some of whom, I imagined, spoke little English. The rest were a mix of whites, blacks, and a few Asians. They toted lunch boxes, big thermoses of coffee or tea, and carried hard hats tucked under brawny arms. I admired these men—

like my dad, they showed up every day, worked an honest eight hours, and built our homes and communities.

One man in jeans, boots, and a plaid jacket made a beeline for us.

"Here's Pete now. He's been running the job," Graham said.

Dog let out a welcoming "woof," wagged his tail, and presented himself for a petting.

"Pete, I'd like you to meet Mel Turner, the general director of Turner Construction."

Pete had the ropy muscles common to those who spent their lives on jobsites, but his slightly batty, wide-open eyes and blond hair, worn long and frizzy, lent him a crazy-professor vibe. A knowledgeable foreman was worth his weight in gold and was allowed to push the conventions a little. Construction tended to attract off-beat personalities—like me. It was one of the reasons I liked the business so much: I met a lot of real characters.

On the other hand, construction also attracted a lot of people with criminal records. Perhaps that was no coincidence.

"Heck of a nice thing to meet you, Mel," Pete said. "I've heard a lot about you. You're the ghost gal, right?"

"I'm . . . uh . . . Sure. Yep," I stumbled. "That's what they call me, the 'ghost gal.'"

Graham winced.

"Here's the situation," said Pete with a nod. "A lot of folks in this business, well, I don't gotta tell you that they don't care much for woo-woo talk. And I don't either, to tell the truth. But what can I say? I can't deny something's going on, and it's interfering with getting this building done."

"And what might that be?"

"There's a . . . a something. An apparition, I guess it's

called. At the back of the sacristy. He's got a, uh—What's that really big sword called? Real broad?"

"A broadsword?"

"That's right! He's chased out more than one crew, swingin' that thing. These are good men, Mel. They don't scare easy. Also, the folks up at the house have seen lights on down here at night when there shouldn't be, and sometimes there's music."

"Speaking as a professional . . . ," I said. "That sounds like ghostly behavior to me. It surely does."

Graham gave me a dirty look.

"Anything else?" I asked.

"Well, there is that, uh, red thing."

"There's something red?"

"It's . . . well . . ." Pete's Adam's apple bobbed. "Some of the guys think they've heard a woman in there somewhere. They go in to look around, and . . . they end up staggering out of there, crying."

"Crying?"

"I swear, they come out, sit down right on the ground, and sob like their dog died. I tell you what: That's a little, whaddayacallit, disconcerting."

"How do they describe it?"

"Like I said, it's . . . red."

"What else?" I knew from experience that folks who'd had an encounter of the ghostly kind were often unwilling to relate all the details, for fear of sounding foolish. I had learned to be patient.

Pete shrugged.

"Just to clarify—they haven't seen any fireballs, have they? I mean, we're not talking dragons here, right?"

I didn't have to look to know they were both gaping at me. People come to me begging for help, but when I

ask a few simple clarifying questions, they act like I'm
making it all up.

"Dragons are a stretch, it's true, but you were talking
about a man with a broadsword. According to ancient
lore, that could be a knight out to slay a dragon. Dragons
breathe red fire." I shrugged. "Just a thought."

"Maybe we should get back to the construction issues." Graham turned to address Pete. "Mel was wondering how you're getting around the local codes."

"I'm surprised to see unreinforced masonry in earthquake country," I clarified.

"Ah, but it's not unreinforced," said Pete. "That's one
of the reasons it's taking so long. We're drilling through
each stone to insert rebar. Let me show you."

We walked over to a pile of stones near some heavy
equipment, including a massive drill.

"Clever," I said as I inspected the process. "But it
seems a shame to alter the ancient stones at all."

"I hear you. Ellis—uh, Mr. Elrich—has been adamant
on this point: We're to do the least damage possible, even if
it takes extra time and money. We've got an army of stonecutters on-site—from Mexico and Europe, mostly. There
aren't enough locals with this kind of specialized knowledge of masonry. The master stonemason is from Poland."

I nodded. It was common in historic restoration to
employ master artisans from Latin America or Europe.
Most construction in the United States was of recent origin and utilized new materials and new methods. Proper
historic renovation construction required traditional skills
and techniques.

"And the rebar reinforcement will pass code?"

I noticed Pete and Graham exchange a glance. Finally,
Graham spoke.

"The county inspectors—all except one—have been

cooperative. Wakefield will be a pilot project for the inclusion of green techniques in building. The county commissioners figure if the techniques can be folded into such an ambitious project gracefully, they will be able to convince other builders to follow suit."

"Makes sense," I said. "It would be great to make this sort of thing a priority—good for the local guys for supporting it."

"As for the rest . . . ," Pete said. "Well, I don't ask too many questions. Elrich seems to have a way of getting things done."

Pete's smiling, easygoing facade fell away. I followed his gaze to a red-faced man hurrying toward us, huffing from the effort. Dressed in a three-piece suit, a white shirt, and shiny black shoes, the man was overweight and jowly. He carried a clipboard in one hand and a black computer case in the other, and he did not look happy.

"Who's that?" I whispered.

"Larry McCall," said Graham. "County building inspector."

"Damned thorn in my side, is what he is," grumbled Pete.

"*Mr.* Nolan," shouted McCall. "A word with you, if I may."

"You're not supposed to drop in unannounced, *Mr.* McCall," Pete replied.

"I'll drop in anytime I see fit," McCall retorted, scowling. "Just because Mr. Elrich considers himself above the law doesn't mean I'm willing to go along with it. I'll sign off on the preliminary inspection when I think it appropriate, and not one moment sooner. This project is *not* adequately reinforced, as you know very well."

"As *you* know very well," Pete said, "we've experienced some setbacks. We're addressing them as fast as we can. It just so happens we've brought in a new consultant, someone experienced in this sort of building."

Three sets of male eyes turned to me. Only then did I realize Pete was talking about me.

"I . . . uh, yes. Yes, indeed. I'm here to make sure things are done right and proper. Wouldn't have it any other way. That's me."

There's an informal code among builders that says inspectors are the enemy. We know full well that a good building inspector can improve public health and safety, foresee problems down the line, and even save lives. I, for one, follow building codes with a religious devotion. Still, when it comes to dealing with inspectors while on the job, builders maintain a united front. If we agree something is wrong, we'll fix it just as soon as Mr. Snoopy leaves the jobsite.

"Who might you be, may I ask?" Larry McCall demanded.

"This is Mel Turner, the general director of Turner Construction," Graham said. "She has years of experience with historic renovations in the Bay Area. You've no doubt heard of her."

"Can't say that I have," McCall said sourly.

"Nice to meet you," I said, holding out my hand.

After a moment's hesitation, McCall shook it. His hand was cold and clammy, and he appeared so agitated I feared his blood pressure might be spiking.

I couldn't decide whether to talk about my ghosthunting credentials or to spout some bullpuckey about my (virtually nonexistent) experience with ancient structures. Happily for me, McCall turned his attention back to Pete Nolan.

"I ordered this project shut down," McCall said to Pete. "You might as well send those men home."

"It was my understanding Mr. Elrich had that stop-work order lifted," said Pete.

The tension between the two men flared like a spark held to dry timber, and within seconds they were chest to chest, like a baseball player arguing with the umpire.

"*I'm* the one with the authority here," said McCall. 'Not Ellis Elrich. If you continue building while the project is under review, I will have you arrested for inter-fering with—"

"You will do no such thing! You will get off this prop-erty or I'll—," Pete yelled in reply.

"Everybody simmer down," Graham said, his tone quiet but firm. Stepping between them, he placed a hand on each man's chest and pushed them apart. "We're all professionals here. Surely we can work something out."

"You listen to *me*, McCall," said Pete, jabbing a finger at the inspector. "I need this job. You hear me? I got a mortgage to pay and kids to feed. You screw this up for me, and by God, you'll be sorry."

Dog started barking. I held his collar tight and hushed him.

McCall stared daggers at the foreman, but to his credit appeared to be trying to rein himself in. "I'm going to check out the mortar mix. If you're still leaving out the latex admix, I'm shutting this site down. I've found some remarkable inconsistencies. . . ." He waved his clipboard full of papers. "Let's just say I don't care *how* rich and powerful Ellis Elrich is."

McCall nodded to Graham and me and, after straight-ening his tie, stalked down the hill toward the arched mouth of the monastery. After a moment, Pete followed, flyaway hair streaming behind him.

Dog let out another yelp, and Graham quieted him by stroking his silky head.

"You sure those two should be left alone together?" I asked, watching as the men disappeared into the darkness beyond the monastery's entrance. "Maybe you should go with them."

Graham shook his head. "It's not like I'm running things here; I'm just the green consultant. I've done a couple of presentations for the building department so they understand the new techniques we're using, but it's Pete's show. He's got to learn to work with the county inspectors or McCall's right: The site will be shut down until he or Elrich can find a way to accommodate the code."

This was the way construction worked: You dealt with the personalities and laws of the city or county in which the jobsite was located. Some permit offices were notoriously difficult to work with, others more easygoing. It depended on individual temperaments as well as on whether the town or county wanted to promote a bigger tax base, or was concerned for the environment, or if the mayor had significant ties to real estate developers.

"So what now?" I said.

"I'll let Elrich know McCall's back. Maybe he can intervene before those two kill each other. Do me a favor? Do a quick walk-through of the building. Let me know if you see or hear anything that could help us get a handle on whatever's going on, spirits-wise."

I smiled. "You really do think I'm a ghost whisperer, don't you? I hate to disillusion you, but I don't actually know what I'm doing where ghosts are concerned. I mean, they find me sometimes, but I'm really just flying by the seat of my pants."

"What about that ghost-busting class you took?"

"I learned a lot, but . . . it was more focused on proving the existence of ghosts than figuring out how to get rid of them. Or how to keep them from killing you, which is what I wanted to know."

"You always insist ghosts can't hurt us."

"That's true. Probably."

As we spoke, I watched burly men moving in and out of the building. At the moment, the day was bright and sunny, and the suspicious activity was mostly a problem after sunset. And there was no denying that I yearned to take a look around the monastery, run my hands along the stones, soak in the atmosphere of the ancient corridors and chambers through which so many souls had passed over the centuries. "All right. I'll go see if I pick up any vibrations. Maybe see a ghost about a broadsword."

My phone started ringing. Because I'm a contractor, my phone is a lifeline, allowing me to run simultaneous projects from afar. I answered a plumber's question about the modifications we'd made to the century-old piping in a Castro neighborhood bed-and-breakfast and then returned an earlier query from my foreman on a small greenhouse we were finishing up in Piedmont.

The second I hung up, the phone beeped again, and I confirmed an order for lumber for a project in the Mission. While I was answering a text message about blown insulation, Dog started barking and wagging his tail in ecstatic ferocity.

This wasn't a simple yelp. This was the semihysterical bark Dog let out whenever . . .

I looked up to see men running from the cloister, shouting, white-faced with fear. When one slowed to look behind him, two others plowed into him, and all three flailed their arms to keep from falling.

It would have been comical, had they not been clearly terrified.

"What happened?" I called out to the fleeing men. "What is it?"

I had grown up on my father's construction sites and learned at an early age how many things could go dangerously wrong on a job. Slippery surfaces, wobbly ladders, power tools, heavy materials—they could maim or kill in seconds, without warning. "What happened?" I repeated. Now that they were safe in the open air, they shrugged, chagrined. The men glanced at one another, and a couple of them quite literally kicked at the dirt with their boots.

Out of the corner of my eye, I caught a flash of red. It had crossed in front of the arched doorway that led into the cloister. By the time I realized what I had seen, it was gone.

Dog yanked free of my grasp and ran into the building.

I took off after him.

"Hey, lady! Don't . . . Lady, don't go in there!" I heard someone yell as I paused in the doorway.

I ignored the warning. I wanted my dog. Besides, I knew the biggest impediment to dealing with ghosts was getting freaked-out by the very thought of them. My ghost-busting mentor, Olivier Galopin, had taught me ghosts retained their essential human characteristics. They might be sad, or angry, or tormented. Dead, I'll grant you; confused, most certainly. But fundamentally human. And as fallible as ever.

I reached up to rub the gold wedding ring that hung on a chain around my neck. My mother had given it to me; she had inherited it from her own mother. It was the closest thing I had to a talisman, and touching it helped keep me centered and focused, connecting me to two generations of strong women.

Finally, I breathed fresh early-morning air deep into my lungs, released it slowly, then walked through the antechamber and into the chapel.

The chapel's walls were still being built, the space covered by a temporary roof of corrugated metal held up by tall steel beams. Daylight shone through the gap at the top of the walls. Stone pillars supported nothing, arched niches sat empty, and several carved portions of what I imagined were ceiling vaults remained on the ground, in groupings scattered throughout the cavernous space.

Following the sound of Dog's bark, I crossed the chapel to the rear of the sacristy and ducked into a passageway that led to a series of tiny, cramped chambers. The doorways were low, the walls the beefy thickness of the stones. While the main chapel featured the graceful arches of Gothic style, the farther I went into the heart of the reconstruction, the cruder the structure became.

I stepped into a large antechamber.

Out of the corner of my eye, I saw a man.

Larry McCall sat in a stone niche, looking as unpleasant as he had a few minutes ago. But this time he was still. Silent.

"Mr. McCall?"

When I looked straight at him, he was gone.

Uh-oh.

Chapter Two

I searched my peripheral vision.

McCall sat hunched over. Unmoving, silent—just staring.

Standing perfectly still, I listened for sounds of breathing but heard only the harsh rasp of my own accelerated panting.

My breath hung in the air in foggy puffs. The temperature had plummeted.

And then I heard a woman crying. Weeping. Sobbing as though her heart were breaking. An overwhelming sadness washed over me.

I took another deep breath, clasped the ring at my neck, and walked in the direction of the sobs. Passing through a carved vestibule, I emerged into a round room, reminiscent of a turret but only a single story tall. It was made of golden stones that retained bits and pieces of colored plaster and stood out from the dark gray of the rest of the building. To one side was a huge stack of bags of mortar, and on the floor were several mixing troughs, trowels, and knives.

Dog cowered against the far wall.

A body lay on the ground. Three-piece suit, white shirt, shiny black shoes.

I could see from where I stood that Larry McCall's head had been crushed by a sixty-pound bag of mortar, and blood was pooling on the stone floor.

I recoiled in horror, hardly believing that a man I had been speaking to just moments before was now dead. Murdered.

I reached for my phone, dialed 911, but there was no reception.

Something moved. Spooked, I jumped, plastering my back to the wall.

When I looked straight at it, it disappeared. But in my peripheral vision I could see a woman in a long red dress. An old-fashioned gown, festooned with lace and trim. I'm no fashion expert, but I was thinking seventeenth or eighteenth century. She held a long string of beads in her hands.

She was crying. With each sob, I could feel myself sharing in her despair and emptiness. I felt famished, nauseated with a deep, gut-wrenching hunger.

I tried to fight off the sensations, but it was no use. They were overwhelming. I felt wetness on my cheeks, only realizing then that I was crying.

I doubled over, then sank to the floor and sobbed.

It seemed an eternity before Graham found me and led me out of the cloister.

The only positive thing I could say about finding Larry McCall's body was that we were in Marin County.

That's not saying much, I know, but at least I didn't have

to contend with the one-raised-eyebrow, I-think-you-must-somehow-be-involved-in-this stare of Homicide Inspector Annette Crawford, of the San Francisco Police Department. Sooner or later, she would no doubt find out I was involved, and I would have some 'splaining to do, but for the moment, I could pretend to be the kind of person who didn't stumble over dead bodies with alarming frequency.

It wasn't hard acting rattled, though, because I wasn't acting. Besides the visual of the body on the floor, I kept remembering the powerful feelings stirred up by the Lady in Red's weeping. Even as Graham led me past Larry McCall's glowering ghost and through the stone chambers, our work boots ringing loudly on the stone and cement floors, I felt a near-debilitating sense of grief and a deep, gnawing hunger. I was famished, sick with hunger and hopelessness.

The sensation finally ebbed when I emerged from the cloister, stepping into the bright sunshine.

I shook my head, as though to dislodge the memory from my brain.

"Just one more time," Detective Bernardino said, misinterpreting my gesture. "Then we can wrap this up and you can go. Heck of a day, huh?"

"You can say that again."

Detective Bernardino was about my age and height; pear-shaped, with an olive complexion, he had dark curly hair, and full, sensuous lips that would have been attractive on a different sort of man. "You say the victim and"—he checked his notebook—"this Pete Nolan person were fighting?"

"They were arguing. Not fighting, exactly."

"What were they arguing about?"

"They were discussing the proper admix for the mortar, but I certainly wouldn't characterize it as a 'fight.'"

"And what about this Graham Donovan person?"

"He's the green consultant on the project."

"He a hippie type?"

"Um, not really, no. He's a green consultant type who—"

"Was he fighting with the victim as well?"

"Nobody was actually fighting. I mean, I don't think McCall was Graham's favorite person. After all, nobody likes building inspectors. But—"

Bernardino's beady eyes bored into me. "Nobody likes buildings inspectors?"

"I didn't mean that, exactly. It's just . . . In fact, Graham used to be an OSHA inspector, himself. So he understands the need for regulations. Besides, he was with me the whole time, so unless you think we worked together to drop a bag of mortar on that poor man's head, I—"

Apparently I had opened up a whole new avenue of investigation because Detective Bernardino fixed me with an interested look. *Shut up, Mel,* I told myself. *Shut up, shut up, shut up. The detective doesn't know you from Adam and has no reason not to think you're an upstanding citizen who just happens of see a lot of ghosts.*

I was starting to miss Annette Crawford.

I began again. "Sorry. I'm not being clear. What I'm trying to say is that Graham—who is an honest, upstanding businessman—was with me the whole time. He had no reason to harm Mr. McCall, no motive, and no opportunity. Neither of us did. That's what I meant to say." I sat back and tried to relax.

Detective Bernardino's gaze rested briefly on my chest. Now I *really* missed Inspector Crawford.

"Okay, so what you're saying is the DB—'scuze me, that's cop talk for dead body—was threatening to shut down this job," Bernardino said. "That about right?"

"It didn't get that far—"

"So the owner of the project would have plenty of motive. Am I right?"

"I . . . um . . ." I wasn't sure what to say. Annette Crawford never asked my opinion about whodunit. "I can't imagine Ellis Elrich would risk everything—and he has a lot—just to rid himself of a pesky building inspector. There are much easier—not to mention less homicidal—ways to take care of something like that."

Now Detective Bernardino gave me the stink-eye. Apparently, I wasn't supposed to have *that* much of an opinion.

The once-peaceful scene was a whirl of activity, with squad cars, unmarked police cars, the medical examiner's wagon, and the CSI van littering the meadow, and dozens of police officers and other officials milling about. Could Pete Nolan really have killed Larry McCall? Last I'd seen him, he was following the inspector into the building, but then I'd spent several minutes chatting with Graham and on my phone. For all I knew, Pete had stormed out of the building even as someone else entered, found McCall, and crushed his head with a sixty-pound bag of mortar. But who? That took strength, and a lot of it. I was reasonably strong, and while I could probably drag a bag that size from point A to point B, maybe even carry it if someone handed it to me, there was no way on earth I'd be able to hoist it up, much less throw it at someone. It took a lot of force to move sixty pounds of dead weight.

"What I meant to say is that if Mr. Elrich had a problem with a building inspector, he has more than enough money to bribe someone. Or at the very least, to pay one of his employees to take care of it."

Sheesh. I couldn't believe what was coming out of my mouth. I was implicating people left and right. I was the opposite of the kind of person you wanted in your fox-hole when hell started raining down.

"So you think Ellis Elrich had motive and opportunity."

"I actually don't think anything, really. That must be obvious by now."

"You seem awful nervous."

"I'm not used to finding . . . to, uh, being around . . . I mean . . ." Could I be any more suspicious? I took a deep breath and let it out slowly. *As far as this paunchy fellow is concerned,* I told myself, *you are an innocent bystander. Start acting like one.* "I'm sorry. It was a very unsettling experience."

"I can imagine," the detective said, seeming more sympathetic.

"Let me start again. I'm a contractor. I'm not at my best around murder."

"You think it's murder?"

Well, yes, Detective, I thought. *I assume the man did not drop a bagful of mortar on his own head in a rather inventive suicide.*

But I was finally getting smart. I kept my mouth shut and shrugged.

"So. A lady contractor." Bernardino looked me up and down again. I was beginning to think he wasn't attracted to me as much as he couldn't wrap his head around the idea of a "lady" contractor.

"Actually, we just refer to ourselves as contractors. The 'lady' part seems kind of unnecessary. Superfluous, even."

He nodded, as though he'd finally figured me out. "Gotcha. You're a libber, then."

"Sure, that's me, a lady libber."

"Huh." There was a hint of a smile on the detective's

ruddy face, but it wasn't particularly friendly. His eyes ran over me one more time, and I lost my patience.

"Do you have any other questions that might help you figure out what happened to poor Larry McCall? Because if not, I'd like to go."

"Well. *Somebody's* got her knickers in a twist, doesn't she?"

"My knickers are none of your—"

Bernardino's eyes flickered over my shoulder, and he seemed to nod to someone behind me. "Okay, I guess that'll do for now. Just one more question: Why didn't you call nine-one-one right away when you found the body?"

"I tried, but my phone didn't work. The guys say it's the thickness of the stones, or something, but cell phones don't work inside the monastery."

"Huh. This your current address and phone number?"

I nodded.

"All right. You can go, *Ms.* Turner," he said grandly.

I headed over to where Graham had been speaking with some of the construction crew. He looked grim.

"You okay?"

I nodded.

"Did you tell him about the fight between Nolan and McCall?"

"I may have mentioned it."

I could see a muscle work in Graham's jaw as he scanned the hectic scene. It was a tableau I had encountered too often in the last couple of years. It always amazed me how many people were involved in the processing of a crime scene. Especially since I suspected Marin County didn't see a lot of such crimes. Ellis Elrich's celebrity status no doubt also guaranteed the full-court press.

"I think I managed to implicate just about everyone in McCall's death, up to and including myself," I continued. "Given how often I've been through this lately, you'd think I'd be better at dealing with the police. The detective was kind of an ass. As much as Annette Crawford scares me, I'm starting to pine for her."

Graham gave a humorless chuckle.

"Are you worried about Nolan?"

He nodded. "They were asking a lot of questions about him, and given how many witnesses overheard his argument with McCall . . . I don't know. It doesn't look good."

"Nolan does seem to have a temper."

"Yes, he does." Graham inclined his head.

"Still . . . do you really think he could have done it? Practically right in front of everyone? I mean, that would be pretty stupid, wouldn't it?"

"Anger can make people do some pretty stupid things. But I don't know. . . . I've known Pete for years—your dad knows him, too. I've never seen him become violent. Not unless . . ."

"Unless what?"

"Unless he's been drinking."

"Surely he wasn't drunk this early in the morning?" Pete Nolan had seemed sober enough to me, but I hardly knew the man and hadn't been close enough to him to detect the odor of alcohol.

"No, not that I could tell. He got sober a couple of years ago, and as far as I know, he's been on the wagon since. But he's got a couple of priors, bar fights from back when he was still drinking. I hope they don't dig those up and draw some conclusions."

"I hate to say it, but Detective Bernardino wouldn't be much of a cop if he didn't."

Graham's eyes were shadowed with worry. I understood what he was feeling—the first time I'd seen a ghost was when my friend Matt stood accused of murder. Matt and I hadn't been particularly close then, but I remembered the urge to prove his innocence and the frustration of not knowing how. The justice system can be relentless, and there's nothing quite like having someone look at you as if you're a killer to throw you off your game.

"It could have been a freak accident," I suggested. "Maybe Pete was threatening him with the bag of mortar—you know, just to scare him—and it slipped out of his hands. . . ."

"And landed on McCall's head?" Graham shook his head. "*Dammit*, I should never have let them go in there alone."

"You couldn't possibly have foreseen something like this. And you can't police everybody on a jobsite."

"Still, I wish I'd followed them." Graham blew out a breath and ran a hand through his hair. "I hate to think Pete did this. But it happened so fast, and it's true he's always been a hothead. Anyway, I expect we'll know more after the police review the security tapes."

"What security tapes?"

"Elrich had the site wired for security."

"He bugged a monastery?"

"And his home," Graham said with a shrug. "He has an extensive surveillance system. That's not unusual these days for folks with lots of money. Factor in Elrich's personality, and well, it's safe to say there's not much going on around here that Elrich doesn't know about."

I made a mental note not to do anything on the jobsite that I didn't want Elrich to watch and possibly share with others—I could only imagine some lame construction folly going viral—then followed Graham's gaze to where the man in question was speaking to Detective Bernardino. The police officer appeared to be smiling and nodding obsequiously.

Ellis Elrich was okay-looking, though a bit bland for my taste: Of average height and build, he had light brown hair cut short and was clean shaven. A recent photo on the cover of *Forbes* magazine had indicated he had brown eyes, thin lips, small ears, and a mild expression. Altogether ordinary, though clearly there was a lot going on beneath the surface. One doesn't build a motivational-speaking empire and become a self-made billionaire without having at least a few unusual qualities—or being unusually ruthless.

"What's he like, for real?" I asked.

"Elrich?" Graham shrugged. "Pretty much what you'd expect: charming and very much in control. But if you're asking me whether he had a pain-in-the-ass building inspector killed to get him out of the way, I would find that hard to believe. There are always ways to get around an uncooperative inspector. And even if McCall did somehow pose an insurmountable threat, I imagine Elrich's methods of dealing with it would be more subtle than murder right here on the worksite, which would be guaranteed to trigger a police investigation."

We stood in silence for a few moments. It was hard to know what was appropriate after a loss of life, even that of an unpleasant stranger. Not for the first time, I wondered how first responders coped with the awful situations they faced on a daily basis. Go home and hug their kids? Find a favorite bar and hoist a few? Catch a matinee and tamp down the emotions with an extra-large tub of buttery popcorn?

"So what are you up to now?" I asked.

"I should probably check in with Elrich, see if there's anything I can do. Why don't you head on back to the city? I'm sure you've got plenty of work waiting for you. Should I assume this puts the kibosh on your taking over this project?"

"The money's tempting and the building is beautiful, but I think I'll pass."

"Had enough encounters with dead bodies, have you?"

I nodded. Not to mention beautifully dressed specters who made me break down and cry. I had enough on my plate as it was. And I was not a pretty crier.

Chapter Three

The next day I found myself fighting the urge to throttle a stubborn building inspector who was holding up a job at a bed-and-breakfast in the Castro because he wanted yet another engineering review of an already overengineered garage addition.

I tried not to think about what had happened yesterday, but the scenario put me in mind of poor Larry McCall.

The truth was, there weren't a lot of us general contractors who hadn't wanted to kill an inspector from time to time. Of course, that was where it ended, and a responsible contractor knew it was necessary to find a professional way to work out differences.

It had been unsettling, to say the least, to find a dead body. Especially of someone I had been speaking to only moments before. Such a tragic and violent loss of life. But if I were to be brutally honest, the overwhelming sadness I had felt in that moment, the profound grief,

also had something to do with the weeping figure in the
red dress.

Who was she?

Her gown was far too antiquated to have been from
the United States. She must have been attached to the
imported stones somehow; it was the only explanation. I
knew from experience that ghosts hated renovation
projects: The disturbance to their surroundings could be
profoundly upsetting for them. So what would happen if
a ghost's home was dismantled, stone by stone, shipped
overseas, and rebuilt in a new land?

Talk about confusing. And that wasn't all; Pete Nolan
had said workers had been chased out of the cloisters by
a man with a broadsword. So maybe there was even
more paranormal fun to be had at the Wakefield Retreat
Center.

Graham had called last night to tell me that, indeed,
the police were holding Pete Nolan as a "person of interest" in McCall's slaying because the evidence pointed to
his guilt. Graham also mentioned he was going to take
advantage of the work stoppage to follow up on some
new wind-energy technology being developed by a small
firm in LA, so he was flying down for a couple of days
and would return on Thursday.

After dealing with the stubborn building inspector at
the bed-and-breakfast conversion, the next item on my
to-do list was to check in with the B and B's ghosts—the
family that had built the house a century ago and who
had wanted to remain. Fortunately, the B and B's owners
were happy to have them; they delighted in showing me
a recent article about their haunted bed-and-breakfast
that had come out in *Haunted Home Quarterly*. My name
was mentioned prominently as the builder—and ghost
buster—on the job.

I made a mental note to warn my office manager, Stan, who had been fielding an increasing number of query calls more interested in ghosts than in renovation. It was a worrying trend.

Once I settled things in the Castro, I met with Raul at an Art Nouveau house in Bernal Heights. Raul was by far my best foreman, and though I dreaded the day he would move on, I knew it was only a matter of time before he started up his own company. There had been spirits in this house once, too, but after an intervention, they appeared to have departed.

Raul and I went over the double-paned glass we were installing to increase the old home's energy efficiency. This was tricky. If the existing sashes weren't thick enough, or the window structure itself wasn't sturdy, we could end up replacing the original glass as well as remilling the sashes and sills; by the time we were done, there might be nothing left of the original. I understood the energy-saving reasons behind it, but it hurt my heart to dump the wavy old window glass. Historic renovation demanded creativity and compromise.

Even while hashing out these details with Raul, my mind kept wandering back to Pete Nolan. True, I didn't know him, and he had been upset with Larry McCall, but it was hard to believe that a quick fit of temper could result in such a tragedy. Still, as SFPD inspector Annette Crawford so often reminded me, most murders were the result of exactly this sort of scenario: some stupid disagreement that got out of hand.

Way out of hand.

Thinking about my last couple of big jobs, I realized that both the Castro B and B and the Bernal Heights house had contained entire spirit families that were trying to tell me something about crimes in the present. At

least in the case of the Wakefield project, I didn't think
the spectral Lady in Red was connected to the building
inspector's death. There was too much separation of
time and space; if the spirit had come here with those
ancient stones, what possible connection could she have
to Larry McCall?

Once I wrapped up my day, I headed to Pacific
Heights to pick up my ex-stepson, Caleb, whom I had
talked into joining me, my dad, and our friend Stan at
Garfield Lumber's annual barbecue.

"I don't know why I have to go to this lame barbecue," grumbled the seventeen-year-old. His chestnut hair
fell so low over his forehead it almost covered his near-
black eyes, which was probably the idea. I tamped down
the urge to brush his hair back so I could see his expression.

"It's . . . fun," I said. Which was sort of a lie. "Anyway,
it's tradition."

"Not the same thing."

The truth was, Garfield Lumber's operation was old-
school. The nails were kept in the same bins they had
been in since 1929; the long wooden counter was scarred
and gouged; the slower-selling items on the shelves ac-
quired a thick layer of dust. And if you stepped into Garfield without knowing what you were doing, the staff
could be downright rude. There was no Helpful Hardware Man here. "Don't Waste My Time" was Garfield
Lumber's unofficial motto. If you valued your life and all
your body parts, you didn't mention a certain huge store
that catered to the DIY crowd.

On the other hand, once they got to know you, the
folks at Garfield would go the extra distance to make
sure you had what you needed to get the job done right.
In a rapidly growing and ever-changing region like the

Bay Area, Garfield Lumber was untouched by trends and entirely predictable.

I loved it. Probably because it was a place I always had been—and would always be—"Bill's girl Mel."

"You have to eat," I continued. "Right?"

"Stale hot dogs? Oh, yum," Caleb said in a snarky tone that reminded me a little too much of myself.

There was no denying the barbecue was no great shakes; at Garfield Lumber, even their hot dogs tasted like they'd been around a while. But no one seemed to mind. It was a rare chance to mill around with folks who were normally in a rush, to chill out and knock back a beer or two while swapping jokes, tales of construction mishaps, and the occasional bits of delicious gossip.

"Besides," I said, "it's important to Dad. He wants to show you off, introduce you to his friends."

That got him. Caleb was sullen as all get-out lately, but my dad's opinion mattered to him.

It had taken a while, but my dad had finally welcomed Caleb into the Turner clan. I had married Caleb's father, Daniel, when Caleb was five and had been his proud stepmother for eight years. I adored him, and the hardest thing about leaving Daniel had been accepting that I would no longer have any legal ties to Caleb, who felt like my own son. My heartbreak was lessened when I realized that Caleb was as loath to give me up as I was to let him go. Caleb's mother and I had always gotten along well, and she was happy to allow Caleb to spend time with me when she had to travel for business, especially because Daniel's new wife was not enthralled with the idea of being a stepmother. Now that Caleb was seventeen—a difficult age—I was in the peculiar position of being able to speak to him not as a parent but as a trusted adult one step removed.

We headed over the Bay Bridge, which connected San Francisco to Oakland and the East Bay. The bridge consisted of two spans that met at Yerba Buena Island, and the eastern section was brand-new, the old one having failed in the last serious earthquake to hit the area. Its single tower soared skyward in a dramatic sweep.

I enjoyed the novelty but held my tongue. The last thing Caleb wanted to talk about was architecture.

"So we'll pick up Dad and Stan at the house and then head on over to the barbecue. I'll take you back after, or your dad says you can spend the night if you want."

"Whatever."

But his interest was sparked when we turned the corner onto the street where I lived in an old farmhouse with Dad and Stan.

"Who's *that*?" asked Caleb, nodding at a shiny black stretch limousine parked at the curb.

One didn't see a lot of limos in my neighborhood. It wasn't prom season, and unless my dad had become a high-rolling drug dealer while I wasn't looking . . .

As we pulled up, I recognized Ellis Elrich—flanked by two muscle-bound, unsmiling men, who could only be bodyguards—on the sidewalk, talking to my father and Stan. Dog was bouncing around, barking wildly and ineffectually while wagging his tail, as was his wont.

Dammit.

When Dad had asked me last night how the trip to Marin had gone, I'd kept it vague, and soon enough his attention was captured by trying to figure out his new smartphone, with one eye on a baseball game.

It wasn't that I had been keeping Larry McCall's murder a secret, exactly. But I was a little tired of having to explain why someone died whenever I got near a construction project. It was downright eerie, when I stopped and thought about it.

And since I hadn't been planning to sign on to the project anyway, I didn't see the point.

I climbed out of my Scion with caution.

"Here's my girl," said Dad in the kind of booming, cheerful voice he reserved for Very Important Clients. My father wasn't easily impressed, but he did feel that the client was king and took that to its logical extension.

Dad wasn't a large man, but even now he retained the muscles of a life lived on a construction site, though he had a prominent beer belly and thinning gray hair. Today he was wearing his usual outfit of worn blue jeans and a formerly white T-shirt.

Ellis Elrich, for his part, was wearing what I was certain must be a very expensive suit.

"Ah, the famous Mel Turner." Elrich turned his attention to me, and I understood why everyone was so gaga over him. Charisma. The man had it in spades. There was an intensity to his gaze, a keen intelligence that was apparent from the start. Or maybe it was just his aura—now that I was in the ghost business, it was easier for me to imagine that we all emitted energy, some more clearly than others, and that the people around us sensed and reacted to that energy. "May I call you Mel?"

"Of course. But what—"

"And allow me to introduce my driver, Buzz, and this is Andrew, and Omar."

"Hello," I said. Buzz nodded in reply, but Andrew and Omar remained silent and stoic, flanking Elrich, their eyes hidden behind sunglasses.

"And who's this young man?" Elrich asked.

"I'm Caleb."

Elrich put out his hand, and to my surprise, Caleb shook it, standing up straight and nodding in a sort of "hail-fellow-well-met stance.

"Nice to meet you, Caleb," said Elrich. "You look like you play soccer."

"Yeah, and baseball." Caleb nodded. "Too short for basketball."

"Ah, well, soccer's more poetic, anyway. And remember what Satchel Paige said: 'Never let your head hang down. Never give up and sit down and grieve. Find another way.' There's always another way." Elrich gave Caleb a warm smile before turning back to me. "Mel, it is *such* a pleasure. I was so disappointed we weren't able to talk yesterday."

"Well . . . it was understandable. Under the circumstances, it would have been awkward to keep the sherry hour going."

He held my gaze for a long time, then nodded. "In any case, I know this seems sudden, but in fact, I had spoken with Graham previously about whether Turner Construction might take over the Wakefield job, or even work together with Pete Nolan. Now, with what happened yesterday . . ." He trailed off, his expression somber. "Anyway, we're in a real race with time, and I hear you've done joint projects in the past."

"Only one, and it was a highly unusual project."

"I think you'll agree this project is pretty unusual, too," said Elrich. "Not only will Wakefield serve as a retreat center for the Elrich Method, but it is a pilot project for incorporating green techniques in historical renovations. I understand that's a particular interest of yours."

I nodded. Clearly, Graham had been talking. "Why do you call it 'Wakefield'? Is that the original name of the monastery?"

"Yes, it's a rough translation from the original Gaelic. But it's perfect for a retreat center — don't you think? As 'waking up to the world . . .' And speaking of history, Graham mentioned you're an anthropologist, which is ideal for this project. It combines history, culture, and architecture. It's an archaeologist's dream."

"I'm not really that kind of anthropologist."

Elrich smiled. "But you are the best in the business, are you not?"

"Among the best. There are other talented folks out there." But would they do as good a job as my crew? And more to the point, would they be able to cope with spirits on-site?

"I really need your help, Mel. I can't just let this project grind to a halt. Nolan's workers don't deserve to lose their jobs over this. And combined with your own crew, you can employ all those people and accomplish a great reconstruction. Win-win. Not to mention it'll give Graham Donovan the chance to work on the most exciting project of his career, and be a prototype for green construction in the future. I don't have to tell you that this is the kind of building that can make history. Also, and perhaps most importantly, I'll make sure you have the resources you need to do it right."

Stan and Dad hung back, following the conversation with avid interest but not chiming in. I appreciated the way they were letting me make this decision, as head of the company. When I had taken over Turner Construction after my father fell apart at the sudden loss of my mother, it had been for only "a few months." I'd assumed Dad would pull himself together, step back in to run the company he had built, and I would take off for Europe to drown my sorrows or kick up my heels, whichever struck my fancy. But it hadn't worked out that way. After several years of acting as interim head of Turner Construction, I finally had come to accept that my dad was permanently retired.

The company was now mine, for better or worse.

Still, both Dad and Stan had a stake in the health of Turner Construction and were as nervous as I about the lack of work in the pipeline. Here stood a fabulously wealthy client with a project seemingly custom-made for Turner Construction, and I was balking? Since I hadn't filled them in on the details of what happened yesterday, they were bound to be bewildered by my attitude.

"I don't know the first thing about reconstructing an ancient building," I said. "Our company does historical reconstruction, but that's in a San Francisco context—we're talking a hundred years, not six hundred."

"Not a problem," said Elrich with a confident shake of his well-coiffed head. "I have a special consultant on retainer. Florian Libole, have you heard of him?"

"Of course," I said. No one in my line of work would fail to recognize the name. Florian Libole was world famous in the historic reconstruction business, the go-to man for the British aristocracy.

"He's very anxious to meet you."

"To meet *me*?"

"There aren't many firms that specialize in this sort of thing here in California, as you know. If you refuse me, I'm afraid I'll have to import someone from back east, or worse, from Europe. They would take time getting their bearings, not to mention a job of this magnitude should be handled locally as much as possible—don't you think?"

"I don't know. I have several other jobs going, and with the commute to Marin County . . ."

"You're welcome to stay at my place," he said. "It's huge, built to house plenty of folks. I've got several people staying there now, and I've invited Graham as well. As a matter of fact . . ."

Ellis paused, and I noticed he had everyone's full attention, even Dog's. This guy was *good*.

"According to my assistant, the house could use some sprucing up. It's a Victorian on the outside, but inside it's sort of Spanish Revival, Mission style, lots of hand-painted tile—you didn't get a chance see it yesterday, but I think you'll like it. Don't forget your bathing suit; we have a beautiful pool and sauna. And feel free to bring the dog—he'll love running free on the fenced grounds."

Elrich reached down to pet Dog. The canine wagged his tail and leaned his considerable weight against the billionaire's leg, leaving long brown hairs on the fine suit. Buzz looked annoyed on his boss's behalf, but Elrich didn't seem to mind; on the contrary, he seemed determined to make everyone—even the dog—like him, and appeared to be succeeding.

I looked at Stan's face, at my dad, at Caleb. They all seemed to be in favor of Ellis Elrich's proposal. Eccentric clients with more dollars than sense were my specialty. And there was no doubt Turner Construction needed a big job like this.

But only Dog knew what I'd seen yesterday, and he wasn't talking.

"I'll think about it," I said. "I do appreciate the offer, but I need some time to think it through. I hope you didn't come all the way here just to talk to me."

"I had some business in San Francisco anyway, and I rarely take time to explore Oakland. Florian tells me I simply must stop by and see the Chapel of the Chimes while I'm here. He says it's a hidden gem. Built by Julia Morgan, right? Oakland really is a beautiful city."

That was very politic of him. My dad's house was nowhere near the Chapel of the Chimes; instead, we live in the Fruitvale section of Oakland, a neighborhood once chock-full of orchards but now jammed with small bungalows all in a row, with the exception of the big old farmhouse that was our home. Locals called it "working class"; outsiders referred to it as "gritty."

"In case you decide to join us." Elrich signaled to one of the burly men next to him, who reached into his breast pocket and extracted a plain manila envelope. He handed it to Elrich, who offered it to me. "This contains some documents that will fill you in on a few of the details, and most importantly, a check for the deposit."

I peeked at the check and gulped. There were a whole lot of zeroes. It didn't take an accountant to realize it was enough to keep Turner Construction—and all the people we employed—solvent for a good six months. And this was just the "deposit."

"Give it some thought," said Elrich. "And let me know by tomorrow? I'm sorry to rush you like this, but we don't have any time to lose. Even with yesterday's tragedy, it's essential we keep on schedule to the extent possible."

"Do you have the go-ahead from the police to start construction again?"

"That won't be a problem."

"Okay, I'll think about it," I repeated. I wasn't promising anything, but I hadn't seen a check that big since . . . well, since never, actually.

Ellis thanked us, patted Dog, and climbed into the limo with his entourage. We watched the huge car glide down the street. The sight of the luxury vehicle had coaxed several of our neighbors out onto their porches, and a trio of laughing kids chased it for a block before giving up.

"A limo like that's even more exciting than when the

garbage truck fell into the sinkhole right there. Remember that?" observed Stan. He explained to Caleb: "It took three industrial tow trucks to pull the lumbering truck out of the hole, and it forced the city to finally fix the problem."

"Seriously?" said Caleb. His two homes in San Francisco were in fancy neighborhoods; he still found Oakland's less-than-posh approach to urban life to be intriguing.

We waved at the neighbors, and when the limo turned the corner and zoomed out of sight, Dad turned to me.

"I thought you said the site meeting in Marin yesterday didn't result in anything."

"I wasn't planning on taking the job."

"Why the devil not?"

"It's sort of a good-news, bad-news situation," I explained.

"I can't wait to hear this," he said, and I imagined he was mentally rolling his eyes.

"The good news is, someone died at the Wakefield jobsite yesterday. Was killed, actually."

Dad, Stan, and Caleb looked at me like I'd lost my mind. Dog looked at me as though waiting for me to drop some food, but that was his typical stare.

"Someone *died*?" asked Caleb. "Who?"

"No one you know," I said. "A building inspector."

"Well, no one likes building inspectors," Dad observed with a grunt.

"Even so," said Stan, "I would have thought a murder would count as the *bad* news."

"Yes, well, obviously, if you were the one killed. Or his family, or . . . Okay, clearly it's tragic. Horrible. All I'm saying is that in terms of *me*, at least the place is now pre-disastered."

They weren't following my logic. I tried again.

"You know how, lately, I have a tendency to stumble across dead bodies on my jobsites? Well, this jobsite already has a dead body. What are the chances I'll come across another one?"

"That's . . . random," said Caleb.

"We sure could use the work, babe," said Dad with a shake of his head. "But I don't want you on yet another job with yet another murderer running around."

"That's more good news, actually—the killer's in custody. He was the general on the job: Pete Nolan. Graham said you know him?"

"Sure, I know Pete," said Dad. "They say *Pete's* the one who killed this guy?"

"He's a loose cannon, all right," said Stan. "That SOB sucker-punched me once when he didn't like what I said about the Oakland Raiders' chances for the Super Bowl. Remember that?"

"That was when Pete was a drunk," said my dad. "He hasn't had any problems like that for years now."

Stan shrugged, unconvinced.

"Anyway, he's in custody," I continued. "So I guess that's the end of that. That's what I mean about the place being pre-disastered."

"So if a dead guy on-site is the good news," said Caleb. "What's the *bad* news?"

Ghosts, I thought to myself, but did not say aloud. I remembered the sensation I had felt in the presence of the Lady in Red. It gave me a knot in the pit of my stomach, just thinking of it. On the other hand, maybe I needed to help her. Maybe that was my special role: to find buildings full of miserable ghosts and either banish them, or help them cross over, or negotiate a settlement between them and the living.

"The bad news is, it's too far for me to commute. Raul

could step in on the day to day finishing up our current projects, but I'd have to take Elrich up on his offer to stay up there for a while. At least until we get things running smoothly."

The truth was, I could use some time away. I adored my father, and his friend Stan, and this old farmhouse. But Elrich was offering me the chance to have some time to myself as his guest at a beautiful estate complete with pool and a view of the ocean? *Yes, please.*

"Well, you gotta do what you gotta do, babe," said Dad.

I had to admit, he didn't appear exactly broken up over the prospect of my being away for a while. I supposed it was possible *I* had become a bit annoying, what with nagging him to eat organic vegetables and to stop watching so much TV.

Probably we could both use a little time apart.

"But I don't know. . . ." Dad trailed off, his attention seeming as divided as Caleb's usually did. He kept fiddling with his new smartphone. "Maybe if you're gonna go on up and stay at Elrich's house, you should take a gun, just in case. You're a good shot with that Glock."

"Um . . . okay."

He looked up, surprised. "You're getting smart now, are you? Change your mind about gun control?"

Stan, who had a few decided opinions about gun control, gaped at me.

"No, no, it's nothing like that," I said. "I just . . . Just in case, it might not hurt to have a little extra protection."

"You think you'll be in danger?" asked Stan. "Mel, no job is worth putting yourself at risk."

"No. Not really. Not at all. I'm just . . . I thought it might be a good idea. Considering my track record. Besides, Graham will be there, so I'll have plenty of protection."

"Still . . ." Dad trailed off again. This was not like him.

"What are you *doing*?" I demanded, annoyed.

"This 'smart' phone isn't near as smart as a person would hope." Dad only recently, and quite reluctantly, had upgraded from a flip phone. He had been waiting to make sure it wasn't just a fad, he explained. Now that he had bought the newfangled device, he appeared to be enamored with its many features and apps. "I'm trying to look up directions to the barbecue."

"Dad, you've been going to Garfield Lumber for thirty years," I pointed out. I felt a sudden stab of worry. Dad wasn't *that* old, was he? "You need to look up the directions?"

"Don't be ridiculous. I just want to hear the voice tell me how to get there. See if she's right. I like her voice. Sounds like a real nice gal."

Caleb rolled his eyes but smiled and held out his hand. "Here. Give it to me, Bill. I'll show you."

"Okay, everybody ready?" I asked, wanting to get the show on the road. "Shall we take the van?"

Stan was in a wheelchair following a construction accident years ago. It was best to take the specially outfitted van so he didn't have to get out of his chair.

"Sure," Dad said, tossing me the keys. As we were climbing in—he, Caleb, and Dog in back, Stan riding shotgun—he asked: "Hey, when are you and Graham gonna make me a grandfather again?"

Stan hooted with laughter.

Wow. That was out of left field. I was just beginning to inch past my I-hate-all-men phase; no way was I ready to move on to procreation.

"You've got Caleb," I said, trying to ignore the strange butterfly sensation at the base of my throat. "That's all I'm guaranteeing at the moment."

"Well, now, I guess he'll do just fine," Dad said.

Caleb pretended to be absorbed in programming Dad's phone, but when I glanced at him in the rearview mirror, I could tell he was smiling.

"Hey, Bill," Caleb said. "What do you call a ridiculous old man?"

"I give up. What?"

"A fossil fool."

Dad chuckled.

Garfield Lumber's stale hot dogs and cheap beer had never tasted better to me.

Unfortunately, construction workers are big on lame anecdotes; after Dad blabbed about what had happened at Wakefield, I spent the rest of the evening listening to jokes that culminated in dead building inspectors.

Maybe it was just too soon, but I didn't find them at all amusing.

Chapter Four

After a day of soul-searching, I told Stan to cash Elrich's check.

We needed the money. But, as usual, it was more than that. The chance to work on this kind of historical building didn't come around every day. I'd worked with a few eccentric billionaires in my time, but this was the only one who had decided to import an entire monastery. It was extraordinary, and despite its echoing sadness—or could it be because of it?—Wakefield fascinated me.

In any case, I made arrangements for Raul to oversee our existing San Francisco projects, packed my bags—with my bathing suit—and Dog's food, bowl, and leash, put a Pink Martini disk in the CD player, and headed for bucolic Marin County, north of San Francisco.

Unfortunately, I made the mistake of driving up to Elrich's decorative wrought-iron front gate instead of the far more utilitarian construction entrance a quarter mile down the road.

A dozen picketers lined the way, carrying signs and shouting at me to turn back.

As I waited for the gates to open, I had to fight the urge to explain myself to the protesters; normally, I respected picket lines. Most of the signs appeared to be about employment issues with one of Elrich's smaller subsidiary companies. A few apparently didn't like his contributions to particular political causes.

But there was one protester who stuck out: He was wearing a kilt with a thick leather belt, boots with tassels at the top, and a tartan cloth flung over one shoulder. He had the sandy-haired good looks of a poet, with romantic bright blue eyes and a boyish face.

His sign demanded REPATRIATION OF THE WAKEFIELD STONES.

Huh.

"What do you think, Dog?"

Dog's head lolled over toward me. He thumped his tail, and then his head rolled back toward the protesters.

"I'm only asking because one of them appears to be in costume. You don't see *that* every day."

The gates swung open, and I started to edge my car through the crowd. One pretty young woman banged on my hood.

"Hey!" My boxy Scion was a working car and was hardly pristine, but physical contact seemed over the line. "Back off."

"Why are you crossing the picket line?" she demanded.

"I don't work for Elrich Enterprises," I said. "I have nothing to do with his company."

"What are you doing here, then?"

"That's really none of your business."

"She's working on the new construction," said the man in the Scottish costume. "Let her be."

"She is? How do you know?" demanded the young woman.

Their attention diverted, I drove through the gates, which swung shut behind me. A glance in the rearview mirror told me the protesters did not try to follow.

My tires crunched and popped as I proceeded slowly along the long, yellow, crushed-granite drive. After nearly a quarter of a mile, the drive formed a loop around a fountain in front of Elrich's beautiful two-story grand Victorian home.

Painted in various shades of cream with gold gilt trim, the massive Victorian was fronted by an ample porch. The building formed a U shape around a courtyard, at the center of which was a melodious fountain. A round turret was accessed by winding stairs, and a balcony featured a finely crafted wrought-iron railing.

I looked down toward the building site for the soon-to-be Elrich retreat center. The way Wakefield was situated on the hill, it really did seem like Ellis Elrich fancied himself a modern-day reincarnation of the famous but controversial newspaperman William Randolph Hearst.

It was hard not to draw the comparison: Like Elrich, the newspaper magnate lived in a grand home high on a hill overlooking the ocean—though Hearst's Castle down the coast at San Simeon was much larger and grander than Elrich's house. But it was the circumstances of the construction that really brought home the similarities. Hearst was in the habit of buying entire buildings, having them disassembled, and shipping them to the United States to be reassembled for his various interests. It was the sort of outrageous yet inspired thing only the extremely wealthy and rather flamboyant could pull off.

"I was thinking about taking a vacation at a Club

Med," I mumbled to my canine companion. "But I guess this is pretty close."

Dog agreed. He didn't talk or anything, but I could tell by the way his head lolled.

The home was gorgeous and seemed welcoming, but as I parked, I had second thoughts about being here without Graham.

And in fact, he hadn't been pleased when I called to tell him I'd had a change of heart. How ironic that in the end, the one most opposed to my getting involved in the Wakefield project was the one who had tried to entangle me in the first place.

"I don't like it," Graham had said on the phone last night.

"Which part?"

"The part where you're working for Elrich."

"I thought that was your grand plan when you introduced me to him. Now you're changing your mind?"

"That was before a man was killed."

"You don't seriously think Elrich did it?"

"No, but I'm not convinced *Nolan* did it."

"Okay . . . but why should I be worried? I mean, McCall was a building inspector. No one likes building inspectors."

Graham, a former building inspector for California Office of Safety and Health, or OSHA, didn't deign to reply.

"Seriously, though, maybe it was an accident. McCall seemed like the type to poke his nose into everything. Who's to say the bag of mortar didn't slip off that big pile?"

"That seem logical to you?"

Not really. "I'm just saying that since we don't know

what happened to McCall, there's no reason to let it affect my business decisions."

"Listen, Mel, at least wait until I get back to town. We'll move into Elrich's place together."

"There's a meeting tomorrow with Florian Libole, and I don't want to miss it. It's just one night, Graham. Even *I* don't manage to attract problems that quickly. It's like I was telling Dad and Stan: This place has already experienced one murder, so I figure we're safe for a while."

"I'm beginning to worry about you."

"This is why you like me so much, though, right? I keep you guessing."

"No, actually, that's not why. Not even close."

I was too smart to take that bait. I thought about telling Graham that I had borrowed my dad's Glock, but rejected that on the theory that in this case, discretion would be the better part of valor. Somehow I didn't think knowing I was armed—without a license or carry permit— would make Graham feel better.

I left my car in the shade, rolled down the windows halfway, and told Dog to be a good boy. I would come back for him after I checked out the scene.

My suitcase banged as I rolled it up the steps to the porch, the noise mingling with the cheerful splash of the water in the fountain.

I knocked on the large wooden door, checking out the architecture. Given decorative details like the fan light over the front door and the carved crests and angels along the roofline, I estimated the house was built around the turn of the twentieth century. The house's aesthetics were well-done, but there were some visible issues: The wood siding was sagging and warped in spots, and there were cracks along the joints of the window lintels and sills. No big deal, but such issues needed to be addressed before they led to water damage and dry rot. Even with environmental risks like termites and carpenter ants, wood-frame buildings held up well in California's temperate climate, but all aged structures required maintenance and repair from time to time.

"Yes?" The woman who opened the door frowned, looking me over as if I were a trick-or-treater on the day after Halloween. She held a massive key ring in one hand, a large notebook in another.

She was tall, strong-looking, and tanned a rich mocha brown, which was unusual in the SPF-soaked Bay Area. Her auburn hair was cut in an attractive style that brushed the tops of her shoulders with a feminine élan yet still managed to seem businesslike. A small scar under her right eye, and another that split her top lip, somehow highlighted her appearance. Her dress—short, chic, and cocoa brown with bright blue piping—reminded me of a chocolate Easter egg.

But then again, I'm a little food-fixated. Dog and I have that in common.

"Hi. I'm Mel Turner."

"*You* are Mel Turner?" she demanded, unsmiling.

I nodded. "Nice to meet you."

"I'm Alicia Withers, Mr. Elrich's personal assistant. He informed me you would be arriving and asked me to help you settle in."

"Oh, great. Thanks."

"I expected you to be a man."

"I . . . um . . ." I'm never sure how to respond to this sort of thing. I'm clearly not a man—at least, I hope it's clear; otherwise I'd best get me to a beauty parlor—but my nickname and the fact that I'm in the trades tend to lead to these kinds of assumptions. However, upon visual confirmation, I would think people would figure it out without further explanation. "Sorry. I'm . . . not."

"So I see." Clearly perturbed by this turn of events, Alicia looked me over once again.

I glanced down surreptitiously. I endured a good amount of ribbing over my usual wardrobe, which included any number of spangled and fringed outfits not normally seen on construction sites. Or, really, anywhere outside of Mardi Gras or a costume party. But I'd spent so many years unhappily encased in proper, respectable (read: boring) clothes that upon my divorce I had embraced my sartorial freedom. I did have limits, though, and since I was arriving at an extremely wealthy client's home, I hadn't worn one of my offbeat outfits. Today I was wearing a simple patterned skirt, camisole, and cardigan sweater. I even wore sandals; I had been feeling a mite frisky-free—and *feminine*—without my usual steel-toed work boots.

"So." Alicia's eyes narrowed and her mouth pressed tighter. "You're with Graham Donovan?"

"I, uh, we're . . . Well, when you say 'with,' I mean . . ."

"That explains a lot." She let out an exasperated sigh, closed the door, and started off. "This way."

As I entered the tiled foyer and looked around, I experienced a kind of architectural dissonance. Elrich had mentioned that the interior and exterior didn't match, but the significance of this hadn't fully registered until the moment I walked in.

The interior was right out of a Spanish Revival home: white stucco walls, beehive fireplaces, tiled floors. The heavy furniture was dark carved woods upholstered in rich brocades. I love Victorian architecture, and I adore the Spanish Revival style. But together . . . ? It made me think of going to the Gilroy Garlic Festival and trying their famous garlic ice cream. Separately, I'm a big fan of both. Together . . . they make me feel a little queasy.

Amazingly enough, however, Elrich had not hired me to work on this house beyond making a few small repairs. I was here to finish building Wakefield.

I followed Alicia past a lovely sitting room that overlooked a sparkling pool and the meadow leading down to the worksite, and down a spacious corridor. The key ring jingled as she walked.

"Since I thought you were a man and a professional colleague, I assigned you your own room, here."

Alicia paused outside an open door made of heavy dark-stained wood, the hinges pounded iron.

The room was decorated in a classic Spanish style: Heavy, carved dark woods stood in stark contrast to the snowy white stucco walls. In one corner was a raised beehive fireplace, its hearth doubling as a small bench. Colorful painted tiles covered the hood and hearth and made for a brilliant display. The bed was a large four-poster, adorned with a mound of satin pillows in a rainbow of deep hues. Hefty wooden candelabra in graduated heights marched along in front of the windows, topped with tangerine and ruby pillared candles. An antique trunk sat at the foot of the bed.

I walked slowly around the room, taking it in. Dad was a big fan of old Westerns, and this house could have been a set for one of those movies. Except in reality, those old haciendas had probably smelled a lot like beans, livestock, and sweat. Here in Ellis Elrich's house, everything was potpourri, scented candles, and oranges. And as long as I ignored the fact that it was all wrapped up in a classical Victorian exterior, I could appreciate it.

"This is beautiful," I said.

"I decorated it."

"It's gorgeous. You've got a great eye."

Alicia shrugged. My compliment was sincere, but either she didn't believe me, or she didn't care. I was getting the distinct impression that Alicia and I were not destined to be besties.

"Anyway," she continued, "this was the room assigned to you. But if you'd rather share with Graham—"

"*No*, no. Thank you," I said. Whether or not Ellis Elrich was aware of my personal relationship with Graham, I preferred to separate business and pleasure. A jobsite romance had never been on my bucket list.

She fixed me with a stern dorm-mother look. "It would be best if there is no late-night sneaking around. It's very disruptive to the household."

"I assure you, I almost never sneak around late at night. So, Mr. Elrich mentioned that I could bring my dog with me. He's very obedient. . . ." That was a bald-faced lie. Any and all attempts to train Dog had crashed and burned. Still, he slept eighteen hours a day and didn't bother with much of anything but food and squirrels.

"A dog?" Alicia's voice scaled upward.

"Mr. Elrich invited him. Personally."

"Will he need anything?"

I shook my head. "I brought his food, and his bowls, and even a mat to set them on so he doesn't make a mess. He's all set. Okay if I bring him in?"

She gave a nod and handed me a piece of heavy-stock paper with a printed itinerary. "Here's today's household schedule; the new one will be slipped under your door each morning. I would appreciate it if you would attempt to adhere to the hours posted. I have circled the events at which you are expected."

The schedule broke the day down into half-hour increments, with blocks of time marked off for meals, as in a full-service hotel. Ellis Elrich's meetings were highlighted, during which, an asterisk noted, "household guests shall kindly observe silence." Sherry hour was indicated prominently, to be held in the front parlor. My first obligation, circled in red, was a meeting with Ellis Elrich, his chief financial officer, Vernon Dunn, and designer Florian Libole, at ten. I felt as if I had been summoned to the Oval Office.

"Okay, thanks."

She gave me another suspicious glance. "It's very important for Mr. Elrich to have a harmonious living arrangement. Please respect the household hours."

I wasn't sure what it was about me that gave Alicia the impression I would be whooping it up at three in the morning, or sneaking out on sherry hour. The sad truth was that, as a contractor, I usually woke before dawn and put in long, hard hours. I was rarely ambulatory, much less in the mood for drunken revelry, after nine at night.

Clamping down on my irritation, I delved deep, looking for a little compassion. Being Ellis Elrich's personal assistant could not be an easy job. He was incredibly wealthy and probably expected to have his needs anticipated and met at all times, even while surrounding himself with wild cards like me. That was a lot of responsibility without much authority.

No wonder poor Alicia was wound a little tight.

"I will try my darnedest to comply," I said. "I see the schedule indicates that breakfast is served at seven—I'm usually on the jobsite by then, and since we'll need to work twelve-hour shifts to meet Mr. Elrich's requests, it might even be earlier, around six. I don't really eat breakfast, but I do need to have some coffee, if possible."

"Earlier than seven?" Alicia frowned.

"If that's not possible, I'd be happy to brew my own." I'm a coffee addict, and like most addicts, don't want to depend on others for my fix. "I travel with my own French roast, plastic cone, and filters. A little hot water, and I'm good to go."

"You most certainly will *not* brew your own," said Alicia, jotting down a note to herself. No doubt some remark about troublemaking sexpots who demanded coffee at ungodly hours.

"Mr. Elrich doesn't get up early?" This surprised me; most powerful people I knew were early risers.

"He is typically up by five. But he does not drink coffee. He has no need of chemical stimulants."

"Oh. Well, good for him." I wasn't going to ask what might be served at sherry hour. "Well, then, thank you so much for allowing me and Dog to stay in this beautiful room."

"You're Mr. Elrich's guest."

If Alicia had her way, I'd no doubt be pitching a tent at a KOA somewhere.

"Yes, true. Oh, hey, I do have a question: What's the deal with the protesters at the gate?"

I would have thought it impossible, but her lips pressed together even tighter in disapproval.

"Malcontents," she said. "People who are unhappy with one very small aspect of Mr. Elrich's Elrich Enterprises. He has nothing to do with it directly and has ordered the management to negotiate the matter with the employees, but the worst offenders have decided to bring their argument directly to his doorstep, so to speak."

She paused and fixed me with a look that indicated I should react.

"Ah," I said. In truth, I admired the protesters for taking their grievance to the top of the corporate ladder: I imagined they'd get some results if Ellis Elrich himself picked up the phone and directed his managers to make a deal.

"I suggest you come and go through the construction gate from now on. It is located on the lower level, closer to the building site." Alicia ducked into the bathroom and flicked on the lights, her dispassionate eyes surveying the scene as though to be sure the toilet paper had been stocked.

"Thanks. I will. So what's with the costumes? Something about repatriation?"

She turned toward me so fast I took a step back in surprise.

"Costumes? What's this about costumes?"

"Um . . . I noticed one of the protesters wearing what appeared to be a costume: a kilt and a plaid tartan? Unless that's what he wears every day. One person's costume is another's self-expression. Am I right?" I should know. "I mean, this is the Bay Area, after all."

Bright little flags of red painted Alicia's cheeks, and she mumbled under her breath, something about ". . . foreign activists and local press . . ."

"I'm sorry?" I asked for clarification.

"Never mind. Some rabble-rouser from Scotland who is intent on halting the progress of the Wakefield Retreat Center."

From malcontents to rabble-rousers in just a few seconds? On top of a murder committed by a "hothead" the day before yesterday? Maybe Graham was right; maybe getting involved with this project was a bad idea. Maybe I should turn and flee back to Oakland. Surely if I shook enough trees, I could scare up a project or two in San Francisco, enough to keep my guys employed.

But Elrich's words rang in my head: What of Pete No-

Ian's men currently working on the project? Would they all be sent packing? Would Elrich bring in a crew from Europe to get this thing done, and would someone else get to work with Florian Libole, historic renovator extraordinaire?

And . . . what was the story behind that weeping woman?

"You'll notice there are no TVs in the rooms. Mr. Elrich doesn't believe in people sitting by themselves watching the programming dictated by the whims of Hollywood's elite. However, there is a well-stocked library full of worthy books in the east wing and a large-screen television in the rec room for gatherings."

"Thanks. I'm not a big fan of television either." Still, I hoped I didn't sound as morally superior as Alicia here.

"The renowned French chef Jean-Claude Villandry is in charge of the kitchen, which is strictly organic and locally sourced to the fullest extent possible. Do you have any special dietary demands? Gluten-free? Vegan? Religious concerns?"

"I'm pretty much an equal-opportunity eater."

She nodded and made another notation on her clipboard. "If you consult your schedule, you'll see that you have a meeting with Mr. Elrich in fifteen minutes."

I consulted my schedule. Yep, there it was: a meeting with Mr. Elrich in fifteen.

"You might want to"—her eyes raked over me—"freshen up."

So much for good intentions; it was clear I didn't measure up to whatever it was that Alicia wanted to see in a general contractor. Starting from having the gall to have ovaries. My admittedly weak attempts to win her over were clearly not working.

"I'll be there. Where's the, uh"—I consulted the schedule—"Discovery Room?"

"Turn the schedule over."

I flipped it over and saw a map of the house and grounds, including the retreat center building site and a helipad.

"Ellis has a helicopter?"

"Sometimes he needs to travel quickly. It's a long drive to the airport."

"How about that? I've never known anyone with his own helicopter."

"Is there anything else, Ms. Turner?"

"Call me Mel. No, thanks. I'm set."

"Don't be late to the meeting."

"I think I can manage it."

"I'll let you settle in, then." Alicia stalked off down the corridor, leaving me to unpack and "freshen up."

I sat on the side of the bed and bounced a little, wondering whether to get Dog out of the car now or wait until after the meeting. I had parked in the shade, the windows were rolled down, it was a nice cool day, and he was no doubt sleeping. I decided to wait until after the meeting, so I would have time to help him accommodate to his new surroundings before leaving him alone in the room. With my luck, he would pee on a satin pillow or discover a new fascination with chewing and eat the bed, and how would I explain *that* to the already morose Alicia?

Wakefield was only a little more than an hour's drive from Oakland, which meant I hadn't worked up much of a sweat during the early-morning drive, and since my current outfit was the most conventional thing I had to wear, I busied myself by unpacking my suitcase—coveralls, jeans, T-shirts, a couple of inappropriate dresses designed by my friend Stephen, the only son of a Vegas showgirl. I shifted my underthings into a dark wood dresser and stashed my shoes in the ample closet. I hadn't brought much: a pair of flip-flops, running shoes for when I wasn't wearing my work boots, plus the sandals I had on.

I put my toiletries in the bathroom . . . and that was about it.

Despite Alicia's dubious ministrations, I felt a thrill. I hadn't spent a lot of time in nice hotels, and just beyond the French doors the pool sparkled, sending ripples of light onto the ceiling. The en suite bathroom was rimmed in cobalt blue glazed tiles, roomy and attractive. It featured a huge "Italian" shower, which meant there was no shower curtain. European style.

It wasn't the worst place in the world to spend a few weeks.

Unwilling to mar the "done" look of the bedroom, I decided to stash my suitcase under the tall bed. As I pushed it under, I felt it hit something. I knelt down to look and spied not a single dust bunny. *Props to Alicia,* I thought grudgingly. There was, however, a book. I reached as far as I could and was just barely able to grab it with the tips of my fingers.

It was a beat-up paperback novel.

The cover showed a shirtless man, his long golden hair blowing in the wind. A red-haired beauty stood beside him, her hands resting on his impressive biceps, her lovely face looking up at him in adoration. In the background, a ruined castle loomed menacingly against the sunset sky.

Keeper of the Castle had clearly been read many times and, judging by the crinkling around some of the pages, had been dropped in a bathtub at some point. The book's pine was cracked and splayed open to one section: a lovingly described sex scene that, without becoming too graphic, involved heaving bosoms and thrusting manhoods.

Oh, *my.*

I remembered my sister Cookie used to read romance novels like this when she was a teenager. I had teased her about it, and goaded our youngest sister, Daphne, to follow in my snide footsteps. But one day I discovered Daphne had a stash of similar novels hidden under *her* bed.

Now, upon reading that particular scene, I understood the reason.

The book no doubt belonged to the last guest to stay in this room. But what should I do with it? Put it on the bedside table and let Alicia think it belonged to me? Toss it back under the bed and let the maid or whoever found it assume it belonged to me? Stash it among my things? Sneak it into Elrich's august library and add it to his collection of "worthy" works of literature? And ultimately, why did I care what Alicia thought of my reading habits? Whether I read a trashy novel or Camus in the original French, she still wouldn't think much of me.

For the moment I placed it on a small shelf, which, I noticed, held not a single book but instead a classy glass bowl full of shells, a framed decorative tile, and a couple of brightly painted ceramic vases.

I checked the clock: time to meet with Ellis Elrich and his minions.

I consulted the map and located the stairs leading down to the Discovery Room. I pushed through a heavy wooden door off the main foyer and began to descend. Though the door doubled as a fire block, it was well appointed, like everything else in the house, and closed behind me with a muted *snick*. The house had been well insulated; when the thick doors were closed, hardly any sound escaped.

The basement was as attractive as it could be, given that the only source of natural light was narrow slits near the ceiling. They brightened up the space a bit but did nothing to assuage the discomfort of a claustrophobe.

Discreet brass plaques indicated an exercise room, sauna, and Jacuzzi were to the left and the Discovery Room was to the right.

I turned right, wondering what I would discover.

Chapter Five

The Discovery Room was apparently named for the hand-painted frescoes that covered the four stucco walls. Each wall depicted a different theme of discovery: one was of Hernán Cortés encountering the Aztecs, another depicted Neil Armstrong walking on the moon, and I thought a third represented Madame Curie. I never could figure out what the fourth was, as my attention was diverted by the handful of men sitting around a gleaming mahogany conference table. In front of each place was a notepad—engraved with *Elrich Method*—and a pen, a glass of water, and a muffin. A beautiful floral centerpiece added freshness to the virtually windowless room.

"Ah, here she is now. Mel, welcome. I'd like you to meet my chief financial officer, Vernon Dunn," Ellis said as he gestured to a large, constipated-looking man in his sixties. "And I believe you know Florian Libole, at least by reputation."

Libole's pencil-thin mustache and long gray hair re-

minded me of a musketeer, a connection I had the fee
ing he played up given his outfit of loose linen shirt an
leather boots—not work boots, mind you, or motorcyc
boots, but nice leather boots that hadn't see a day of la
bor in their lives.

"It's a pleasure to meet you," I said, shaking the
hands.

"And these are two of the men you will be workin
with on-site, Tony Esparza and Jacek Miekisz. Tony ha
stepped in as foreman, and Jacek is our master stonema
son, direct from Poland."

"How ya doin'?" Tony asked. He looked to be in h
early thirties, a big guy with navy blue tribal tattooir
not only on his hands and neck, but also on his face. Tor
looked ill at ease, which I could understand. His boss ha
just been arrested for murder, and he'd been saddle
with the lead on this project.

Jacek looked dusty, as most stonemasons do, a
though he had come to the meeting directly from h
workshop. He also looked bored, and though he nodde
politely, he said nothing.

The sour Alicia sat in one corner, taking notes. Sh
did not look up.

"I am so thrilled that you've joined our team," co
tinued Elrich in a warm voice. "Now that you're on th
job, I feel confident we will be able to do justice to th
reconstruction of Wakefield, keep all these people en
ployed, and make our deadline."

"Which, uh, deadline is that?" I realized we migh
have skipped a few of the details when I dove headfir
into this project. I hadn't made it all the way through th
thick sheaf of papers in the manila envelope. Once I sa
the size of Elrich's check, I had been blinded by dolla
signs.

"Our grand opening is scheduled in three months."

"Three *months*?" I asked, unable to keep from squeaking. On some projects, just getting the paperwork through the permit office took that long. Constructing a modern building out of stone was one thing; assembling a bunch of medieval stones into a habitable building that would pass inspection in earthquake country? Quite another. Not to mention introducing wiring and plumbing to meet current standards of safety and convenience. A project on this scale would typically take years, not months. "Do you think such a time frame is, um, realistic?"

Vernon Dunn smiled. "Exactly! I do believe that setting the date that early might be difficult. Perhaps we should push it back, take our time. . . ."

Ellis gave Vernon a look that combined patience with annoyance. "Your objections have been noted. There is no need to repeat them."

"It's not an *objection*, per se," said Vernon with an obsequious smile. "No, not at all. This is a marvelous project, simply *marvelous*. Why, Wakefield will be a wonder to which visitors will flock for generations to come. I merely think, well, as they say, art cannot be rushed. Good things come to those who wait, and all that. Why hurry?"

"The drawings have been worked and reworked, and all supplies are on-site or in the warehouse," said Florian Libole. "I have conducted meticulous research on Wakefield. The men are in place, including a master stonemason and his Polish crew, and they're eager to work two shifts: from six in the morning to six at night. Isn't that right, Tony?"

"Uh . . ." Tony looked like he had been called on in algebra class without his homework. "Yup, that's true. Two shifts."

"So, everything is in place," Libole reiterated with a final nod. "Waiting would be folly."

Libole and Dunn glared at each other through the spray of flowers in the centerpiece.

The discussion continued along these lines. I spent a lot of time not saying anything, which my mother had long ago taught me was the best way to deal with tense situations stemming from overinflated egos. It occurred to me to wonder whether my host and boss, Ellis Elrich, would think less of me for my silence, but given that the man had driven all the way—actually, had had his driver bring him all the way—to Oakland to persuade me to take over, I figured my position was secure, at least for the moment. Elrich was trying hard not to show it, but I believed the man really was sweating a little.

I would be, too, if my grand opening was scheduled less than three months out. The stone building still looked like ruins rising on the horizon, nothing like a fully functioning retreat center.

Tony managed a few less-than-articulate statements, whereas Jacek just sat and glowered, playing with his crumpled cigarette packet, giving the distinct impression that all he wanted in this world was to slip outside for a smoke. Though I don't smoke, I would have taken up the habit in a New York minute just to have an excuse to leave the room.

At long last, Elrich said, "That's settled, then," and asked everyone to go "with the exception of Ms. Turner."

I watched the others file out of the room, feeling like a scolded kid told to stay in and talk to the principal. I longed to follow everyone else out to recess.

But I turned back to find an amused expression on Elrich's face.

"Did that make you nervous?"

"Your problems with your employees aren't any of my business," I said.

Now he smiled and inclined his head. "True enough. And as I'm sure you noticed on the way in through the main gates, I've got plenty of problems with my employees."

I couldn't think of anything to say, so I just nodded and looked around the room. My eyes alit on a credenza sporting large framed photos, pictures of a smiling Ellis Elrich handing over huge gifts to charities ranging from the March of Dimes to the Humane Society to the United Nations High Commissioner on Refugees.

Elrich noted my interest.

"It wasn't my idea to display those," he said, sounding rather abashed. "But Vernon and Alicia . . ." He inclined his head slightly. "They convinced me it was good for my image—more importantly, for the image of Elrich Enterprises. And I'm facing a harsh reality, Mel: My corporation employs hundreds of people. What started out as Ellis James Elrich standing onstage, talking about overcoming personal adversity, has somehow morphed into a major employer."

"I know how it is to feel responsible for other people's jobs," I said, surprised to find anything in common with this billionaire.

"I thought you might," he said, intelligent eyes studying me. "That's why you agreed to come work for me, isn't it? I have the sense that you wouldn't have done so if not for the good of your workers."

This was how Elrich had made his money, I thought. Whether or not he was sincere, he sure came off as honest and forthcoming . . . and perceptive.

"Vernon Dunn doesn't share my vision, I'm sorry to say," Elrich continued. "Even Florian is only here because I am paying him to be."

"To be honest, so am I."

He nodded. "Fair enough. But I have the sense that once you sink your teeth into a project, it becomes more about the love of the building than about the paycheck. Am I right?"

True. I did my job to the point of obsession sometimes. "Still, this project is quite different from what I usually work on. . . ."

"Only in the sense that it's not yet a building," said Ellis, sitting forward. His hands were clasped on top of the table, large, surprisingly graceful, unadorned by rings or the heavy watch so common to wealthy men. His skin looked richly tanned against the pure white of his cuffs, his wrists thick. "Once it starts to feel more like a building, I do believe you'll fall in love with the project, just as I have. And just think: Combining history with the forward-thinking green concepts of Graham Donovan — the possibilities are endless."

I nodded.

"The retreat center will house the followers of the Elrich Method most of the year, but I am setting aside six weeks in the summer to provide a summer camp for underprivileged children from Oakland and San Francisco. They're only a short drive away, and yet many of them have never had the opportunity to breathe good country air, to see the ocean, and to understand how a farm works."

"That's . . . very generous. I know there's a lot of need."

He smiled and ducked his head. "So what I need from you is help proving the naysayers wrong. When you have a chance to spend some time with the stones, I think you'll fall in love with them, just as I did when I first came upon them in Scotland. As Helen Keller said, 'The best and most beautiful things in the world cannot be seen or even touched — they must be felt with the heart.'"

I was beginning to understand how Ellis Elrich had gotten where he was. He was a motivational speaker, after all, and I was falling under his spell, feeling quite motivated. On the other hand . . .

"So, about the murder . . ."

He shook his head. "Such a tragedy. Did you know Larry McCall personally?"

"I met him just moments before . . . the, um . . . incident."

"I've arranged for a memorial service to be held in the chapel—such as it is—tomorrow evening."

"Really. I didn't realize you knew him."

"I didn't. Only tangentially. But given the tragedy, I think we could all use a little closure. Saying good-bye allows us to move on."

I nodded, wondering whether Elrich knew about my experiences with ghosts. And if he did, whether that had anything to do with his invitation to come take over this enormous, profitable project. I was trying to think of a way to form the question, when he continued.

"There will be no sherry hour tonight, given the circumstances. I understand Graham's due back from LA tomorrow?"

"Yes, probably by lunchtime."

"Wonderful." He clapped his hands together and gave me a broad smile. "I can feel it, Mel. We're coming together. We're a team now. You think we should get some T-shirts?"

Even as I smiled at his joke, I couldn't help but wonder: Had McCall's death—and Pete Nolan's incarceration— cleared the way for this team?

"Ms. Turner!"

I jumped. After leaving Elrich in his Discovery Room,

I had been so preoccupied with my thoughts that I hadn't noticed Florian Libole lurking at the top of the stairs. In addition to his musketeer outfit, he wore a large leather bag, much like a woman's purse, slung over one shoulder.

"Please call me Mel. May I help you?"

"Quite the opposite, I expect. Mr. Elrich had suggested that I take you on a walk-through of the site, help you to get your bearings. Heaven knows poor Tony isn't capable of running this motley crew, so I fear the future of this project rests upon your shoulders." He squinted at me, mustache twitching, as though assessing whether or not my shoulders were up to the task.

"I'm looking forward to getting started." There were plenty of aspects to this project that made me nervous, but getting my hands dirty, starting the work, was always exhilarating. My mind was already racing with possibilities.

I took time to pull on my work boots, then got Dog out of the car and attached his leash. Libole waited for us, literally tapping his foot, at the entrance to the path that led from the house to the jobsite. The top of the walkway was lined with little solar path lights and landscaped with carefully placed boulders and native plants that hugged the rocks.

"I'm honored to be working with you on this project," I said when we started down the hill. What began as a paved walk turned to gravel and then to hard-packed dirt.

"Thank you. I believe it will be a true legacy, if I do say so myself. Indeed, this locale reminds me a bit of Marshcourt, home of the seventh Earl of Hampshire. Do you know it?"

"I'm afraid not," I said with a shake of my head. "But I'm not really familiar with British aristocra—"

Apparently, I had no need to know anything, as Libole was more than happy to fill me in. He launched into a long and involved description of the myriad ways in which he was connected to British royalty and of the numerous noble manors he'd worked on over the years. I listened politely but felt like telling him that the name-dropping was wasted on me. I don't give a hoot about the royal family—typical colonial that I am—and knew nothing of the British aristocracy, though Libole's renovation résumé was undeniably impressive. Unfortunately, he delivered his self-important monologue with such a pompous air I found it hard to enjoy, even though he was talking about one of my favorite subjects. Did I sound like this when I talked about my projects? I wondered.

". . . but ah, yes, the bones of Gertrude Jekyll's design survived, in the exquisite sunken garden, the long begonia path, the rose and vine-covered pergolas, the herringbone redbrick paths, and the boxwood and yew hedges . . ."

"Gertrude Jekyll?" I interrupted. "Really?"

"You know her?"

"No, I'm sorry. I don't. I just . . . That's quite a name," I said with a smile.

He looked down his nose at me, his mustache aquiver. "She was a very well-respected designer in her day."

"I'm sure she was. And she had a heck of a handle. Bet 'Gertrude Jekyll' wasn't her stripper name, eh?" At Libole's startled expression, I changed the subject. "So tell me, what's Vernon Dunn's objection to this project?"

"The man cares for nothing but money. He has absolutely no poetry within his soul."

"Ah. I—"

"It is a nest of vipers, Ms. Turner. Beware Alicia Withers, as well."

"Okay . . ."

He leaned toward me and dropped his voice. "She's a snoop."

"Oh?"

"I lock my doors. Still, she has the skeleton key. I'm sure you've seen that key ring she carries around. I can hear it clanking after I retire every night. I fear there is no privacy where she is concerned."

As we grew closer to the jobsite, the noise level increased. Between the compressors, the saws, and the banging, we had to raise our voices. The crew was in full swing.

"I'm surprised the police have already released the scene," I said.

"Elrich has friends in high places. The room where the body was found is still off-limits, I'm afraid. But the rest of the building was released yesterday."

Just as Elrich had promised.

Tony greeted us in front of the small trailer that served as the site office. I introduced him to Dog, and he introduced me to his second in command, Miguel, a bear of a man in his forties. I found a shady spot out of the way to tie up Dog, filled his water bowl from the site's big yellow thermos, and followed Tony to the temporary shed where Jacek was overseeing the stonecutting. As before, the master stonemason remained mute, nodding and smoking while his assistant, Cesar, explained the specialized stonecutting equipment.

I was beginning to wonder whether Jacek's apparent surliness was the result of limited English language skills, which did not bode well. I spoke a little construction-site Spanish, but my Polish was pretty rusty.

Jacek, Cesar, and two other assistants were covered in so much gray stone dust that they looked like walking statues, and dozens of cigarette butts littered the ground.

Between the smoking and their daily exposure to dust, I couldn't help but worry about the state of their lungs.

"Shouldn't you be wearing respirators?" I asked.

Jacek shrugged, and Cesar rolled his eyes.

I had also noticed that only about half the men were wearing hard hats, even though they were working on a jobsite featuring masonry.

Regrettably, a lot of construction guys feel their manliness is challenged by commonsense health and safety guidelines. And if the man in charge was cavalier about the subject, the others fell in step. The only way to get these macho types to do the right thing was to lay down the law and then allow them to grouse and grumble about bureaucrats. At least some of them would be secretly pleased that they could care for their health without losing face.

I felt a little awkward—I hadn't been formally presented to these folks as the general in charge yet. But there was no time like the present.

"Tony, call the guys together, will you, please? There are a few things I need to say." Tony obligingly summoned the crew, and I climbed onto a large block of stone.

"Starting tomorrow," I said, my voice rising to carry over the whine of a compressor, "I'll be in charge of this worksite. I'm Mel Turner, of Turner Construction. Please call me Mel. And yes, before you even bring it up, I'll say that I have an odd style of dress. You'll see tomorrow. Feel free to snicker and make jokes behind my back, but I'll be signing your paychecks, so get used to it. Several of my men will be joining you tomorrow, and as you know, we'll be working double shifts in an effort to bring this project in on time. But just so we're clear, Turner Construction follows basic health and safety guidelines, no exceptions. Stonemasons will wear respirators while cutting, and everyone will wear a hard hat at all times. Anybody has a problem with that, feel free to leave. We've got a big job ahead of us, and we don't need to waste time with accidents."

The men shifted on their feet and stared at me with cold, flat eyes. Had I been less experienced with construction crews, I would have thought they hated me. But this was just how it went. They were holding back, evaluating me. I wouldn't be surprised if they tested me a little in the next few days. I was not only the new kid on the block. I was the new *girl* on the block. They'd put me through my paces.

Complicating the situation, these men were working on a site plagued by sabotage, spirits were running them out of the building, and their former boss had just been booked on suspicion of homicide. Was it any wonder they were feeling a bit insecure?

"Any questions?"

"You heard about these . . . ghosts?" asked one slim young man who didn't look much older than Caleb.

There were a few snide exhalations of breath, and his colleagues looked at him askance.

"Just sayin'," he mumbled, looking down at his hands covered in heavy leather work gloves.

"Yes. I have heard about that," I said. "I'll be looking into it."

"Also, someone's been stealing food," said a big fellow.

"Stealing food?"

"It's got to the point where we need someone to watch the lunch boxes. I locked mine in my truck, but this is ridiculous."

Others jumped into the discussion. Ghosts were one thing, lunches another. These guys worked hard, they got hungry, and they were out in the middle of nowhere, with no easy access to cafés or stores. I wondered why Pete Nolan hadn't made arrangements for an on-site canteen, as was common on remote locales. A canteen would not only keep the workers fueled but would contribute to a team mentality, an esprit de corps. If the crew thought they couldn't trust one another not to steal lunches, the whole project would be affected.

"I'll check that out," I said. "We should at least be able to get some fresh coffee and energy drinks down here for you guys. I'll see what I can do."

It pleased me to see a few heads nodding. Heck, throw in a dozen glazed doughnuts and they'd be eating out of my hand. I wasn't averse to bribing my way into the hearts of men. Besides, up at the house we had a twenty-four-hour snack bar supplied by a famous French chef. It didn't seem quite fair.

I handed out my Turner Construction business card, which included my cell phone number, shook a number of hands, and assured everyone that payroll would be met, as usual, on Friday. I would see to it personally.

Finally, I joined Florian Libole, who had been lounging on a stone bench by the entrance to the chapel, watching.

"Are you quite ready to speak about architecture now, Norma Rae?" he asked, mustache aquiver.

"'Norma Rae'? Because I think the guys should have coffee? Or follow basic safety procedures?"

He gave me a scathing look. So much for my plan to win over the distinguished Florian Libole. I was beginning to feel discouraged. Ellis Elrich might like me, but so far his entourage appeared less than impressed. I looked forward to the arrival of my guys on-site tomorrow, not to mention Graham. Murderer on the loose or not, I needed some friends at my back.

"Shall we begin?" Florian asked.

I handed him a hard hat and put on my own.

"After you," I said, and watched him duck into the main entrance to the chapel.

I hesitated for a moment, thinking about my less-than-dignified departure from this building yesterday. The vision of Larry McCall's ghost, then seeing his body on the floor; the weeping; that strange Lady in Red. The sensations of despondency and nauseating hunger.

But as I had assured the men in my life just yesterday: Surely this place was now pre-disastered, and I could go about figuring out what the ghosts were trying to tell me and get this job done. Right?

Besides, workers were scuttling in and out of the building, pushing wheelbarrows and mixing mortar. Men swarmed across scaffolding like honeybees on a hive, soldering and sawing and laying stone.

I paused in the archway and stroked the ring around my neck before stepping inside.

Chapter Six

Florian launched into full-blown tour-guide mode, pointing to a wall here, a section of ceiling there.

"The building was abandoned centuries ago, and half of it had long since been dragged off by the surrounding villagers, who used the stones to lay the foundation for their own homes or in landscaping and walls."

"I saw someone demonstrating at the gate," I said as I trailed Libole through one stone chamber after another, in varying degrees of completion. "I take it there have been issues of repatriation?"

He grunted and waved one large hand in the air. "Stuff and nonsense. This is the classic case of wanting something only after someone else has invested in its salvation. No one wanted this monastery; it had been falling apart for aeons. Elrich paid the village and the Scottish government handsomely for it. They can do much more with the money than they could ever have hoped to do with the building. It's different over there, you know: They have more ruins than you can shake a shillelagh at. Worse, the monastery was on a small island off the coast; nothing there but rocks and sheep."

He handed me a manila envelope containing photos of the ruins in their original location on an island off the bleak, forbidding coast of Scotland. The monastery did, indeed, look like an abandoned ruin, consisting primarily of haphazard piles of tumbled stones scattered about the rocky ground. Only one tower and a few exterior walls remained standing.

"Why is Elrich so intent on this building in particular?" I asked. "Wouldn't it have been easier to build something new, or to renovate an existing historic building in the area? There's the old mill in Mill Valley. . . ."

"Ellis Elrich doesn't believe in taking the easy path. He took a trip to Scotland long ago and apparently had what he refers to as a 'spiritual awakening.' I believe he fell in love with the place at that time." Libole shrugged and pointed out an area of stone joinery where the walls met the ceiling. "You can see that this part of the building, here in the back, featured thick, bulky walls and small, rounded windows that didn't let in much light."

"Was that on purpose or due to the engineering of the time?"

"Excellent question! Windows and other openings had to be small and narrow to support the weight of the building. But with advances in engineering, building methods changed. The front of the chapel, which was built more than a century after the rear portion, is Gothic; the walls are taller and thinner, with large openings to allow in light through pointed arches. Graceful, isn't it?"

I nodded as I took it all in. Gothic architecture was revered for a reason: The arches seemed to soar into the heavens. Perfect for a house of worship.

"Also within the cloisters are a chapter house, a warming house, and a refectory. Claustral buildings include a night stair, the sacristy, latrines, cellars, and a piscine."

My mind reeled. What had I gotten myself into? I didn't even know what half those things *were*. It looked like someone would be hitting the books at night to get up to speed with her medieval building project.

"A, um, 'piscine'? Would that be a . . . pool?" Hard to imagine monks taking a dip on the chilly coast of Scotland, but one never knew.

"Don't be silly," said Florian. "A piscine was a special room reserved for washing the goblets and plates used for saying Mass."

"Oh, I see." Just as I thought, being a monk wasn't much fun.

"Notice the cresset lamps and the hunky punks."

"I'm sorry. The what?" I was starting to wonder if Florian was pulling my leg. Was I being hunky punked?

"Cresset lamps are indentations in the stone, into which oil was poured and a wick was placed. Some were portable, and used to awaken brethren who dared fall asleep during midnight Mass. And hunky punks are carved little squat fellows, often with funny faces. They have no purpose I can see, but they are entertaining. I have more in the warehouse."

"Like gargoyles?"

"Something like that."

He led the way outside to a rough patch of land that was ringed by a temporary wood security fence. Foundation stem walls had been laid around it.

"This area will be surrounded by a colonnaded walkway, called the promenade. The second story was where the monks copied books. Before the invention of the

Gutenberg printing press, all books were written out and illustrated by hand. It was a primary occupation of the brethren."

I nodded. This much, I did know.

"Mr. Elrich would like to utilize those spaces as guest bedchambers, each with its own en suite. The cloister surrounds an herb garden, called a garth. We will plant the garth with traditional plants. We're to consult 'Harper' in the matter."

The way he said the name left no doubt as to his opinion of her.

"Harper?" I asked.

"Harper Elrich."

"Is that Elrich's wife?"

"He isn't married. It's his daughter."

"Oh, I see. Is she a landscape designer?"

He sneered. "In her dreams. But as you know, the client gets what he wants. Especially this client."

Next Libole led the way into the refectory, otherwise known as the dining room. It was attached to a large space that would become the kitchen. Libole handed me paperwork showing the proposed floor plan, as well as receipts for the industrial-sized refrigerators, freezers, cookstoves, and other appliances that had already been ordered according to the instructions of the chef, Jean-Claude Villandry.

I slowed my pace when we neared the round room where I'd found McCall's body. As Libole had mentioned, it was still cordoned off with yellow police crime scene tape. It felt somehow comforting to know that Elrich's influence didn't extend to compelling the police to set aside a proper homicide investigation for the sake of the Wakefield Retreat Center.

But now that I saw this room without being distracted

by ghosts or a dead body, I realized that not only was the room incomplete, but these stones were unlike the rest of the monastery.

"Why are these stones different?" I asked, looking in the doorway.

Libole shrugged. "Different quarries, perhaps. And as you know, parts of the building were built at different times, sometimes centuries later."

"These stones appear to still have bits of plaster on them. Were the walls often plastered, back in the day?"

"Apparently so," he said, his tone making clear what he thought of questions with self-evident answers. "Again, they were probably from a different time."

"There are several pigments," I said as I looked more closely, then stepped back to get the big picture. "Almost as though there was a mural here. But I don't think the stones are placed properly or we might be able to make out the painting—"

"It's lost to us." Libole waved a hand in the air, impatient. "There's far too little of it remaining to interpret what used to be here. But I *will* say the people of the time believed very firmly in hell and divine retribution, and many of these walls would have been covered in frescoes depicting such horrors. Best to have it replastered, perhaps by a fresco artist who can re-create something typical to the period. I have been visiting monasteries from the same era, ones that have been preserved or artfully restored, and I have notes as to appropriate themes."

"I'd love to look at your ideas, of course," I said. "And I know a muralist who does wonderful work. Though obviously we're putting the cart before the horse. We still don't have the electrical roughed in, much less dictating final wall finishes and the like."

"Of course."

Giving in to temptation, I reached into the room to drag my fingers across the ragged bits of plaster clinging to the stone: In some places it was shiny and smooth, cold but inviting to the touch; in others it felt ready to crumble under pressure.

Just then I felt a sudden wave of hunger and sadness overtake me. I was so ravenous I felt faint, so sad I had to fight back tears.

"Do you know what this room was used for?" I asked, taking a deep breath and trying to tamp down the sudden sensations.

He paused so long I thought he wasn't going to answer. "Not really. It was probably merely another sort of storage room."

"It's an unusual shape, isn't it? Are there a lot of round storage rooms?"

"Not really, not at that time. Now, I'd like to hear your opinion about a problem we've been having. . . ."

He led the way outside to a stone outbuilding with walls constructed only a few feet off the ground. Several men stopped their work when we arrived, leaning on their shovels and pickaxes.

They fixed me with a steady gaze. It dawned on me that this was a test, for which I was unprepared. Luckily, I was no novice.

"So this area won't have a new foundation laid for it?" I asked. "You're laying these stones directly on the ground?"

"It's a low outbuilding," said Libole. "Mr. Elrich would prefer to have authenticity preserved wherever possible."

"A stone foundation won't pass code in earthquake country," I pointed out.

Libole actually rolled his eyes. "Code *again*? You are worse than a building inspector—you know that?"

Those were fighting words on a jobsite, but I wasn't about to take the bait. I'd been living with my father for years. Crotchety old men didn't faze me.

"Just fill me in on the work-arounds," I said.

One of the men started detailing the bracing and connecting they'd done to be sure a stone foundation would function properly in earthquake country. The bracing wouldn't be adequate for a larger structure, but it should suffice for a small outbuilding.

Still, it seemed like a lot of extra work just to avoid pouring a simple concrete foundation and stem walls. But then again, I supposed it made sense to keep the historical feel as much as possible in areas where there was a little leeway.

"Here's the problem," Tony said as he joined us, his silver earrings sparkling in the sunshine. Back in the day, when I used to follow my dad around as a kid, it was rare to see long hair, much less tattoos, on the jobsite. Construction workers were, by and large, a conservative lot. But times had changed. "See this chalky residue? It keeps happening, and we can't figure out how to stop it."

"This is pretty standard stuff for an old stone building," I said. "It's a problem of capillary moisture and subsequent efflorescence."

"Right," said Tony. "That's what I was thinking."

"Stone wicks moisture up from the ground," I explained. "No big deal in the Southwest, or even more inland areas of California, but in a place like this, on the coast? There's so much moisture in the ground and air, we'll be fighting chalky residue forever."

"What about a plastic membrane base of some sort?"

"I don't think we need anything that complicated. In a building this size, a stainless steel flashing would be sufficient."

There were some subtle nods among the men. I had passed this simple test. I was sure there would be other, much more difficult ones, but for the moment I would take what I could get.

As much as I enjoyed the history of the building, I felt relieved when we came to the end of our walk-through, emerging from the shadows of the stones out into the sunshine of the late afternoon. Once outside, I felt brave enough to ask Libole the question that was weighing on my mind: "Would a woman ever have been brought into the cloisters?"

"A woman? Never." Libole shrugged. "There were, however, guest accommodations separated from the monastic cloisters, sometimes quite sumptuous. Because of our space and locale, we have moved such chambers closer to the monastery, when in fact there would have been more of a distance."

"So a woman might have stayed here, but outside the cloister where the monks lived?"

"A noblewoman, with her entourage, quite possibly. There were no hotels in those days, so nobles were offered shelter on their journeys."

Whereas the peasants could shiver in the cold, I thought.

I took another look around at the great piles of stones yet to be used. One group appeared different from the others.

"These . . . these are from the round room?"

"Perhaps," said Libole. "Or from a similar part of the structure, yes. From the same era."

Out in the sunshine, I could see things more clearly. Much of the plaster was tinted with typical shades for old frescoes: ocher, terra-cotta, the colors of pigments taken from the earth. All were pale, and other than a curl here or a line there, it was impossible to make out what the picture must have been. But I was now sure they had once constituted a mural.

There were also flecks of something decidedly modern: bits of bright blue chalk here and there, as though the stones had once been marked. The stones reminded me of something, but I couldn't put my finger on what, exactly.

"You mentioned that many of the stones have gone missing?"

"Cretins, Ms. Turner."

"I'm sorry?"

"We are surrounded by cretins. Villagers dragged pieces away to build farms and whatnot. I have been forced to search high and low, but finally found an adequate quarry to replace what's missing. As luck would have it, the quarry was not in the hills of Italy or the mountains of Afghanistan. Oh, no. It was in Texas."

"Well, that will save on shipping costs."

"We have a veritable legion of stonecutters working with us. We needed so many that we brought them in from several countries. They're staying at local hotels and motels and bed-and-breakfasts." Libole let out a long sigh. "As I'm sure you realize by now, much of this process is being invented as we go along. The monastery was too far gone to re-create it exactly as it was, though we can, at the very least, bring authenticity and veracity to the project through proper study and research."

Libole was undeniably brilliant, but he was also a pompous priss. He served as a reminder not to be so self-important when I indulged in one of my spiels about re-using old lumber or finding just the right stained glass for a curved stairwell window.

"I say, isn't that your dog?" Libole asked.

I looked over to see an empty leash lying on the ground, then caught a flash of the brown plume of a tail as Dog disappeared into the building.

Dammit.

Chapter Seven

He would probably be okay; construction workers were notoriously canine friendly. But Dog wasn't the sharpest tool in the shed. He had his charms—chief among them that he saw ghosts, just as I did—but common sense and keeping out of harm's way weren't among them.

"Sorry. I should go after him, make sure he doesn't get into trouble."

"Certainly."

The chapel was empty except for a trio of men on scaffolding, carefully placing a stone corbel at the top of one wall. I hurried through a series of chambers until I emerged at the vestibule where I had seen Larry McCall's ghost two days ago.

Dog was sitting attentively, wagging his tail the way he did when someone was offering him food, with the excited pseudo-patience of a hungry dog.

I searched the dark stone walls, checking out my peripheral vision. Just in case.

"Hello?" I ventured.

A slight echo, "*o . . . o . . . o,*" was my only response.

An eerie light was shining from the next room—the round room. The room that had been empty of everything but bags of mortar only a few minutes ago.

I crept along and peeked through the vestibule, into the round room.

The crime scene tape lay limp on the floor. Food had been laid out on a plank supported by bags of mortar. An apple, a sandwich, a bag of ranch-flavored Doritos. A cup of coffee, still steaming. And several small tea candles.

What in the world?

"Are you quite all right?" came Florian's voice from behind me.

I jumped at the sound, then stood with my hand over my pounding heart. "Sure. Yep, I'm great."

"Did I scare you?"

"Just a tad."

"Don't tell me you've been listening to the ghost stories."

"I may have listened to one or two, yes."

"Surely you don't believe in such things?"

"I take it *you* don't?"

"I'm a realist, my dear, not a fantasist. A building this old, well, it's seen its share of history. War, love, famine, birth, disease, the drama of human life. I will grant you that such goings-on can give a historic building a certain je ne sais quoi, a sense of something *other*, another place and time, the way a new building never can. But ghosts? *Tsk-tsk.*"

His eyes flickered over the food.

"Is that an . . . offering?"

"Sure looks like it."

"This is ridiculous. The men have been taken in by that ghost story as well. *Doritos*." Libole *tsk*ed again.

"Doritos do seem like an odd choice, but ranch flavor . . ."

"It's idle heresy." And with that he stepped into the room and dashed the food and candles to the floor. Then he stormed out.

I remained in place, shocked. The odd altar and food offerings, the mess Libole created on the spot where McCall's body had lain just two days ago—the whole scene felt bizarre, unseemly.

As I hesitated, I noticed Dog's panting started to cause clouds in the air. A wave of cold air, then a bone-deep chill, enveloped me.

"Let's . . . get out of here," I whispered to Dog. Dragging him by the collar, I could have sworn I felt something behind me. Something more than cold, something . . .

Don't turn around.

My hair was in its usual ponytail, leaving my neck vulnerable to ghostly exhalations. . . .

And then I felt something much worse. That same sensation of hunger: deep, aching hunger pangs so strong that for a moment I almost doubled over. And on top of that, a gut-wrenching sadness.

Don't turn around.

Dog yelped.

Then we ran.

Outside, the sun shone, the sky was filled with puffy white clouds, and a peaceful Pacific Ocean sparkled in the distance. A small army of men bustled around the jobsite. My ears were assaulted by a cacophony of stone being cut, compressor motors pounding, a pneumatic drill whining, the noises blending into a comforting sym-

phony of organized chaos that reminded me of being a
kid, working with my dad. The smells of the jobsite were
soothing to me, too: sawdust, axle grease, and fresh concrete. Here at Wakefield those scents combined with
eucalyptus and the briny ocean air.

I leaned over, hands on my knees, and took a few minutes to soak it all in, trying to get my bearings. Dog,
quicker to rally than I, trotted over to lift his leg on a tuft
of grass.

Libole was nowhere in sight. I saw Tony, the foreman,
studying blueprints at a makeshift table made of planks
laid over sawhorses.

"Tony, talk to me about food going missing."

"Not much to tell," he said with a shrug. "Just that
Guys are losing things from their lunches."

"Their whole lunch pails, or . . . ?"

He shook his head. "Just stuff out of them. Like an apple
or a cookie, like that. You know, the kind of thing that happens in grade school? But it's rare on a jobsite, right?"

I nodded. "Could this be a practical joke of some sort?"

"I doubt it. No one's sitting back and laughing—if
that were the case the guys'd be finding their sandwiches
behind the walls; you know the drill. Guy opens up a
wall, finds a shrunken head."

On my debut job for Turner Construction, the guys
had placed a full skeleton behind a wall I was about to
open up. That was how I knew they liked me.

"It's got to the point where guys are keeping their
stuff locked up in their trucks," Tony continued with another shake of his head. "Not only is that inconvenient,
but it's a damn shame when you can't trust a member of
a crew; you know what I'm saying? Hey, speaking of that,
have you heard anything more about Nolan?"

"No, sorry."

"I still can't believe it. I worked with the guy for six months. I mean, what a shock, right? And that it happened right here, so fast . . ." He let out a loud breath. "I tell you what. I think this place might be cursed."

"Cursed?"

"Like . . . like the guys were talking about ghosts, or whatever? We've all seen some stuff. . . . I don't really know if I want to stick around. It might not be worth it."

I couldn't afford to lose good workers, not with the timeline Elrich was insisting on.

"We need you, Tony."

"I know, you're new on the job and all. I mean, I'm not gonna bail right away. I'm just . . ." He left off with a shrug.

"I know things feel unsettled," I said. "But give me a few days and we'll see if we can get things back to normal. Okay?"

He nodded.

"Did you hear about the memorial service tomorrow evening?"

"Yeah, I already told the guys. I feel bad, but the truth is, McCall was a real jerk. The way he ran around here with that Clipboard of Doom, like he got off on finding problems. You ask me, he was sort of asking for trouble. All due respect."

"I'm not sure he meant to be a jerk. I mean . . . he was a building inspector. No one likes building inspectors."

"I guess," he said. Then he brightened up. "Hey, did you hear the one about the building inspector who walks into a bar with a rabbi?"

"Yup, I just heard it," I said, cutting him off. "Good one."

It really was too soon.

But as I walked away, I wondered about McCall's

Clipboard of Doom. I didn't remember seeing it with hi
body. What could have been on it? And . . . what ha
happened to it?

I spent the next few hours familiarizing myself with th
men, the site, and the drawings but couldn't bring mysel
to venture back into the cloister. Not yet. I wasn't the
only one a little nervous about the place: The me
started packing up by six, anxious to get off-site befor
sunset. So far I'd seen plenty during the daylight hours
I could only imagine what went down after dark.

I decided I'd been brave enough for one day, so
gathered up the paperwork Libole had given me
grabbed Dog, and headed up the hill to the house. Do
sniffed around our bedroom while I put down his ru
and his bowls. Once I brought out his bowls, I had to pu
something in them, of course. So I went to the car an
lugged in a big plastic bin of dog food, topped by a ba
of treats.

Dog devoured his food in approximately two inhala
tions, and I sat with him on his rug, petting him for a fe
minutes. Despite his propensity to carsickness—whic
was getting better now that we had been doing therapy—
Dog had one very important trait of a constructio
hound: He fit easily into new environments.

Dog and I had found each other at the first construc
tion site where I had seen a ghost. I hadn't planned t
adopt him—at the time I had been planning to move t
France and fought against more responsibility—but Do
was so skinny and pitiful and . . . *abandoned* that I woun
up taking him home. When it turned out he could se
ghosts, just like I could, having him around made me fee
less like a crazy ghost-seeing lady. Besides, Dad love

ogs, and the pup had made our offbeat household—
Dad, me, Stan, my semi-but-not-really-stepson, Caleb—
eem more like a family, as beloved pets were wont to do.

It was pretty pathetic that we still hadn't given the
oor mutt a real name. It was still on our to-do list, but
ve hadn't managed to find one we agreed on. In the
neantime, Dog seemed to have learned his current mon-
ker, and it was by no means assured that he would be
ble to learn a new one. Not the brightest bulb in the
handelier.

After a few minutes, Dog began to snore. *Not a bad
idea*, I thought with a yawn. But I checked the clock: It
vas only seven thirty. If I started going to bed at this
our, I would be even more of a social pariah than I was
lready.

I made my obligatory evening phone call to Stan, and
ve went over the plan to take over Pete Nolan's payroll
nd be sure the men were paid, as usual, this Friday. I
lso called Dad, but he didn't answer. Instead he texted
ne: *Cooking. Spaghetti. ROTFLMAO. LoL!* Texting with
Dad. *Oh, boy*. I was going to have to brace myself for this
ew aspect of our relationship.

Finally, Graham and I chatted for a while, and I as-
ured him I was safe and sound. I didn't mention what
Libole had said, about stumbling into a nest of vipers.

While we spoke, I noticed one of the decorative tiles
ver the fireplace was loose. I picked at it a little, and it
ell right off into my hand. The ones on either side of it
vere moving, as well. By the time the phone call was
ver, five of the historic glazed tiles were off the fireplace
ood, and of course the plaster around them was crum-
ling. I would have to fix that. I'd bring my tools in to-
norrow.

When I hung up, I looked past the swimming pool and down the hill, to the Gothic ruins glowing pink in the dying light of day. I supposed I could go for a swim, but that sounded awfully ambitious, and what if my splashing constituted what Alicia would consider disturbing the peace? Besides, I should use this evening to bone up on Scottish history in general, and the story of the Wakefield stones in particular.

First, I studied Florian Libole's drawings, curious to see how he had envisioned updating this ancient building. A reinforced concrete envelope held the remains of the old cellars, and steel would be cleverly inserted into the antique stones to form a skeleton. Various small rooms would house modern essentials such as the furnace and hot-water heaters. The electrical and plumbing would be incorporated into new and existing troughs in the stone, or disguised by soffits when necessary. Libole was clever, I thought. He had earned his reputation.

Then I started reading through the history of the place, but my eyes lost focus. I was beat. I wasn't up to thinking through deadlines and schedules, much less about despondent, ravenous ghosts.

Speaking of hunger, where was that snack bar, again?

I looked for the map of the house and the daily schedule that Alicia had provided, but couldn't find it anywhere. I could hear my mother's voice saying: *Melanie Ann Turner, you would lose your head if it wasn't attached.*

Okay, this house was big, but it wasn't *that* big. Surely I could find my way to food. And the library—I'd love a good book to read in bed. I gave Dog a pat and slipped out.

Before I even got to the end of the corridor, I ran into

ernon Dunn. He was big enough that it was awkward
assing him in the hall. The overhead light shone down
his shiny bald spot and glinted off his aviator glasses.

"Hello, Mel," he said with a smile. Or maybe it was a
leer; it was hard to tell.

"Hi, Vernon. I didn't realize— Are you staying here as
ell?"

"Ellis likes to keep us all close at hand."

"Oh, I see."

"Florian is next to you."

"Is he?"

"Next to your bedroom, I mean."

"Ah. Anyway, I was just on my way to the snack bar," I
replied, wishing I weren't here, or *he* weren't here. Ei-
ler way. Vernon gave me the creeps. Florian had men-
oned a lack of poetry in the man's soul, but something
bout the chief financial officer made me think he lacked
ther things, as well.

"You know, Ellis has reasons for wanting you so badly."

"Excuse me?"

"This project is absurd. Ellis has poured an obscene
mount of money into it already. Libole seems deter-
ined to bankrupt him. It will be a disaster for our bot-
om line; you mark my words."

"Perhaps he's motivated by something other than a
ottom line," I said, wondering why I was defending Ellis
lrich to his chief financial officer.

"Ah, yes. I suppose you are referring to his so-called
piritual awakening' in Scotland?"

"I don't know—"

"I see how it is." Vernon smiled, but there was no hu-
or in his eyes. "You're falling for him, too, aren't you?
ypical."

"I imagine Ellis Elrich has many admirers," I said "The man's a motivational speaker, after all. That's sor of his currency, isn't it?"

"Yes, it is. And you would do well to keep that i mind."

"Okay . . ." What was going on here? Vernon Dunn was a sycophant when Elrich was around yet spoke thi way behind his back? "So, are you trying to warn m about something? Why do you think he wants me on thi job?"

"Don't trust Libole. That's all I'm saying."

There was a sound of someone coming down the hal Dunn turned on his heel, stalked into his room, and slammed the door.

It was Alicia, looking agitated, as always. "Are you lost? May I help you with something?"

"I was looking for the library."

"Down past the parlor, first door to the left."

"Thank you."

"We're not serving a formal dinner tonight, but i you're hungry, there is always food in the snack bar, a indicated on your map."

"Oh, super. You know, I might have misplaced my—

Before I could finish, she whipped another copy o the map out of her notebook and handed it to me.

"Thank you," I said.

"The chef is excellent. Everything's organic, of cours much of it grown right here on the estate. I'm sure you' want to confer with Mr. Villandry when you begin to se up the herb gardens around the Wakefield center. Wit Harper Elrich's input, too, of course."

"Okay, great. Thanks."

She gave a final little nod and turned to leave.

"Good night," I said to her stiff back as she stalked down the corridor.

I passed through a parlor set up with several easy chairs and a sectional sofa, as if to invite conversation. Here, too, there was a stucco "beehive" fireplace, decorated with brightly painted Spanish tiles and a raised hearth for extra seating. Broad French doors on one side of the room opened onto the courtyard, while on the other side of the room a twin set of doors led to the pool and meadow and the path to Wakefield. If only the exterior of the building had been Spanish Revival instead of Victorian, it would have made quite a harmonious milieu.

Clouds streaked with pink, gold, and orange hung low over the ocean, announcing the imminent sunset. Beyond the French doors was another terra-cotta-tiled terrace, with a stone balustrade, more conversational groupings of outdoor furniture, and a *chiminea*—a freestanding iron fire pit.

When Graham arrived, I promised myself, I would spend at least one evening on that terrace or lounging in the pool, after-work drink in hand, watching the sunset over the ocean. Even a cynic like me could see the romance in that scenario.

But for now I continued down the hall. The next door, to the left, was marked with another discreet plaque that read, simply, LIBRARY.

I stepped inside. It was beautiful, a fantasy library: two stories tall, with a spiral staircase and a catwalk around the second story. There was even a whiff of must so common to old bookshops and junk stores, which made me feel right at home. A quick glance at the first shelf at hand proved it was full of classics: *Moby-Dick, Jane Eyre,* and *The Iliad.*

I was enamored, looking at the titles on the shelves, when I came around the side of a plush red leather chair and saw a mass of curly hair.

I jumped back and swore.

What were the chances I'd find two bodies in as many days?

Chapter Eight

S he opened her eyes.

A sullen gleam reminded me of my teenage step-son. But she must have been in her twenties—young, but not a child. And apart from the blond hair, she looked a lot like her father.

"Hi. Sorry. I didn't mean to disturb you," I said.

She shrugged. "Whatever."

Yep, she and Caleb had a lot in common.

But I hadn't become one of the few women running a construction company in California—not to mention an up-and-coming ghost buster—by being easily put off.

"You must be Harper? Ellis Elrich's daughter?"

"Yeah. Who are you?"

"I'm Mel. I run Turner Construction. I'm staying here while I work on the Wakefield Retreat Center."

"The 'Elrich Method' retreat center?" Harper rolled her eyes and made a rude noise. "This is so bogus."

"Why's that?"

"Kieran says my dad practically stole that whole building from Scotland."

"Kieran?"

"He's . . ." I could have sworn she blushed a little. But the sullen mask descended and she shrugged. "A friend. So if Daddy Dearest wanted a retreat center so badly, why didn't he just build a new one?"

"He said something about preserving the building for posterity."

"I'll just bet he did," she said with another eye roll. "That sounds just like him."

"Anyway, this house is really something, though, right?" I said in a lame attempt to make conversation. "I can't wait to take a swim in the pool."

She shrugged again, unimpressed. "You know what? If you're a remodeler, you should totally put TVs in the bedrooms. That would be an improvement, for sure."

"Actually, there's a difference between a remodeler and a renovator . . . ," I began, but trailed off as I saw the look of utter boredom on the young woman's face. "Never mind. I hear there's a TV in the rec room?"

"Yeah. But then Dad always comes in, or one of his creepy colleagues, and they always want to watch something educational and engage me in erudite conversation so Dad will be impressed."

I imagined any young woman who used the word 'erudite' in casual conversation probably had more to say than she'd like to admit.

"So, your dad's colleagues are creepy?" Now that someone had been murdered on the grounds, I figured I should keep my eyes and ears open, just in case Pete Nolan wasn't the perpetrator. "In what ways?"

"Whatever. Just normal creepy. I gotta go."

I watched her leave. Her hair was unruly, curls gone

to frizz, but her wardrobe looked new and expensive. She was clearly still in an awkward phase, and I decided maybe she was younger than I'd initially thought: late teens or very early twenties. Still finding her place and her voice.

I remembered that age well. That was when I had been dazzled by the man who later became my husband, and then—in hindsight, entirely predictably—my *ex*-husband. It was also around that time that I was trying to get over my crush on Graham Donovan, the wild young man who worked for my dad.

Speaking of whom . . . Graham was no longer so young or so wild, but I sure wished he were here. I missed him, and I wasn't sure I wanted to spend many more nights under this roof without him. Even assuming Larry McCall's killer was behind bars, there was a lot of tension in the Elrich mansion. Creepy tension.

But for the moment I had the library all to myself, which suited me fine. Plop me down in a bookstore or library and the hours zoom by.

I started circling the room, head tilted, reading the spines as I perused the shelves. Ellis—or whoever had put this library together—had done a wonderful job. There was a large selection of literature, where Nathanial Hawthorne's classics rested alongside Stephen King's latest. I plucked a couple of novels I hadn't yet read from the shelves before turning to the large nonfiction section. This collection featured some standard reference books as well as numerous self-help books, several of which had been penned by none other than Ellis Elrich himself, promoting the Elrich Method. I added one of those to my pile of books to read. Elrich was such an enigma that I thought it would be helpful to learn more about how my client's mind worked. As my mother, an avid reader, had taught me, *If you want insight into someone, read what they write.*

I tucked several others—one on medieval architecture and one on Scottish history—under my arm, consulted the map Alicia had given me, and headed for the snack bar. This turned out to be a well-stocked pantry next to the house's industrial-sized kitchen. The pantry had a microwave, a hot pot, a drip coffeemaker, an espresso machine, and a toaster oven. Shelves displaying salty and sweet snacks lined the room, and the granite countertop offered bowls of fresh fruit. An oversized refrigerator was stocked with fruit and soft drinks as well as yogurt, kefir, a variety of cheeses, and a stack of prepared single-serving meals. I took a look at one, labeled "Pan-Seared Tuna with Avocado Remoulade." It was like shopping in the prepared-foods section of a pricey, upscale grocery store, except it was all free.

I opted for a caprese sandwich—mozzarella made from organic milk, organic basil, locally sourced organic tomatoes, on San Francisco sourdough bread—a bottle of spring water to refill the aluminum water bottle in my room, and, prompted by today's discovery, a bag of Doritos. After a moment's hesitation, I grabbed what looked like a fresh-baked chocolate chip cookie. Wouldn't want to risk waking up hungry in the middle of the night.

On the way back to my room, I thought about the food that had been set out, like an offering, in the monastery's mysterious round room. I had felt a deep, gnawing hunger when in the presence of the Lady in Red. Was someone trying to assuage the ghost by feeding it? If so, why risk the violent wrath of really buff construction workers by pilfering their food? Why not just bring something from home?

Dog was waiting for me at the bedroom door, whapping himself in his face with his own tail in an ecstatic display upon my return. Not to cast aspersions on his loyalty, but it was unclear whether he was more interested in my arrival or in my sandwich. I set the books down on the desk, switched on the gas fireplace, and enjoyed an impromptu picnic by the fire, sharing a couple of bites of the sandwich with Dog. He would have liked the Doritos and cookie, too, but since they weren't good for him, I sacrificed myself. Once the food was gone, Dog took a long drink of water, curled up on the rug I had brought from home and placed in front of the fireplace, and started to snore.

I love real wood fires but could easily get used to this: One flick of a finger and the flames roared. I changed into my pajamas by firelight and found myself relishing the solitude. I adored my father, and Stan, and Caleb, and Graham, too, but my life was so jam-packed with men and their needs and opinions and energy; it was fun to have an evening all to myself. I crawled into the king-sized bed and snuggled into the fluffy pillows, the thousand-thread-count cotton linens, and the goose-down comforter, with my dog snoozing in front of the leaping flames and a sweeping vista out the French doors. . . .

On second thought, I got up and closed the heavy brocade drapes. If I could see out, others could see in. And that, as Harper Elrich would say, was just plain creepy.

I cracked open *Wuthering Heights*, which I'd never read, though I'd always pretended I had. The Gothic tale seemed fitting, given the moonlit but fog-shrouded ruins down the hill. But though I was determined to enjoy Emily Brontë's spooky tale, I found the prose a bit dense and dated. Well worth the effort, I was sure, but it took more concentration than I had at the moment. *Jane Eyre* was almost as challenging, and despite my best intentions, I wasn't really in the mood for *The Iliad*. I paged through Ellis Elrich's biography for a few minutes and noticed a photograph of him in a kilt in Scotland. The caption mentioned Elrich had trekked through the Scottish Highlands and isles and had stumbled upon the ruins of the Wakefield monastery.

That helped explain his attachment to the place.

I closed the book. I really should read more about my host and client, but at the moment, nonfiction didn't suit my mood. I was yearning for an engrossing story.

My eyes alit on the vivid cover of *Keeper of the Castle*.

Maybe just a few pages. Just to see what it was all about.

An hour later, the penniless daughter of the laird and the poor-but-scrappy serf were arguing about nothing in particular, and you could cut the sexual tension with a knife.

I was utterly absorbed in the tale when I heard an odd sound.

Music. Or something like music. Was that a flute? Eerie, ethereal, it was a simple tune played over and over, as though the musician didn't know the next notes.

One of Elrich's many guests, perhaps?

I sat up and listened. The music was coming from outside.

I pulled on a robe, grabbed my aluminum water bottle, and went out the French doors to the terrace. The cool night air was fragrant with eucalyptus and damp earth. Though this area didn't see a lot of rain per se, the fog gave everything a good dousing. California's famous redwood trees flourished along the misty coast, absorbing water through their leaves as well as their roots.

I took a long swig from my water bottle and looked

down over the meadow toward the ocean, the moon shining so brightly I could see the blanket of low-lying fog gliding this way, having already enveloped the piles of stones and building materials down below. As I watched, I saw a flicker of light in the half-built chapel.

Was someone down there? Or had I imagined it?

Were the ghosts wandering those stone corridors, looking for their lost loves? Had the evil laird refused his daughter permission to marry a commoner, and now . . . *Get a grip, Mel,* I chided myself. I was going to have to stop reading that book; it was putting ideas in my head. Like I needed fiction, given the life I led.

There it was again: a flicker illuminating one arched window, then the next. I saw the glow of yellowish light, as though from a candle, and then a flash of red. The lilting notes drifted up from the ruins. And was that a . . . a plaintive wail? Was the woman in red still crying?

"Pretty, isn't it?" came a voice from behind me.

I jumped a good six inches and dropped my aluminum bottle, which clattered loudly on the terra-cotta tiles as it sprayed its contents across the terrace. I swore a blue streak as I crouched to pick it up.

"Sorry," said Ellis Elrich with a chuckle. He held a snifter of amber liquid in each hand. "Guilty conscience?"

"No, I . . ." I looked at the monastery. The lights were gone, and the flute had been silenced. "Just absorbed in thought. I thought I saw something at the construction site."

Dog finally roused himself to bark as he trotted out to the terrace, tail wagging, and made a beeline for Elrich.

"Some guard dog you are," I muttered.

Elrich held out one of the brandy snifters. "Cognac. Very old cognac."

"Oh, um, thank you," I said as I took it from him.

I swirled the amber liquid and breathed in the heady aroma. A beautiful moonlit night, a lovely snifter of cognac on the terrace of a gorgeous estate—what a perfect romantic setting. My flannel pajamas spoiled the ambience a bit, but that was the only off note. But surely Ellis Elrich wasn't interested in *me*? Rich men who were ugly and old had their pick of beautiful young women; I could only imagine the romantic prospects available to a rich man who was handsome and young. Besides, I wasn't the kind of woman who inspired men to spout poetry, much less to flout their lawyers' advice and date an employee.

Once more I wished Graham would hurry up and get here.

Ellis petted Dog. "He knows a dog lover when he sees one. What's his name?"

"He doesn't really have one, sad to say. We just call him Dog."

"Let me guess: He was a stray, and you refused to name him for fear of becoming attached."

I had to laugh. "How did you know?"

"Experience. I remember the first time Harper swore a kitty had 'followed her home.' But," he said with a shrug, "since it was pretty clear there was no way that kitten was ever leaving, I let her name it right from the start. Fluffy. Silly name for a short-haired cat—for any cat, actually—but Harper was only six, so we let it go."

After giving Dog a final pat, Ellis peered down the hill at the monastery, lit by the nearly full moon. As he studied the vista, I studied him. Ellis had the bland good looks of a B-movie actor or a successful motivational speaker: easy on the eyes but nothing too out of the ordinary. Still, he had a certain charm, an appeal that grew the longer I knew him.

"I don't see anything," he said.

"I don't either, now. Must have been my imagination."

"It's possible someone broke through the perimeter fence. One of the protesters, maybe. I should notify security." But he stayed where he was, sipping his cognac, apparently feeling no sense of urgency.

"Has that happened before?"

"From time to time." He shrugged. "A while back, some kids were found camping in the woods. You can hardly blame them, with this view, right?"

"What were they doing there?"

"Kid stuff: getting high and playing their guitars. Badly, I might add. If memory serves, they favored Neil Young. Got to admire their taste, though no points for originality."

"Tony was telling me about sabotage on the jobsite. Do you think the protesters could have anything to do with that? Maybe they're accessing the site, and . . ."

He shook his head. "I seriously doubt it. They're protesting a situation in one offshoot of Elrich Enterprises. It has nothing to do with Wakefield."

I nodded, though it seemed to me Elrich was missing the point: If the sabotage wasn't the work of trespassers, then the culprit had to be one of the crew.

Or a ghost.

I wondered if I should broach the subject. Elrich seemed open-minded, and was no doubt already aware of my reputation. A businessman of Elrich's caliber would have done his due diligence before hiring me for such a critical position. Probably knew where I went to elementary school and the combination to my locker at John F. Kennedy Junior High. So my raising the topic of ghosts should not have come as a shock to him. What's more, I had a sense that something was mounting. I'd encountered the monastery's unpleasant ghost twice in as many days, which suggested she wanted to tell me something. And even if she had no interest in chatting with me, I might soon be in the position of having to oust her from the ruins. This job would never get finished if she kept chasing people out of the building.

Still . . . This was my first day on the job. Maybe it would be wise to wait until Graham arrived and I had a little backup.

"Do you . . . ? I heard someone mention you have cameras at the site. Did they record what happened to the building inspector?"

Elrich hesitated. "Alicia has the footage on the computer, but the visual cut out just moments before the murder."

"That's unfortunate." Or convenient, if you happened to be the killer. "How did that happen?"

"We're not sure. There was no power surge, no sign of tampering with the equipment, nothing to account for the lapse. The recording just . . . stopped. And that's not the oddest thing."

I was afraid to ask. "Oh?"

"There is some audio, but it doesn't appear to be related to the homicide. There's some muttering, nothing intelligible. The police suggested it may have been an errant radio signal, though I'm not sure how that would happen. Very strange."

"Indeed," I said. *Very* strange.

Dog was leaning against Ellis's leg. I've always heard that dogs are good judges of character, though I wasn't convinced. I knew for a fact that Dog would like anyone who smelled like or appeared in any way to be a conduit to food.

"I hear you met Harper."

"Yes, just briefly." That was fast, I thought. Had Harper mentioned it to him? Or did Elrich have surveillance cameras throughout the house, as well as on the jobsite? "She's charming."

Ellis let out a mirthless chuckle. "She's spoiled rotten, with few social graces. Don't get me wrong. I adore my daughter, but I should have drawn the line more when she was young. After I lost her sister, I couldn't bear to deny Harper anything. I realize now I didn't do her any favors. She's smart and has a good heart, but I'm afraid the world's going to knock her around a little. As a father, it's hard to sit back and watch."

"You say you 'lost' her sister?"

"Childhood leukemia. Adrienne was only five years old; she was a year and a half younger than Harper."

"I'm so sorry."

"I was devastated, as you can imagine. My marriage didn't survive. The pain was so bad, I didn't think I could bear it any longer. For a while there, I even considered killing myself, and might have done so if not for Harper. She was my lifeline." He cleared his throat and took a sip of cognac. "After finally coming through that dark period . . . that's when I started speaking to others. It began with my own grief support group; then I went on to talk with other grieving families, and it sort of grew from that into the current enterprise. Amazing where life will take you, isn't it?"

I nodded, thinking of the unexpected twists and turns my own life had taken lately.

"It's so odd. . . . In a way, my daughter's death brought me all of this." He swept his arm to show the estate. "And yet I'd give it all up for another day with her. One single day."

The flute music started up again, weaving through the air like there were fairies playing around us.

"I have a stepson, Caleb—you met him the other day," I heard myself confiding to Ellis. "He's not technically my stepson, but I married his dad when he was five, and we were together for eight years. He's seventeen now, and he's struggling a little."

"Drugs?"

"No. At least, I don't think so. But he's unhappy at school, seems to be searching, trying to find himself. He grunts a lot."

Ellis smiled. "Even grunting is communication. I'm sure I don't have to remind you of this, but cherish every moment with him, grunting or not. The future is never guaranteed. Time is a gift, and life is fleeting. There's no amount of money that can buy more, and there's no way of knowing when it will be taken away."

His words made me think of Larry McCall's murder. We had been speaking to the man one moment, and just a few minutes later, McCall's life was snuffed out. Like the flame of a candle.

I was becoming maudlin, I thought.

"Well," Ellis said as though reading my mind, "Thank you, Mel. This has been a lovely way to end the day. I'll let you get some rest now. Alicia tells me you're planning on getting up with the birds tomorrow. I appreciate your work ethic."

It was on the tip of my tongue to ask about what Vernon had said—about Ellis hiring me for reasons other than my abilities as a contractor—but I held my tongue. Ellis had shown me nothing but faith and friendship so far. I should give him the benefit of the doubt.

As I watched him walk across the moonlit terrace, he seemed neither powerful nor rich, but profoundly lonely.

He had lost a child, surely one of the most difficult sorrows for a person to survive. My heart went out to him.

I was surprised how much I liked him.

Then again, I reminded myself, it was his business to make others like him.

Chapter Nine

The next morning, I was up before dawn, fed Dog, showered, dressed in a fringed dress topped by a sweatshirt, pulled on my work boots, and took my canine pal for a quick walk through the meadow, fresh with dew. We returned to the room, and I was about to venture out in search of coffee when I saw a piece of paper on the floor near the door.

It was today's schedule: Coffee and breakfast would be served from six to nine in the breakfast bar; lunch would be available from eleven thirty to two in the dining room. Elrich was in a couple of meetings, the memorial service for Larry McCall was set for five o'clock in the Wakefield Chapel (construction would stop early; men would be paid for their time and invited to join the service), and sherry hour was scheduled for seven o'clock (late to accommodate the memorial service). Dinner would be served late as well, at nine.

No way could I guarantee I would make it through a

nine-o'clock dinner. Not if I was getting up at five and working a twelve-hour day. It was far more likely that I would stuff myself on canapés at sherry hour, become inarticulate and combative by eight thirty, and fall asleep within the hour.

It occurred to me that if Graham wasn't already having serious doubts about me as a girlfriend, a little too much togetherness at the Elrich mansion might do the trick.

The house felt hushed when I ventured out of my room, putting me in mind of Alicia's response to my early-coffee request. Probably no one else—besides the inimitable Ellis Elrich, of course—would bother to roll out of bed for another hour. On the other hand, given how soundproof the house was, I supposed it was possible all sorts of activities were going on behind closed doors.

But not, apparently, in the breakfast bar. There wasn't a soul in sight, though a big urn of coffee had been set out, along with silver platters full of a number of other food items: pastries, doughnuts, muffins. I'm not a big pastry gal, but even *I* was tempted. These weren't the dried-out baked goods laid out at the free Continental breakfast offered by midrange hotels. On the contrary, it looked as though someone had gotten out of bed much earlier than I in order to roll out buttery croissant dough.

Which reminded me: I had forgotten to talk to Ellis Elrich about arranging for coffee and snacks for the men. General contractor fail.

I started filling my large travel mug at the urn, grateful when a rich aroma wafted up, indicating excellent coffee. Not that I would expect anything less from such a classy joint.

"What would you like for breakfast?"

Alicia was standing in the doorway, looking fresh as a daisy in a turquoise linen shift dress and matching shoes. If it hadn't been for the perturbed expression she habitually wore, she would have been darling.

"All I need is coffee. Thanks," I said as I struggled with the cap of my mug, which always gave me fits. It was the only travel mug I'd found that didn't drip, but the cap was a bear to get on.

Alicia took the mug from me unceremoniously and—without apparent effort—snapped on the lid and handed it back. "You don't want anything at all? Not even a muffin?"

She held out something that looked made of whole grains and would probably fulfill my dietary fiber needs for an entire week. I tried not to take it personally that she wasn't offering me a frosting-laden doughnut.

"I'm good, thanks," I said. "I think I mentioned yesterday that I don't really eat br—"

"The chef is standing by, available to cook any hot item you might want. Omelet, eggs, bacon . . . sausage?"

"I'm not really a breakfast person. I'm more a caffeine-driven, let's-get-this-show-on-the-road kind of person."

Alicia looked at me as though not entirely understanding what I was saying. I almost suggested she trade notes with my father, who appeared heartbroken every morning when I declined what he would call "a hearty breakfast." The man had made it through two tours of Vietnam with his good spirits intact, but I feared one day my refusal of "the most important meal of the day" would cause him to break down and cry.

It was on the tip of my tongue to ask Alicia about getting some coffee and snacks set up for the jobsite, but she had looked about ready to crack when I asked for early coffee yesterday. I decided to take it up with Ellis directly, or arrange for a truck to come by myself.

Alicia was still staring at me.

"I guess I could take a croissant with me," I conceded.

She wrapped up two croissants, along with the bran muffin, and tucked them into a brown paper bag. She added a paper napkin, folded the top of the bag over neatly, and handed it to me.

"Thank you," I said, feeling like a child going off to school with her lunch bag.

Alicia nodded, frowned, and didn't wait for me to leave before turning back to rearrange the platters of pastries, straightening up the already spotless breakfast bar.

My new commute was great. The sun was coming up by the time Dog and I started down the path that led from the house to the construction site, and seven minutes later we stood on the jobsite.

I was pleased to see the area was still deserted. New as I was to the project, I wanted a few moments alone before the men started to arrive, the day's commotion shifted into gear, and the steady stream of construction questions began.

There is something mysterious and beautiful about a ruin, and something magical about laying a new structure on those shattered remains, breathing new life into the old. Like an archaeologist sifting through layers of soil, peeling back the layers. Except I was doing the opposite, trying to restore what once was, without much of a road map.

And besides, I'm really not that kind of anthropologist.

I walked along the outside wall of the chapel, my fingers trailing along the stone, feeling the irregular crevices and rough texture under my fingertips. I was beginning to see the building in my mind, to *sense* it, and I knew my psyche had been at work while I slept: thinking how I might use epoxy resin to reinforce fragile supports, imagining simple double-pane glazing to infill window gaps and stainless steel frames to hold the walls together. Lighter materials like fresh finished wood, white plaster, and reflective glass would provide a welcome contrast to the heavy stone. In contrast to my usual approach to historical buildings, this place was so old that rather than return it to its authentic original state, we would update it and leave distinctions between the old and new: sleek black-powder-coated steel window trim would meet crude stone arches; new wood supports would hold up ancient ceiling vaults. It would be a glorious mélange.

Assuming, that is, that I could get all the interested parties on board. Ellis Elrich had the last word, of course, but I was certain he relied on Florian Libole's counsel in issues of architectural design. And if Vernon Dunn had much of a say, we were in trouble.

I tied Dog up to a post of the canopy, so he could choose sun or shade, and put out a bone and his water bowl. I wished I could let him run free, but the truth was that while some construction pups could be counted on not to run into the path of a bulldozer, Dog wasn't one of them.

He was sweet and good-looking, and had on occasion saved my life, but he really was not the brightest light in the harbor.

Six of my men showed up for work, and even though it had been only a couple of days, I set upon them like it was old-home week. It was good to have familiar faces on the job, not only as backup, but because I knew what to expect from them. If I asked one of them to set up scaffolding, he took care of it. If I needed wires pulled, it was done.

Probably if I mentioned I needed the moon, they'd grouse a bit, kick at the dirt, talk it over, and then rig something up to lasso it and bring it on down.

I had spent many a sleepless night trying to figure out how not to lay these men off. Seeing them now reminded me why I was here, at Wakefield, dealing with ancient stones and peculiar personalities.

I asked two of them to join existing teams: one with the stonemasons on the scaffolding in the chapel, the other with the guys shoring up the reinforcements to the stone walls in the refectory. In earthquake country, masonry had to be reinforced by inserting rods or providing a metal skeleton, or both.

The other four men came with me to inspect the systems of plumbing and electrical upgrades. Libole's drawings had shown much of the heating ductwork being run through soffits. With the plumbing and electrical, however, I thought the more elegant solution would be to run utilities through the stone walls. We would have to pull wires and place pipes by drilling access holes, which is hard, painstaking work. It seemed almost sacrilegious to drill through such ancient stones, so I damned sure wanted to get it right the first time.

Tommy and Ignacio crawled down into the cellars, while Javier and Brendan stuck with me. Our cell phones were useless within the building, but by shouting and tapping and consulting our drawings, we were able to pinpoint the precise spots to drill. It was a laborious process, but there was no way around it. Medieval buildings had no accommodations for modern conveniences, so we had to do our best.

Graham showed up around noon and brought me lunch; then he and Tony walked me through the green technologies being installed.

"Elrich is implementing some cutting-edge techniques, many of which haven't been applied on this scale before," said Graham. "He has the money and will to make it happen, and I'm documenting our progress every step of the way. If he pulls it off—and I think he can—Wakefield could become a prototype for this sort of building."

There was a lot of talk about "reduce, reuse, recycle." I lived by that mantra, not just because I believe in conservationism, but because I have always adored old things. Why own an old house if you were just going to rip out the insides and replace everything with contemporary finishes and materials? Might as well buy a new place, with all the modern conveniences.

To my way of thinking, those who were lucky enough to live in old houses were custodians of history. Which was one reason Elrich's house jarred me so: Why make a Victorian into a Spanish-style home? It didn't make any sense.

"What's this?" I asked, pointing to a structure located beneath the building.

"An underground cistern for water collection. The runoff from rain and condensation will be collected and used for all gray-water needs: toilets and irrigation, that sort of thing. And I'm developing solar roof panels in imitation slate tiles to match the originals. Three windmills will supply the electricity for the retreat center, as well as for the existing house. The building is north facing and takes advantage of passive green technologies like sun exposure and the natural insulation of the stone; and we'll be composting."

"Composting?"

"Big-time composting. Over to the left will be the farm: organic vegetables and free-range animals to supply the kitchens. But that's stage two. Right now we're just trying to get this structure up."

Clearly, Ellis Elrich wasn't stinting on his dream. True to his philosophy, the man appeared to be nothing if not motivated.

The memorial service for Larry McCall was planned for five o'clock, so by four thirty we started shutting things down and cleaning up. The men were invited to the service but not required to attend. Ellis made it clear that they would be paid for a full day's work either way.

Graham had to run back up to the house but said he would join me in the chapel.

I supposed Wakefield's half-built chapel was a fitting locale for McCall's memorial, given everything these stones had witnessed through the years. Sunlight streamed in through the gap between the top of the wall and the temporary roof, but it was still dim enough inside that work lamps had been strung on a wire like a workaday string of holiday lights. Several of the cresset lamps Florian had pointed out to me yesterday had been filled with oil and wicks and lit. The combination of lights gave the chapel an odd look: part ancient, part modern.

The turnout for the memorial was sparse: Ellis Elrich, Vernon Dunn, Florian Libole, Harper Elrich looking as sullen as she had last night, Alicia Withers, and a handful of folks I thought I recognized as housekeeping staff. Maybe a third of the guys who had been on the job remained, tempted by the opportunity to say good-bye to an unpopular building inspector . . . or by the food; it was hard to tell which.

Wakefield's French chef had knocked himself out pre-

paring an extensive spread of tempting hors d'oeuvres:
finger sandwiches and cheeses and fruit, canapés of pâté
and mushrooms, and tiny cupcakes and petits fours. I'd
been at Wakefield only a little over twenty-four hours,
but it was clear that this place—up at the house, anyway—provided quite the snack symphony.

Which reminded me . . .

"I was hoping to talk to you about arranging for coffee
and snacks for the crew," I said to Ellis, who was munching
on a water chestnut wrapped in bacon. "Nothing fancy,
just coffee, some juice, maybe a few energy bars. The jobsite is some distance from any stores and restaurants. . . ."

Elrich looked surprised. "Of course! I can't believe I
didn't think of that before. Alicia?"

Alicia hurried toward us, looking alarmed.

"Mel has pointed out that the men at the jobsite need
refreshments available to them."

"It was my understanding that the work crews brought
their own lunches," she said. "*Nolan's* men always did, and
he supplied a thermos of water."

"I'd love to provide the crew with coffee and some
snacks now and then. Nothing fancy—just to help keep
them hydrated and to boost morale. A quick snack can
make a big difference when you're working long hours
out of doors."

"That's an excellent idea," said Ellis. "Mel, thank you
for pointing this out. Alicia, I know you'll take care of it
with your usual élan. Now, if you'll excuse me, I need to
speak to the reverend."

As soon as he left, Alicia turned her wide-eyed, serious gaze to me.

"What sort of snacks?"

"A supply of fresh coffee would be the most important
thing. As you mentioned, most of the guys bring their

own lunches, but it would be nice to have a few dough-nuts in the morning, maybe some energy bars for later in the afternoon when their energy's flagging. Turner Con-struction would be happy to defray the costs." I threw this in, knowing full well the cost would be added to the bill I sent Ellis Elrich and knowing that Alicia was equally aware. It was the cost of doing business.

"Are there any known allergies to contend with? Re-ligious constraints?"

"Religious constraints?"

"I hear Muslims and Orthodox Jews don't eat pork. Isn't that right?"

"I don't think we need anything that complicated," I said. "Just a few energy bars and doughnuts and coffee. Maybe sports drinks—some of the guys like those. Frankly, you don't get a lot of complaints about free food and drink on a construction site."

Alicia whipped out her book and jotted down a few notes.

"If you'll all please gather around," a woman called out, and the crowd shuffled over.

There were no pews in the chapel, so we stood in a loose semicircle as the nondenominational reverend climbed onto a makeshift podium and gave a lovely homily for a man she'd never met. While she spoke, I thought about what Florian had said about the monks being roused from their REM cycles to come down the night staircase and into this chapel, to sing and pray and worship, and if they nodded off, a superior would come at them to rouse them with a swinging cresset lamp.

I imagined the scent of incense, the Gregorian chants, the many shadows that might hold secrets. . . .

I think I dozed off for a few minutes, but then I jolted myself back to the ceremony.

Still, my gaze was drawn to the opening that led to the sacristy and the chambers beyond, all the way to the round room. Though the stone arch was dark, I couldn't help but remember what I'd seen there, what I'd felt. Had I really heard a woman crying? What had been that strange hunger?

When the reverend finished, Elrich rose and gave a stirring talk about the love of life, coping with loss, and not taking our lives and health for granted. At the end of his speech, there was barely a dry eye in the house. It made me wish the deceased man's family could have been here; Ellis's words made the grumpy building inspector one of us.

I felt someone come up behind me. Assuming it was Graham, I turned around, but then I saw Graham was standing on the other side of the room, near the entrance.

The man behind me looked vaguely familiar, but it took a moment to realize where I knew him from. The kilt was the giveaway: He had been one of the protesters at the gate. The one in costume, carrying a sign about Scottish history and repatriation.

"You're Mel Turner?" He spoke in a low voice, with a soft accent.

"Yes," I whispered.

"I thought . . . I thought you'd be a man."

"Sorry."

He glanced around, as though worried about being seen, and held out a folded piece of paper. When I took it, he disappeared into the crowd.

Seconds later, Buzz-the-driver pushed through the group, apparently following the mystery man.

I opened the note, hyperaware that Graham was watching me from across the room.

I have information regarding Larry McCall's murder. Meet me at the Pelican Inn after the service. It was signed simply, *Kieran.*

"You're certifiable; you know that?" said Graham as we walked up the moonlit pathway after the service. Dog trotted after us, veering off every now and then to explore some thrilling new scent.

"I'm curious, that's all. Aren't you curious?"

"You know that old saw 'curiosity killed the cat'?"

"I know it ends 'and satisfaction brought it back.' You have to admit it's intriguing, though, right?"

"A man was killed here a couple of days ago. Murdered, Mel. You haven't been able to encounter the ghosts without running, screaming, from the building, but you have no qualms about meeting a stranger in a bar?"

I had told Graham about my less-than-dignified departure from the building after the incident with the food offering in the round room. I hadn't actually even *seen* anything that time, but I'd felt it. And I had *run*.

"I'd hardly say I was 'screaming.' Whimpering, perhaps. Cringing—now, that I'll grant you."

He smiled.

"Besides, this man's not exactly a 'stranger in a bar.' He's a friend of Harper's."

"If he and Harper are such good friends, why wasn't he welcome at the memorial service?"

"Maybe 'friend' isn't the exact right word. Anyway, I don't think you appreciate the poetry of the situation."

He gave me a *look*.

"C'mon, the Pelican Inn's a public place. And they have great food."

"You're still hungry, after that spread?"

"Have you had their fish and chips? With malt vinegar? Besides, this Kieran fellow is wearing a kilt. How tough could he be?"

"You ever see *Braveheart*? Men in kilts are not to be messed with."

I whistled to Dog, who ignored me. "Seriously, Graham—you've doubted Pete Nolan's guilt from the beginning. What if this Kieran has something of value to say?"

"Then why doesn't he tell it to the police? No offense, Mel, but you're a contractor, not a cop. Why would he slip you a note at a gathering to which he was not invited? Come to think of it—how does he even know who you are?"

"I don't know. But he must have some reason for wanting to talk to me. Which is why I want to meet with him—in public, with a big, strong man at my side. Want to come?"

"I'm sure as hell not going to let you go alone," he growled.

"You're a prince, Mr. Donovan," I said, and gave him a kiss. After a long moment, he returned the kiss, deepening it.

It was a warm, moonlit night, and it took us a remarkably long time to make it all the way back to the house.

Chapter Ten

Our mysterious protester had nabbed the corner barrel, the prime seat in the Pelican Inn Pub.

He sat hunched over a mug of ale, and though he was no longer in costume, he had a romantic, tormented look that made him seem as if from another time. He reminded me of a smuggler in his lair. A *romantic*, poetry-spewing smuggler in his lair.

Graham and I perched on low stools at the small oak barrel that served as a table.

"Thank you so much for joining me," he said, rather breathless, in a soft Scottish brogue. "I was beginning to despair."

"I've never been passed a note for a secret assignation at a memorial service before," I said with a shrug. "It was hard to resist."

"Do you want something?" he asked, as though holding a salon in his living room. "They have only beer and wine. But there's a lovely port. . . ."

"Sure, I'll try some port," I said.

"IPA for me," said Graham.

Kieran gestured to the man behind the bar.

The Pelican Inn, a small pub sandwiched between Muir Woods and Muir Beach, was crowded, as usual. During the day, dozens of bicycles would be strewn about the large patch of lawn out front, as cyclists weary from riding up Mount Tam or along the hilly coast stopped in for refreshments. There were other bikers, as well, the kind who let their motorcycles tackle the big grades. Hikers dropped in after strolling through nearby Muir Woods, taking in the soaring redwoods and lush fern-strewn creeks. And then there were the regulars from nearby Mill Valley or Sausalito.

Though it looked like a snug country inn from the British countryside, the pub had actually been built in the seventies, a decade generally noted for its wretched architecture. But the Pelican Inn had been constructed with love and historical accuracy, to the point that the owners had imported pieces directly from English pubs.

In the way of historic buildings, the doorways were too low, the thresholds too high, the stairs uneven, and I had always wondered how the owners had managed to pull permits for the build.

The Wakefield project was having difficulty passing code, as well, though Larry McCall's demise might ease that situation. In that sense, Ellis Elrich would most directly benefit from his death, though I couldn't imagine Elrich would put everything—his empire, his wealth, his family—at risk just to secure waivers and permits for his imported building. Could McCall's death have been caused by one of Ellis's misguided minions? Not Vernon Dunn; he would be happy with any delay. But what of

Florian, Alicia, or even Harper? Ellis appeared to have a lot of suspicious characters in his life.

I should probably take a trip to the Marin County Building Department soon to introduce myself, just as a matter of good construction manners—and to help smooth the way for future issues that were sure to arise. Maybe I could ask around about past permit issues, get a sense of the personalities involved. I imagined the police had already asked questions regarding McCall's death, so a few days' grace would be adequate.

"So," Graham said, rousing me from my thoughts. "Who are you, and what's this about?"

"Oh, excuse me!" the man said as he handed us business cards: *Kieran Lachaidh, Antiquities.*

"Lack-aid?" I said in a weak attempt to pronounce his last name.

"Lach-ee," he corrected me. "Means 'from the land of lochs.'"

I nodded, and steeled myself against asking him what he thought of the Loch Ness monster. The discomfiture I'd felt yesterday when doing the walk-through with Florian came back with a vengeance. I really had to brush up on my Scottish history if I was going to do a decent job with these ancient stones. Surely there was more to Scotland than scotch, golf, plaid, and the Loch Ness monster.

"Antiquities? Is that like an antiques dealer?"

"Not quite. I track down antiquities that are part of our national heritage."

"Ah. So you think Ellis Elrich has something that belongs to Scotland?"

"Yes. An entire monastery."

Graham and I exchanged a look.

"I'm, uh, not the right person to talk to," I said. "I really don't know anything about the building's origins or the legalities involved. . . . Florian Libole is the designer, and he brokered the deal with the Scottish authorities. He's who you want to talk to about this."

Kieran's eyes narrowed. "How much do you know about Libole?"

"Not much, really. I just met him yesterday. But he's well-known and respected as an expert on ancient buildings."

"He's well-known, all right. As to respected, that depends very much on who you talk to."

"That's often the case, isn't it?" said Graham.

"Are you saying Libole stole this building from the Scottish people?" I asked.

"In a manner of speaking."

"He says the monastery had fallen into ruins, and nearby villagers had been plundering the site, and the money went to the village and the government to pay for school and the like. He showed me photos. . . ."

"You've never been to the original site, have you?"

I shook my head. "I've never been to Scotland."

"I used to play there as a lad, with my brothers. It's a special place, and we adored it. Everyone from the area loved it. Don't let anyone tell you different."

"How did you know who Mel was?" asked Graham.

Kieran placed a newspaper on the table and tapped the lead story. The local Mill Valley paper discussed the travails of the Wakefield project, the death of Larry McCall, and named the new builder on the job: Mel Turner, of Turner Construction.

"You're the new leader of this project, right? Or did I get that wrong?"

"I am."

"Elrich's smart. I'll give him that. A woman general contractor is sure to curry favor."

That stung. "Maybe he hired me because I was the best candidate for the job."

"Do you have a lot of experience with rebuilding ancient stone monasteries, then?"

"No one in the United States has a lot of experience with ancient stone monasteries because we don't *have* ancient stone monasteries. That doesn't mean, however, that I'm not perfectly competent to reconstruct one. Now, is there a reason you asked me to come all the way out here to meet you, or did you just want to insult me?"

Kieran blushed. "Sorry. Good heavens, I didn't mean any such thing. Listen, allow me to start again. Could I give you a brief history of the place?"

Graham and I exchanged looks. What the hell—we were here and we had drinks.

"We'll give you fifteen minutes," I said, and took a sip of the tawny port.

"The monastery was taken from the Isle of Inchcolm, in the Firth of Forth."

"The Isle of Inchcolm in the Firth of Forth?"

"Yes, near a place called the Cairn of the Kerr."

I was immediately reminded of an old movie my sisters and I had watched growing up, in which a character played by Danny Kaye is confused by whether it's the Flagon with the Dragon that holds the Brew that is True, or the Vessel with the Pestle that holds the Pellet with the Poison. I tried not to smile.

"I believe Ellis Elrich wanted this particular building for a very good reason," continued Kieran. "I believe it holds a treasure."

"A treasure, is there?" I took another sip of port.

"Aye. Also, there's a curse."

"A treasure *and* a curse? Do tell."

"It's . . ." He looked around, as though the local bicyclists and hikers were eavesdropping, hoping to get a jump on his treasure. "I believe the curse is protecting an ancient chalice."

"The Chalice from the Palace?"

"Sorry?"

"Never mind. Do go on."

"Or perhaps a ciborium."

"A what?"

"It's like a goblet that holds the hosts—the Communion wafers. Either way, we believe Ellis Elrich has robbed us of a cultural treasure."

"So if this place is cursed, why do you love it so?"

"It's *our* curse. We love our curses; we're Scottish. It shouldn't be here—it should be where it belongs."

"But . . ." I shook my head. "All I've seen are solid stones, a few carved decorative items. I can't think of anywhere a chalice, or anything else for that matter, might be hidden."

"Perhaps it's among all the other pieces?"

"Other pieces?"

"Florian Libole has been collecting pieces for several years. Didn't he tell you?"

"He mentioned he had been collecting some items that he kept in a warehouse, but I haven't seen them."

"They might be worth a look."

"Okay, but none of this explains what happened to Larry McCall, which is ostensibly why you asked me to meet you tonight."

He nodded and took a long draft on his beer.

"Pete Nolan isn't the murderer."

"What makes you so sure?"

"Talk to him. He's got some insight into what happened."

"Okay, but I'm not sure what I'm supposed to do

about it. If Pete wasn't the killer— Well, this is a job for the police."

"But if they've got the wrong man, and they stopped looking . . . then the real killer is still out there."

"Still . . . why come to *me* with this?"

"You have a, um, reputation," said Kieran, reaching into a bag and placing a copy of *Haunted Home Quarterly* on the table. "It says right here, you've been involved in resolving several murders. Murders associated with haunted buildings."

"How did you find this?"

Kieran looked amused. "I looked you up on the Internet. It wasn't hard. I was hoping you had access to Ellis Elrich."

"Speaking of whom . . . Harper mentioned your name the other day," I said.

"Harper?"

"Harper Elrich. Ring a bell?"

"Yes, yes, of course. She stopped at the gates the other day after almost running me over with her Suburban. She asked us what we were doing, and why."

I nodded, watching him. He wasn't meeting my eye.

"Isn't she a surer access to Ellis Elrich than I am?"

"I merely explained my side of the story to her and asked her to help explain it to her father." He took a sip of his beer. "After all, a man's gotta use whatever he's got, to get what he's got to get."

A poet, he wasn't. But I got his meaning.

Graham looked straight ahead, concentrating on his driving as he steered us back to Wakefield. Narrow and windy, the roads in this part of Marin County could be treacherous for drivers unaccustomed to the challenges posed by hairpin turns, migratory deer, occasional mudslides, and sheer cliffs. Graham negotiated the turns with the confidence and ease of someone who'd grown up in the area and had cut his teeth on these roads with his motorcycle.

I liked the way Graham drove. It was sexy. It made me feel comfortable, like I could let myself relax, and didn't have to be in charge.

"What do you think?" I asked with a yawn. Unfortunately, once I got comfortable, I started to fall asleep. Yep, I was a real live wire.

"I'm sorry to say it, because it means a murderer's on the loose," Graham began, "but I think this Kieran character has a point. Charging Pete Nolan hasn't felt right from the beginning."

I nodded.

"On the other hand," added Graham, "he didn't provide us with any information we can actually use. No proof of anything, certainly. If he had anything more than suspicion, he'd be talking to the police, not us."

"Which is what makes me think he's more interested in stopping the construction than in ferreting out Mc-Call's killer," I said, struggling to stay awake. "I imagine the more convoluted the search for a killer, the better the chance that the project would be put on hold. Especially, for example, if Elrich himself stood accused of the murder—or some sort of conspiracy to commit murder. Not that I think Elrich is guilty of anything. With his wealth and influence, he could surely find a way to get the permit department to cooperate without resorting to homicide. Just getting McCall fired would do the trick."

Graham nodded. "Ellis didn't become a very rich man just because he's a smooth talker—he did it the old-fashioned way, by being an excellent businessman. It's not good business to choose a complicated and potentially disastrous solution over an easy solution. There would be no reason for Elrich to kill McCall when he could just buy him off or have him fired. Unless . . ."

"What?"

"Unless McCall had discovered something that made killing him the better option."

"Like a hidden treasure?"

Graham shook his head. "I can't believe we're talking about this. Is it just me, or does the notion of a hidden treasure in an ancient monastery sound like something out of an overblown romantic novel?"

"I wouldn't know," I said loftily. "I don't buy over-blown romantic novels." I just find them under my bed. . . .

"And as you pointed out," Graham continued, "where would you hide a treasure among those stones?"

"Have you seen this fabled warehouse full of stuff that Libole has collected?"

He shook his head.

"Maybe I'll ask if I can look around."

"That sounds like a great idea: an isolated warehouse and a murderer on the loose. What could possibly go wrong?" We pulled to a stop, and Graham fixed me with a stern look. "Mel, promise me, here and now, you won't go snooping without me."

"Aye, aye, Captain," I said with a mock salute. "You're cute when you get all macho and dictatorial; you know that?"

He grunted.

We arrived at the Elrich place much too soon for my taste. I had even toyed with the idea of renting a room at the Pelican Inn until I remembered Dog was waiting for me. But I decided to propose a weekend getaway to Graham soon. I kept talking about going to Europe one day, but it wasn't reasonable to think I could take that much time away from Turner Construction. A weekend at the Pelican Inn, though, was doable. There was no cell phone reception out there, so we could eat our English breakfast in the greenhouse, spend the day hiking along the foggy banks of the ocean, and return for port in the pub and a dinner by the walk-in fireplace, as if we were thousands of miles away from home.

As enticing as staying at Elrich's well-appointed estate had sounded, I was rethinking it. Almost everyone I had met so far—Alicia, Vernon, Harper, and even Florian—had been unpleasant. Only Elrich was friendly, and I was still loath to admit how much I liked him. It went against my grain to join what was trendy and popular. Finally, although Graham and I were sleeping under the same roof, the situation wasn't conducive to romantic interludes. What if we were sharing a roof with McCall's murderer?

We pulled in front of Elrich's mansion, parked, and were set upon by Alicia as soon as we stepped into the tiled foyer.

"Where have you *been*?" she asked, her tone urgent. "You've nearly missed sherry hour."

"I assumed it was canceled," said Graham. "What with the memorial and all."

"No. We just moved it back to accommodate the service. Didn't you see the updated schedule?"

"Yes, Graham." I looked at him with wide eyes and a concerned frown. "Didn't you see the updated *schedule*?"

Graham, showing much more patience and maturity than I, said to Alicia, "I'm afraid I'm not yet in the habit of checking the schedule consistently, Alicia. I apologize. Please, lead the way and allow us to make amends."

We trailed her down the hall to the front parlor. A full bar had been set up in one corner, where a bartender in formal attire was shaking a martini mixer with aplomb. All the usual suspects were there, as were Tony, Miguel, Jacek, and a few of the other men from the jobsite, and several faces I didn't recognize.

I asked for a martini. I didn't usually drink that much, but what with Elrich's sherry hours and assignations with Scotsmen who insulted me in bars, I feared I was on my way to becoming a lush.

One man introduced himself as a lawyer for Kieran Lachaidh, on behalf of the people of Scotland.

"I was flabbergasted when I received an invitation to come by for drinks," he said.

"Is Elrich willing to talk about the situation, then?" I asked.

"I don't know yet," he said, sipping a large margarita festooned with a little umbrella. "He hasn't really talked to me about it. . . ."

He, like everyone, seemed in awe of Elrich.

Tony, who earlier had been on the verge of walking off the job, seemed to be placated, as well.

Elrich stood in a corner chatting with Harper and Alicia, and it was as though there were an invisible shield around him. He had the strangest way of making everyone think they were welcome and had access to him, while actually holding himself apart.

I forced myself to chat briefly with Vernon, met the talented chef Jean-Claude Villandry, and was introduced to a structural engineer who had been working with Libole. Florian himself was conspicuous by his absence.

"I thought the costumes were clever," I overheard Ellis saying. "It's always hard to get the press to pay any attention, so he gave them a good photo opportunity."

"But he's a troublemaker, I feel sure," said Alicia. "I had to call the police again."

Ellis shrugged. Harper looked into her drink.

I was trying to think of a polite way to excuse myself from sherry hour—and dinner afterward—when Alicia approached me.

"Mr. Elrich suggested I speak to you directly," she said, handing me a to-do list. "I'd like to have some projects done here at the house while your men are available."

"They aren't exactly *available*," I tried to explain. "We're already running two shifts trying to get ready for the grand opening."

Alicia blinked and starting reading items off her list. I gave her points for dogged determination.

"Sure. Why not?" I said, thinking rather guiltily of the tiles I'd dislodged in my bedroom. "I'll see about bringing Brendan up from the jobsite tomorrow and put him on these house projects. Maybe Graham could help, as well."

Graham shot me a look when he realized he'd been volunteered.

"And I don't think we should simply repair things," continued Alicia, "but take this opportunity to really spruce the place up. I don't really care for all this . . . white."

"White stucco is traditional for the Spanish or Mission style," I said. "Although clearly the house used to be a Victorian—"

"Mr. Elrich and I don't care that much for the Victorian style," said Alicia. "We prefer Spanish."

"I see."

"What about something more . . . exciting on the walls?"

"Naturally, you can paint it any color you'd like. But

traditionally, in the Spanish Revival style they would have been decorated with murals and borders." I thought of the intricate murals in the Discovery Room downstairs. Clearly Elrich was not averse to wall paintings.

"That's exactly what I was thinking!" said Alicia, and for the first time I saw her smile.

I stepped outside for a minute and put in a call to my favorite faux finisher and mural painter. Years ago, Yuri Andropov had done a lot of wall finishes for Turner Construction, but ever since the Tuscan fad passed, I couldn't give him as much work as before. But whenever we needed wood graining or marbling done in old Victorian homes, Yuri was our go-to guy.

He asked me to send him some photos of the work sites along with measurements and said he would come up with some designs that were historically appropriate, though he was as dismayed as I at my description of a Victorian envelope for a Spanish interior. We decided on a few full-scale murals for the main rooms and then smaller decorative accents for others.

In addition, I mentioned that I might have a fresco job coming up for the Wakefield project. Yuri was particularly excited about that: There wasn't a lot of modern demand for true fresco painting.

While I had my phone out, I made a call to Raul to see how our San Francisco projects were progressing. There were a few small headaches, but nothing that couldn't be dealt with over the phone. Then I checked in with Stan, who gave me the office report—he was hard at work figuring out how the accounting was going to make payroll this Friday to all of Nolan's men as well as our own.

And finally I called Dad, who didn't answer the call but texted me: *Stop calling and get back to work. LOL.*

I returned to what was left of the sherry-hour crowd secure in the knowledge that there was no way I would make it through a formal dinner with these folks. Much to Alicia's thoroughly predictable consternation, I begged off the meal and finally managed to slip away. She suggested I grab a ready-made item from the snack bar, but just as I'd prophesied, I had eaten so many of the delectable hors d'oeuvres that I wasn't hungry.

"You're a better man than I am, sitting through dinner with that crowd," I said as Graham walked me back to my room.

"I'm still trying to get a handle on all these personalities. Besides . . . if this Scottish character is right, then one of them might be responsible for McCall's death."

"Just promise to tell me what they're saying behind my back."

"Mel, I know I'm sounding like the voice of doom, but if Pete didn't kill McCall, then we're talking about something much more serious. Someone who not only set out to kill McCall, but who knew enough about the workings of the jobsite, and all of our movements, to do it in such a way as to implicate Pete Nolan."

"Good point," I said, stifling a yawn.

"No, I don't think you're getting my point. My point is that if it wasn't Pete, then you may be in trouble. As usual."

I twisted my mouth a little, trying to think how to respond to that. Of course I knew Graham was right: My being in trouble did seem to be "as usual" lately. I wasn't sure why I could see ghosts, and why they were so often connected to scenes of violent death. But see them, I could; and connected, they were.

Still, I was becoming accustomed to my new status quo; it wasn't freaking me out anymore. I thought of a cartoon that Stan had taped to his computer in Turner Construction's home office. The first panel showed three people panicking as they fell into a bottomless pit; the second panel showed the same three characters sitting back and relaxing—one had brought out her knitting—after six months of falling into the bottomless pit.

In other words, a person could get used to just about anything after a while.

So perhaps I was becoming resigned to my fate. Apparently, I was meant to become embroiled in renovating historic houses, negotiating with their resident ghosts, doing my best to unmask murderers, and when my work was done, riding off into the sunset with a handsome man on my arm, just like the woman on the cover of *Keeper of the Castle*.

I wondered if Graham would be willing to pose shirtless for me. . . .

Given the grim look on his face, I doubted it.

Chapter Eleven

The next day, I was going over supply orders with Tony in the trailer when we heard a commotion outside.

Oh, boy. I had wondered how long it would take for the ghosts to wreak havoc.

But it wasn't ghosts. Instead, Alicia had outdone herself. Under the shed, but beyond the reach of the stone dust, two long conference tables had been set up with urns of coffee and tea, tubs of iced sodas and sports drinks, and covered platters of fruit and crackers, chips and energy bars. Large red coolers held granola and yogurt, hard-boiled eggs, and sandwiches galore.

One comment to Ellis Elrich, and the crew was no longer arguing over stolen food, and I was a hero. Amazing.

Alicia hovered over the tables, straightening things every time one of the guys took something. She seemed nervous around them at first, but relaxed and blushed prettily as they politely thanked her.

"This is incredible, Alicia," I said. "It looks great."

She shrugged.

Biting into a sandwich as big as his head, Tony thanked Alicia, then went to check on the reinforcement rods I had ordered installed at the mouth of the refectory. I lingered with Alicia for a moment, pouring myself a cup of coffee.

"So, I was wondering," I said, oh so casual-like. "Ellis mentioned you had an audio recording from the surveillance system at the time of Larry McCall's murder."

She blinked.

"Do you suppose I could listen to it?"

"Why in the world would you want to?"

I wasn't sure, exactly. "I thought maybe it could tell me something—"

"Why would it tell you something? The police have already listened to the tapes—there was no video, just a gray screen, and the audio seems to have come from some other place."

"Have the tapes been ruined before, at other times? Or did it happen only when Larry McCall was murdered?"

"It does happen from time to time. It's probably because we're so remote, up here on the hill. Stray radio waves, is what the detective said."

I had a little experience with "stray radio waves." Sometimes they were neither stray nor generated by a radio. Sometimes spirits were able to make themselves heard through such devices. I had seen the Lady in Red when I discovered Larry McCall's body; maybe the tape hadn't been erased on purpose, but her energy interfered with the surveillance tape, somehow. And if so, maybe I could make out what she was saying. It was a long shot, but as an "up-and-coming ghost buster," I thought I should check it out.

"It's unintelligible," said Alicia.

"Do you know if the police sent it to be analyzed in a lab? By sound editors?"

She frowned. "I don't think so. Detective Bernardino said it was worthless."

"Did he take it with him, or ask for a copy?"

"No."

"Could—"

My request was cut off by the unnerving sound of men shouting. Workers were streaming out of the mouth of the chapel.

"What is it?" I asked, grabbing Tony by the arm as he ran by.

"I . . ." His eyes shifted to the building behind me. I looked around but didn't see anything beyond the stone walls.

"Did you see something?" I urged. "What was it?"

He swallowed audibly. "If I didn't know better, I'd say it was some guy out of *Highlander*, with a sword and . . ." He trailed off with a few choice swearwords. He took his hard hat off with one hand and ran the other through his sweaty locks.

Highlander? Not my Lady in Red, then.

"You sure it wasn't . . . ?" Could Kieran be responsible for some kind of trick? He'd seemed harmless enough in the pub, but was it possible he was orchestrating costumed protesters to scare the hell out of the workers? "One of the protesters, maybe? Some of them wear kilts."

"I swear, Mel, it wasn't my imagination. I know it sounds crazy, but I wasn't the only one who saw . . ."

"I believe you. Just tell me exactly what you saw, and where. And how—was it there waiting for you?"

"We were here." On the blueprints, he pointed to

demonstrate the spot near the mouth of the refectory. "The men were putting in those reinforcement rods, like you asked us to. But then a few of us were checking out the other side, near that round room. I kept feeling like something was behind me, kinda like that tingling you get sometimes when you're being watched? And then there was that noise—that's why I say he was like out of the *Highlander* movie, because before we saw anything, we heard the sword as he took it out of its whaddayacallit? The sheaf?"

"Sheath."

"Right. And then this . . . yell—it was terrible. Before we could react, he came running at us full-bore, sword drawn."

I tried to process this. I didn't get far before Tony continued.

"And as we were running, I looked behind me, and he . . . disappeared."

"As in, he hid?"

"No. He disappeared. Into thin air. This was no protester in costume, Mel. It's happened before—it's something about that round room. That's when it happens, when we're doing something in that area."

"Every time? It's always the round room?"

"Not every time, but that's the only place guys have seen . . . it. Or him, or whatever."

"All right. Go get yourself something to drink, and take ten. I'm going to check it out."

"Mel, *don't*. Seriously."

"It's okay. I'm a professional."

I put on a hard hat, then grabbed a big flashlight in case I needed to bop someone over the head.

Who was I kidding? Not once had I managed to adequately defend myself in a crisis situation. Especially

considering the course of my life lately, I kept intending
to take a self-defense class, but there were only so many
hours in a day and I was already making time for a ghost-
busting class. Dad's Glock was hidden in my bedroom up
at Elrich's house, of course, because though I wanted to
have it nearby in scary situations, its mere presence gave
me the willies. After all, once we all started running
around with guns, civilization as we knew it was surely
coming to an end. Then again . . .

There was a sound.

I halted and tried to quiet my ragged breathing. What
was that?

Caught up in my thoughts, I hadn't been paying attention to my surroundings. I was still in the main chapel,
nearing the sacristy. The arched windows and stone walls
looked ludicrously out of place with the new cement
floor, at least until the stone was laid. There was an
echoey gloom in here, making me think of the monks
that had passed through, the legions of people seeking
sanctuary within these walls, the wars and suffering this
place had witnessed.

Resolve. Ghosts were merely remnants of humans, I
intoned. Humans in the next dimension. Often confused,
yearning, trying to attend to unfinished business.

They weren't actually out to kill a person.

I rubbed the gold ring on the chain around my neck
and thought about my mother, and her mother before her.

As quietly as possible in my heavy work boots, I started
walking again, passing through a series of cramped chambers, heading for the refectory. As I moved through a low
stone doorway, I paused and listened.

Sure enough, I heard something. But it wasn't a bloodcurdling Highland yell. Or the Lady in Red's heartbroken weeping. It was a sigh.

An audible sigh.

I inched around the side of the doorway antechamber, peering around the carved stone edge.

A man was sitting at the bottom of the stairs. He was powerfully built, wearing a tunic and a kilt and carrying a sword. A yellow-and-black-plaid tartan was slung over one shoulder.

He was leaning over, holding his head in his large hands. Even in the dim light I could see a nasty scar running the length of the back of one hand.

He leaped up.

Then came the singing of his sword echoing off the stone walls as he pulled it from his sheath in one smooth move.

My heart was hammering in my chest, and it was all I could do not to wet my pants right then and there. So much for my big talk about getting used to dealing with ghosts. I braced myself, forcing myself not to run away. If he charged me, I would stand my ground. Perhaps that would confuse him enough to make him talk to me.

But he didn't charge. At the last instant, he seemed to check himself. He tilted his head, and a frown of concentration spread across his broad brow. He was a giant of a man, especially considering he came from a time when people were much smaller than today. He had another scar on one cheek and a puckered one across his chin, which gave him a slightly lopsided countenance.

"I'm, uh . . . Hello," I began, then cleared my throat.

"Who are ye?"

"I was about to ask you the same thing."

"You're a lass."

"Yes."

"I thought at first you were a man."

"I get that a lot."

He frowned again, then approached me. Walking slowly, deliberately, he held his sword at the ready. His eyes flickered left and right, making sure I was alone, that this wasn't an ambush of some sort. Then his gaze returned to me. His eyes were dark, and though I could barely see, they seemed lit with something, as though an internal fire. Something otherworldly. Mesmerizing.

Fear gnawed at my innards, and I forced myself to stand very still as he walked all the way around me, studying me.

When I finally wrested my gaze from his, I realized the rest of him was fading in and out. The image was perfectly clear one moment, ethereal the next. At least he was appearing to me normally, I thought, and not merely out of the corner of my eye, like the other spectral denizen of these stones. It drove me nuts when that happened.

Finally, he returned to stand in front of me. He sheathed his sword, and I relaxed. Theoretically a ghost sword couldn't hurt me. But I didn't want to put that theory to the test.

"What strange sort of lass are ye?"

Hoo boy. That was a doozy of a conversation starter. "I'm Mel Turner."

"Turner? English?"

"American. It's a . . . different time. What's your name?"

"Donnchadh MacPhaidein."

"Sorry, Donka . . . ?"

"Donnchadh," he repeated. "American? I dinnae understand. This place . . . Naught looks familiar."

"I know. Let's talk, and I'll try to explain."

There was a sound. A boot scraping on cement. turned to see Tony in the vestibule.

Before I could say anything, Donnchadh transformed, a look of fury on his face. He unsheathed his sword and let out a bloodcurdling yell as he ran toward the sacristy.

Tony turned and ran in the opposite direction, screaming.

I ran after them, back through the series of chambers and into the chapel. The image of the Highland warrior disappeared as we ran out into the sunlight.

A couple of the men were gathered around, asking what was wrong. Tony shook off their help. But once the men dispersed, he drew me aside.

"I don't think I can take this much longer," said Tony. "Seriously, Mel. I know you're new, and I hate to leave you in the lurch, but I gotta say, this job ain't worth it. One of these days that . . . that *thing* is going to catch me, and I don't want to be here when that day arrives. I got kids."

I didn't point out the faulty logic of his statement; I got the gist. But I would be up a creek if I lost a good foreman like Tony; most of the guys on the site didn't really know me, and therefore didn't trust me. The tone on a jobsite was set by the foreman, and his presence allowed me a certain flexibility that I would otherwise lose. Not to mention, if we were going to get this job done in time for the big opening event, I couldn't afford to lose a single man.

"Look, I don't want to overstate the case," I said, "but I have a certain expertise in these areas."

"What areas?"

"The, um . . . ghost areas."

He stared at me for a long moment.

"This isn't my first rodeo, as they say."

Tony nodded slowly. "Is that why Elrich hired you for this job?"

First Kieran suggested I was hired because I'm a woman, and now Tony was saying I was hired because I was a ghost whisperer. Apparently, the thought that I was hired because I was talented didn't cross anyone's mind.

Irked, I said: "I'm well qualified to bring this project to completion, on time and on budget. Whatever other qualifications I have are just frosting on top."

"Okaaay," Tony said, clearly neither believing me, nor caring. "So, are you going to talk to that . . . thing? Tell him to lay off so we can get this job done?"

"Yeah. Sure. I'll get right on that."

"Right now?"

"No, um . . . not right now. I've got . . . a few details I need to take care of first."

"It's almost lunchtime."

"Right. Can't neglect one's nutrition," I heard myself saying. "Watch and learn, Tony. Watch and learn."

And I strode off, hoping he would be temporarily appeased with the "learn, young grasshopper" school of avoiding the damned issue.

The issue, of course, was that I was scared. I needed a little time to think before chatting with that Highland warrior again. At the very least, I needed something to eat. This ghost-talking business could take the stuffing out of a person.

I decided to visit with Dog for a few minutes. Usually, I didn't invite him to sit in my lap, because at fifty-plus pounds, Dog wasn't anyone's idea of a lapdog. But at the moment I could use a little canine consolation. I sat on the ground and let him make himself comfortable, burying my face in the scruff of his neck. I could hear a couple of the men arguing about their lunches, while Tony tried to calm them down and suggested they grab sandwiches from the table.

"You okay?" Graham asked as he walked up to us.

"Why wouldn't I be okay?"

"Tell me what happened."

"I just had an interesting chat with a heavily armed ghost."

He looked startled. Graham had known me long before I started seeing ghosts, and more recently, he had followed me into enough haunted attics and basements to understand that I wasn't crazy, that there were thin veils separating our world from others, and that at times I could see beyond them. He knew all this, and he backed me up, but he still found it unsettling.

"What happened?"

"Let's go visit Pete Nolan," I said, scooching Dog out of my lap. "I'll give you the details on the way."

Graham drove as I described what I had seen, and the truncated little chat I'd had with Donnchadh. As I spoke, I realized that I hadn't actually gleaned anything useful from my interaction with the ghost: whether there was a treasure he was protecting, what and where it might be, what was up with the Lady in Red, and if he knew anything about Larry McCall's demise. I sat back in my seat, deflated.

"Hey, buck up there, junior ghost buster. I'm sure you'll get another chance. Surely he'll try to kill someone again soon, and you can go in with a list of questions written down on a piece of paper, like you're supposed to do when you go in for a doctor's visit. That way you won't lose your cool."

"Very funny. I never *asked* to be a ghost buster, you know."

Graham chuckled. "So, not to change the subject, but heres' one of those interesting—dare I say awkward?—couples' questions we've never quite gotten to: Have you ever been to jail?"

"Sure I have. How about you?"

"Never."

"Never? Not even to visit friends?"

"I guess my friends aren't as interesting as yours."

"I thought you and Pete went way back."

"I would call Pete more an acquaintance than a friend."

Ever since I'd started tripping over bodies and seeing ghosts, I'd been to jail a few times. As a visitor, of course. Heck, not long ago I'd even visited a prisoner in San Quentin, a maximum-security prison. So while I wasn't exactly an old hand at this sort of thing, I had some idea of what to expect.

Graham and I went through the processing of visitors at the county jail where Pete was being held, and half an hour later were seated at a table across from him.

"I never killed anyone," Pete said. His eyes were red-rimmed, he was ashen, and even his blond flyaway hair seemed subdued. Dark gold stubble covered his chin. "I was framed."

"What happened that day?" Graham asked.

"McCall's been obsessed with the mortar we're using, and with reinforcement of the stones."

"That's pretty important in earthquake country," I put in.

"Yeah, I get it," said Pete, agitated. "I'm not an idiot. But we've been doing a few experimental things, and this is a historic structure—it's not like everything's easy, or evident. And McCall was obsessed with that round room; you know the one I'm talking about?"

I nodded.

"That place has been a damned thorn in my side from the beginning. It just wasn't fitting in anywhere, but Libole was obsessed with it, too, wants it done a very particular way. It already fell apart once, on a day when McCall dropped by the jobsite without warning, of course." He shook his head. "This whole project has been a disaster from day one."

"What do you mean, it fell apart?"

"Just what I said. I don't know if it was sabotage, or what. It was put together, and then it wasn't. And we've got a whole pile of stones supposed to go on top of it—it's not a one-story room; it's a damned tower. But we can't get the thing to stand up. Go explain that one, why don'tcha?"

"Do you have any idea who might be responsible for sabotage like that?"

"The protesters, most likely."

"And do you think . . . ? Could they have been responsible for what happened to McCall, as well?"

"I'd sure like to say yes, but I can't figure why. If I were a betting man, I'd say Ellis Elrich is behind what happened. You mark my words: The man won't stop at anything until he gets what he wants."

"But why would he kill the inspector?"

"First off, a man like Elrich doesn't get his hands dirty doin' his own killing. He has minions for that sort of thing."

I sat back in my chair. "Look, I know the man's charismatic, but are you trying to say he can order his followers to kill? Isn't that . . . a bit much?"

"I think you'd be surprised at how far some of his groupies would go to win his favor. For instance, I'd check into that Alicia woman."

"What about her?"

"For one thing, that's not her real name."

"No?" I was thinking perhaps Mrs. Danvers, after the sinister housekeeper from the classic Gothic novel *Rebecca*, but that was just me.

"I looked her up. Until a few years ago, there was no such person. It's like she invented herself out of the blue. Doesn't that seem suspicious to you?"

"Maybe. Or maybe she just got married and changed her name."

"Anyway, even if it wasn't her, Elrich has plenty of money to make things like this happen. He could have one of his people do the job, maybe Buzz or Tweedle-dum and Dumber—those bodyguards of his—and then send them away to live out their lives in luxury on an island somewhere, while I'm trapped in here, takin' the fall for somethin' I didn't do."

"I still don't get Elrich's motive for killing the building inspector," Graham said.

"Simple: McCall was going to shut down the project. He didn't agree with the rest of the guys in the permit office, who are no doubt getting paid off by Elrich. And McCall, I dunno, he was going on about having found something new about this project, something that was going to blow the lid off this thing."

"That makes it sound like some kind of conspiracy," I said. "We're just talking building permits, aren't we?"

"All I know for certain is that I didn't do it. Hell, I'd been dealing with that pain-in-the-ass Larry McCall for months. Why would I suddenly snap and hit him over the head with a bag of *mortar*, of all things?

"Listen, we went into the round room so's I could show him the mortar mix, but none of the latex admix was there. McCall wanted to see the documentation that we'd purchased it. I went to the trailer to get it, and that's when someone killed him. I wasn't even there."

"I heard there was no surveillance film from around the time of the crime."

"Yeah," Pete said with a bitter chuckle. "Ain't that a

kick in the pants? According to what my lawyer gathered from the police, the security tape was erased, or intercepted or something. You think I'm smart enough to figure out how to do somethin' like that?" He looked at us like we were his lifeline. "Please help me. I didn't do it, and that tape will show I didn't do it. Without it, I'm screwed."

"So you think the killer ruined the tape to keep his identity secret."

"Or *her* identity. Like I said earlier, Elrich has a lot of female groupies," Pete said. "Starting with that personal assistant of his, Alicia Withers."

Chapter Twelve

I fell asleep while Graham drove us back to the mansion. What with getting up at five, working twelve hours, and sherry hour in the evening, I lost consciousness anytime I got horizontal or was a passenger in a moving vehicle of any kind. Such a hot, romantic property.

When we pulled to a stop, I roused myself.

But we weren't back at Wakefield. We were at the Marin County Civic Center. I recognized the building without having to see a sign. Designed by Frank Lloyd Wright, the Marin County Civic Center is a national and state historic monument; it is odd and futuristic-looking enough to have served as the locale for the movie *Gattaca*, starring Ethan Hawke and Uma Thurman.

"Might as well ask a few questions of the permit office," said Graham in response to my questioning look. "Don't look at me like that. It was only a matter of time until you begged me to come here with you."

I had been to the building before, of course; most local architecture geeks had made at least one pilgrimage. Frank Lloyd Wright had railed against "excessive verticality," and believed in following the organic topography and contours of the land. The Marin County Civic Center lived up to these ideals: Its buff walls and blue roof reflected the golden hills and the sky; and the building was long and horizontal, built over the site's natural gullies and creeks.

We parked and passed through the gold gates into the building. Corridors featured second-story catwalks overlooking small gardens and fountains. Finally, Graham stopped in front of a door marked MARIN COUNTY BUILDING DEPARTMENT.

Inside, the room did not live up to Wright's vision, I felt sure. It was full of beige desks and standard office chairs, acoustic paneled ceilings and fluorescent lights. The men wore white short-sleeved business shirts and ties; the only splash of color was provided by a woman standing at a file cabinet in an orange top and a paisley miniskirt.

A framed poster of an eagle maintained that leadership was the result of "unquestionable integrity," and another featuring a windmill focused on the importance of accountability and warned of the consequences of avoidance. Finally, a cute little calico kitty held on to a branch with one tiny paw, and under it was written, "Hang in there, Baby."

Building inspector Don Stickley recognized Graham, who introduced me. Stickley was pleasant to an extreme, which did make a person wonder.

"I don't mean to speak ill of the dead, but McCall was a real hard-ass," Don said. "A stickler for the law. I tried to tell him, the law is only as good as the latest technological invention. It's true that we aren't the ones who set policy, but if Ellis Elrich is willing to foot the bill for trying to implement environmental advances, then we here at the department should support that. I mean, this is *Marin*. Who better to be at the forefront of green technology? And sometimes it's as simple as the Saltillo tile Graham brought in."

"What about the tile?"

"I'll show you." He went into the other room and brought back a terra-cotta Saltillo tile. "Graham treated this tile with linseed oil instead of the standard penetrating sealer. For weeks now we've tried dropping Coke, coffee, everything on it." He knocked on it and shook his head. "Nothing gets through that sucker. I wouldn't have believed it if I didn't see it."

"It's like the straw bale houses," added one of Stickley's colleagues. "A fellow's building a house with straw bale covered in waddle and daub, using clay mud with sand and hay as binders."

"In the old days they used horse hair," I said.

"Right. Really, whatever was handy could be used as a binder. You protect that stuff from the rain with extended eaves on the roof, and it will last for centuries. Once it finally starts to deteriorate, it melds back into the earth—unlike concrete, which goes into landfills unless it's ground up and reused. That stuff's nasty."

By now every person in the office had joined our circle, talking about their favorite green technologies. Graham was playing it deliberately cool, but he wasn't fooling me: He was as excited as I was—even more so. To find building inspectors this invested in green technology made a person hopeful for the future. I guessed it was like they said: Marin really was different.

"Hey, Graham," said Stickley. "I got a joke for you:

How many official green-accredited professionals does it take to screw in a lightbulb?"

"How many?"

"Four: one to tell you how to earn your official green points, one to change it, one to document the change, and one to file for certification."

I didn't get it, but the office staff burst into laughter.

"Good one," said Graham. "How many building inspectors does it take to change a lightbulb?"

"How many?"

"Change? Never!"

The men guffawed.

One more piped up: "How many salvage contractors does it take to change a lightbulb?"

"Two: one to change it and one to sell the broken bulb as aggregate landscaping."

They were laughing so hard now they were wiping their eyes.

After a few more minutes of chatter, the inspectors drifted off and went back to work. Only Stickley remained.

"I really am sorry about McCall. We all are. All I can tell you is that he recently came back from San Francisco excited about something."

"Excited as in agitated, upset? Or happy?"

"It was hard to tell with McCall. He thought he had something on the folks at Wakefield. You know, a couple of us here tried to take over the project, but there was nothing doing. McCall and that clipboard, you couldn't pry it out of his hands."

This would be the Clipboard of Doom, I would expect. Whatever happened to it? I wondered whether Detective Bernardino would tell me if it had been found with the body, and if so, what it might have revealed.

"The really sad part is McCall's daughter was set to get married in January. He was excited about the wedding. And his wife's a real nice gal, too. She came and got his things just yesterday, brought us cookies as a going-away sentiment. I guess she bakes a lot."

"Could I have her address? Maybe I could go pay my condolences."

He wrote it on the back of his business card.

"Please say hello from all of us if you talk to her. McCall was a real pain in the ass, but still . . . what a shock."

"Suppose there's a taco truck around here?" I asked Graham as we drove out of the parking lot. "We still haven't had lunch."

"This is Marin. Probably I could find some organic greens for you to munch on."

I smiled. "As long as we follow it up with some good coffee."

"So, did that visit tell us anything?"

"There's a missing clipboard, and McCall thought he had discovered something. Stop me if this is too crazy, but do you suppose McCall was onto the treasure Kieran mentioned?"

"It's possible," Graham said. "Hard to imagine where that treasure would be hidden, though."

"There's the warehouse Kieran mentioned. I was going to ask Florian about it, but he didn't show up to sherry hour last night."

"I haven't seen him since before I went to LA," said Graham.

"I suppose that might be on purpose. I mean, maybe McCall learned about the secret treasure, Libole killed him because of it, then ran off and sold it for a million dollars, and is even now living on an island somewhere in the South Pacific. *Ta-da*, murder solved, just that easy."

"Why the South Pacific?"

"Because that's where I'd go if I was on the lam with a million bucks."

"Not Paris?"

"That's the first place they'd look for me."

Graham smiled. "But if the treasure isn't in the building, what is the ghost protecting?"

"Darn you, Graham Donovan, for asking the really hard questions. I don't know. . . . The ghost seemed confused. I'm not convinced he *knows* what he's protecting. I guess I should add that one to my list of questions for him."

"Let's go tonight after sundown."

"Let's?"

"I'll go with you."

"I don't think Donnchadh is fond of men."

"Is he fond of women?"

"Not particularly, but he didn't try to kill me. I think we had a connection. Anyway . . . I really don't think you should go in with me. How about you wait at the entrance?"

"I don't like the thought of sending you in there alone."

"I appreciate that, but I'm not sure you understand exactly how scary this character can be. He seemed willing to talk to me, but was only interested in killing anyone with a Y chromosome."

Graham seemed to be mulling that over. "All right. I'll stay in the entrance. But if I hear anything out of the ordinary, I'm coming in after you, ghostly sword or no."

That night Graham and I made short work of sherry

hour and then headed down to the building site. But before I could even do my pre-ghost-gathering resolve ritual, we heard a woman's scream coming from inside the chapel.

This was no ghostly wail; this was human.

We ran in, following the sound, and found Kieran kneeling on the ground, face wet with tears. Harper was in his arms.

"Help. She fainted." He looked as though he was about to drop her.

"What are you *doing* here?" I demanded. Adrenaline surged through me, making me angry. "Breaking into a man's property and putting his daughter in danger is no way to make your case for repatriation, you know."

"I know that. I'm sorry," Kieran said, and he really did look remorseful. "I didn't mean to. . . . I thought we could look around, that's all. But I certainly didn't mean to find a ghost."

"Is she okay? What happened?"

"She—*we*—saw a . . . I don't even know what we saw. There was something. . . . We heard a woman crying, and it was coming closer, and we both started crying, and then there was a man with a sword and . . . Harper fainted."

"Let's get her home and put her to bed," I said with another glare at Kieran. "Poor thing."

"I . . ." Kieran looked at us, hapless, as Graham gently hoisted Harper over his shoulder in a fireman's grip. "Please tell her I'm sorry."

"I will. But seriously, Kieran. This is no way to go about reasoning with Ellis Elrich."

The eerie notes of a ghostly flute accompanied us as we made our way back up the hill, the music floating on the misty night air.

*   *   *

Murphy's Law of Construction states that when disaster strikes, the client is sure to be on-site. A job can go months without a problem, but the moment the client sets foot on the jobsite, workers suddenly put their boots through windows, painters spill buckets of paint, and scaffolding folds like a house of cards. So I should have known that something would happen when I saw Ellis Elrich was scheduled to do a site tour.

But I was feeling pretty confident. With Elrich's ample resources at my disposal, things were developing fast. I'd been on-site for less than a week, but foundations had been poured and metal skeletons had been constructed. Guest accommodations were roughed out, and the kitchen power sources had been finagled. We were still working on drilling all the access points for the plumbing and electrical, but the guys now had their method perfected.

Wakefield was starting to take shape.

It was Saturday, but given the push on this project, we were working six days a week. Only Sunday would leave these stones in peace to their ghosts. Graham and I had an appointment at one to go talk with Jeanine McCall, the widow of the building inspector. Maybe she would be able to tell us if he'd discovered something unusual, oh, say, maybe a mysterious treasure, something important enough to inspire someone to kill her husband. It was a little hard to believe . . . but then again, people had been killed over much, much less.

Elrich wanted to show the site to two of his business cronies. Harper—who hadn't spoken a word to me since she woke up on Graham's shoulder last night—and Vernon were walking silently and sullenly behind, and Alicia was taking up the rear, her notebook in hand.

The city had sent out a new building inspector, Don Stickley, the man I'd met at the Building Department with Graham. Elrich was impressed to discover we were old buddies as I began to lead the group on a tour of the grounds.

"Let me show you the latex admix we're using in the mortar," I began.

Suddenly, there was a great crashing sound, and a plume of dust rose before us in the midday air.

Chapter Thirteen

"Was anyone inside?" I demanded as I reached the scene.

It was the round room, where the men had been working on an exterior steel skeleton for added support. The interior stones had collapsed.

"No, I don't think so," said Miguel.

"Are you absolutely sure?"

"I . . . I'm pretty sure."

"Okay, until everyone's accounted for, let's proceed as if someone's inside. Miguel, gather everyone and take a head count; use the payroll list as a guide. Tony, you and I will implement procedures."

Forty-five tense minutes later, covered in mortar and stone dust, Tony and I were able to attest that no one had been trapped inside.

Just then Graham arrived to take me to our appointment with Jeanine McCall.

"What happened?"

"Just a little . . . building collapse. No one was hurt, and the stones can be used again, of course. That's the good news."

"And the bad news?"

"A room made of stone imploded for no apparent reason." Our eyes held.

"So, I take it you're not going to make it over to talk with Jeanine McCall?"

I shook my head. "I wish I could, but . . ." I trailed off as Elrich walked up, his entourage not far behind him.

"Dare I even ask?" said Elrich, displaying remarkable outward calm. Almost unnatural calm.

"No one was hurt," I said.

"That's the important thing. Do we know what happened?"

"Not yet," I said with a shake of my head. "I know Larry McCall had some questions about the composition of the mortar. It's possible it wasn't adequate, or perhaps there was a small trembler or something that tipped the scales."

"An earthquake?" Vernon scoffed. "I didn't feel a thing."

"Sometimes they're too subtle to feel if you're walking around, but—"

"I'm really quite sensitive," he said, looking around at his companions as though searching for confirmation. Harper rolled her eyes, Alicia kept her gaze on her notebook, and Don Stickley just kept staring straight ahead.

"I think I should wait and do a walk-through on Monday," said the replacement building inspector. "There's no sense in assessing things right at the moment."

You could say that again. On the other hand, Stickley was well within his rights to issue us a stop order until the cause of the collapse was discovered and documented. He was being extremely accommodating.

"Well," said Graham. "Sorry to watch the disaster and run, but I have to go."

"A solar emergency?" asked Elrich.

"I'm going to call on McCall's widow, pay my respects."

"That's good of you. Please, if it seems appropriate, give her my regards as well."

I walked Graham to his truck, which wasn't far from where Dog was tied up. He made a slight detour to pet the pup.

"I wish I could go with you." I heard someone shouting my name, and looked over my shoulder at a group of men, awaiting instructions. "I *really* wish I could go with you."

"No problem. I've got it handled. McCall's place is near a hydroponics store I wanted to check out, anyway, so I can kill two birds with one stone."

"I hate that expression."

"More than one way to skin a cat."

"That's worse."

He grinned. "Softie. Surely there's a similarly gruesome phrase regarding our canine friends?"

"Don't even dare."

He pulled on one of my corkscrew curls, patted Dog, gave me a wink, and strode off toward his truck.

The rest of the day was spent cleaning up and regrouping. When this sort of thing happened on the jobsite, people got jumpy. Especially when there was no obvious cause.

I'd asked Tony to take over for a few minutes and was walking up the path in search of my phone charger, which I'd left in my room. I also needed a few moments away from the site. It had been a hell of a day.

Off to my right, I saw something in my peripheral vision. I felt a wave of anxiety until I realized the man didn't disappear when I looked at him directly. It was Elrich, intent on a task before him.

He was in the garden, in between the pool and the helipad. I watched as he chose one smooth, spherical river rock about the size of a hamburger, held it for a long moment in his graceful hands, and turned it over thoughtfully. Finally, he crouched and very carefully placed it atop three stacked stones. I watched, fully expecting the little tower to fall; it was like a game I used to play with Caleb where we set down pieces one after another until everything came tumbling down in a rush.

But when Elrich carefully removed his hands, stood, and backed away, the rock tower remained standing.

"I wish I could get the Wakefield stones to stand up that easily," I said.

Ellis turned around as though expecting me. He smiled. "Well, I imagine when you put up those Wakefield stones, they'll stay that way for generations. Whereas this tiny cairn? It's ephemeral. It could topple over anytime, or be knocked over by an animal or the wind."

"What's it for? I mean . . . does it have meaning, or is it just a way to pass the time, like whittling?"

Now he chuckled. "I use it to settle my nerves, so yes, I suppose it's a little like whittling. Though, in the old days, cairns had meaning, as markers in the road, or to mark the summit of a mountain, that sort of thing."

"They're called cairns? Sounds Scottish." Now that I was an expert and all.

He nodded. "It's an old Scottish tradition to carry a stone with you when you climb a mountain, and to set the stone upon the cairn at the top. They were sometimes used to mark a grave, as well, and there's an old Gaelic blessing *Cuiridh mi clach air do charn*. I'll put a stone on your cairn."

"You speak Gaelic?"

"I like to think so, but an actual Gaelic speaker would probably disagree. I spent a little time in Scotland—a remarkable time, actually—and I have an almost freakish ability to memorize quotes. You may have noticed that—it's almost like a verbal tic. I'm trying to break myself of the habit. I fear it has to do with a lack of faith in my own thoughts, the need to use references to back up my ideas."

I didn't know how to respond to that.

"Another tradition holds that Highland clans used to place stones in a pile when they went off to battle. Upon returning, they'd each take one stone—the remainder signified the men who hadn't survived. Then those were used to make a cairn to honor the dead."

"That's very . . . evocative."

"But why am I telling you all this? You're an anthropologist. You probably know much more than I do about this sort of thing."

"I used to be an anthropologist, but that was a while ago. And I never studied Scotland. In fact, about all I can think of with regards to Scotland is scotch, golf, and the Loch Ness monster. And plaid, of course. I'm really more prepared to discuss the stainless steel flashing needed as a capillary break in order to forestall moisture and efflorescence in your stone walls."

He smiled again and held my gaze for a moment.

"I did want to ask you one thing, if you don't mind," I said.

"Please."

"There's an antiquities fellow, named Kieran Lachaidh, who says this building was wrongfully taken from Scotland."

"He's been in touch," Ellis said with a nod. "I discussed it with Florian, who has been talking directly to the representatives of the Scottish government. He assures me they don't want the building; in fact, they're already designing a golf course on the land where it was located. Mr. Lachaidh is a lone wolf on this. I'm not sure why he's fixated on it."

"He says he's from there," I said. "He used to play on the ruins with his brothers when he was a kid."

"Perhaps it's as simple as that," said Ellis, looking down at the jobsite. "Nostalgia is a powerful thing, and those stones can grab your heart. They certainly did mine."

"I've heard people mention you had a spiritual awakening in Scotland?"

He nodded. "It was after my daughter's death. I was distraught, and searching for meaning. Something about hiking those hills and going from isle to isle . . . I don't know what it was, but I found peace. Finally. I was sitting on the ruins of Wakefield, and I could feel the peace settle over me. It's a very special place."

No encounters with weeping women or homicidal Highland warriors, I was guessing.

"If he contacts you again," continued Ellis, "tell him Wakefield is here to stay."

"All right. He also mentioned a treasure that might be hidden somewhere. . . ."

"His lawyer mentioned that, as well. I had never heard of such a thing, but if you find anything that looks like a national treasure, please let me know. We can talk about sending it back to the people of Scotland if and when you unearth such a thing."

"That sounds fair. Okay, I should let you get back to your meditation. Nice talking with you."

"And, Mel? Things fall apart now and then. Usually it's more figuratively than literally, but all the same. You know what Winston Churchill said: 'If you're going through hell, keep going.'"

Not half an hour after I returned to work on the monastery, three men came running out of the front entrance.

I blew out an exasperated breath. This was becoming a daily event. What with imploding rooms and all, it looked like it was time to put my ghost-busting hat squarely on my head and figure this puppy out. Donnchadh had seemed approachable—by me, anyway, as an unarmed woman. And if he was starting to tear down rooms, I needed to find some way to negotiate a truce.

Could Kieran be right? Could there be a curse on this place? Could Donnchadh be guarding something, and was there anything I could do about it? And how did the Lady in Red fit in?

"Tony, why don't you have the guys start packing up? They can go home early today."

Tony looked torn. I was sure he was dying to flee, but he was a decent guy and worried about me going in by myself.

"Really, I'm okay," I said. "I'm just going to try to talk to him, so don't come in after me. I'm hoping I can communicate with him, maybe find a way to bring an end to all this excitement. Keep everyone out of the building, okay?"

This time I took a moment to do it right. My friend and mentor, Olivier, had taught me a method to center myself. I stood for a moment with my eyes closed and did a body scan, feeling my feet attached to the earth, the sun on my face, a soft wind along my skin. I reminded myself: *I am of this physical world, whereas they are not.* I delved deep for compassion. The ghost was a soul. He was confused, upset. And I was one of the few people who might be able to talk to him, and to help.

I walked slowly through the chapel, listening. As before, I stepped as quietly as I could through the series of chambers behind the sacristy, then peeked around the corner.

There he sat on a stone bench, sighing, holding his head in his hands. Donnchadh was one depressed ghost. He reminded me of my first ghost sighting, a man I had known while alive, named Kenneth. Kenneth hadn't done much with his life, and he'd felt bad about it after his death. He sat around moping a lot, like Donnchadh, though without a broadsword. And presumably, this poor fellow had been at this for centuries.

Where was ghostly Prozac when you needed it?

I moved slowly, tentatively calling out, "Hello?"

He sprang up, his eyes burning with an almost demonic fire.

I swallowed hard but stood my ground as he unsheathed his sword and it sang through the air. My heart pounded, and I hoped the sound of my gulp wouldn't echo through these stone walls. I didn't want him to think of me as a threat, but neither did I want him thinking I was afraid of him.

"Donnchadh, right? Remember me? I'm Mel." I forced myself to breathe. "I'm a girl, a . . . lass. A lassie. Like the dog, but not really." I was babbling, and tried to get a grip. "I was hoping to ask you some questions. Maybe you can help me."

He looked angry, and confused. But, as before, he stopped short of trying to run me through with his sword.

I didn't think he actually *could* run me through, but I really didn't want to push that envelope.

This time I got right to the subject: "What is it that you're protecting?"

His eyes narrowed. "What mischief is this? Surely ye know I am guardian of the vessel."

Okay. This was good. Now we were getting somewhere.

"And this vessel would be a, um . . ." I tried to remember the term Kieran had used. "A ciborium?"

"I cannae understand ye."

"Like a chalice? Maybe with a lot of jewels . . . ?"

"Mel?" Graham's voice came from the direction of the chapel. "Mel, where are you?"

Not again. What *was* it with all these men wanting to rescue me?

"Graham!" I called. "Get out!"

The singing of the sword rang out again. Donnchadh's face took on his fierce warrior hue, and he ran toward the chapel, screaming his terrible Highland yell. I ran after him. "Graham, get out of here! Run!"

As I reached the chapel, I heard a thudding noise, and then silence.

Donnchadh had disappeared.

But Graham lay sprawled on the floor.

Chapter Fourteen

"*Graham!* Graham, are you all right?" I ran to kneel beside him. His eyes opened for a moment before they fluttered closed again.

There was blood oozing from a wound on the back of his head. I grabbed for my cell phone, only to abandon it when I remembered these damned stones prevented it from working.

I laid his head down on the cement as gently as I could and ran for the door, yelling the whole way.

Several men had been packing up their gear and climbing into their trucks. They ran to the chapel to help. One grabbed the first-aid kit, and another called 911.

"What happened?" asked Tony. "It was that thing, wasn't it? The ghost?"

"I don't know. I . . ."

"Elrich has a helicopter," Miguel said quietly. "It looks bad."

"Great idea. I'll go outside and call him," said Tony.

As we waited, we did our best to stanch the flow of blood. Graham wasn't responding. Miguel's words rang in my head: "It looks bad."

After an agonizingly long time, Ellis's bodyguards arrived. The men loaded Graham carefully onto a strong board, strapped him down, and carried him as quickly as they could without jostling him. I trotted along behind them, up the hill to the helipad, where the chopper was already warming up.

Ellis met us at the helicopter. "I've called Marin Hospital; they're expecting him. Dr. Petralis is the best in the business for head injuries, and he's on his way. I'm flying him in from LA."

I nodded, unable to speak for fear of crying. I was so grateful I hugged him. Ellis held me close for a moment, then patted my back.

"He'll be in good hands," he yelled so I could hear over the helicopter blades. "Go. I'll take care of everything here."

"Dog—"

"He'll eat well tonight. No worries. And I'll send the men home. We'll suspend work for a day, with pay. Just take care of Graham and let me know what happens."

I'm well schooled in first aid. Construction is a dangerous field, and my father had my sisters and me resuscitating Annie the Dummy when we were still in Girl Scouts—or, in my case, still ducking out of Girl Scouts. So I knew there isn't much to be done for a head injury except stop the bleeding. If the brain swelled, surgeons would have to operate to relieve the pressure before brain damage set in. If the brain didn't swell overmuch, you waited and hoped everything got back to normal once the skull stitched itself back up.

Not that I wasn't grateful for Ellis calling in his head-injury expert, but I already knew it was pretty much that simple. Of course, if Graham was going to need brain surgery, I wanted the best in the world operating on him.

Two hours later, I was pacing the floor in the trauma waiting room when my best friend, Luz Cabrera, walked in.

"Luz? How did you . . . ? I mean . . ."

"You dropped your cell phone at the construction site," she said. "I called to say hi, and Ellis Elrich answered. Could have knocked me over with a feather."

"He told you what happened?"

She nodded. "He said you could probably use a friend right about now. And get this—he offered to send a limo to pick me up. I told him I would drive myself, but he still sent a guy named Buzz with your phone to meet me." She dug around in her expensive purse and handed it to me. "And he says to tell you Buzz will be outside with the limo in case you need a ride somewhere."

She hugged me, and I broke down and cried as soon as her arms were around me.

"What are the doctors saying?" Luz asked after a long while. "Do you have any news?"

I shrugged and tried to pull myself together. "It's pretty much a waiting game at this point. They're watching to see if the brain swells. If it does they'll have to operate."

She nodded. "And if it doesn't . . . ?"

"They can't do much more than wait and see. And send the poor guy for CAT scans and PET scans and a million X-rays. Assuming he heals from the head injury, he'll probably die from radiation sickness."

Luz smiled at my weak attempt at humor.

"Has he . . . ? I mean, is he conscious?"

I sniffed loudly and shook my head. "Not really. He goes in and out, but nothing seems to register. Dr. Petralis says that's par for the course for this sort of thing."

"He a good doctor?"

"He's supposed to be the best. He just arrived and is examining Graham now. Ellis flew him up from LA."

"I tell you what: You are dealing with a better class of client these days. It must be nice to have more money than God."

I nodded, thinking of what Ellis had said to me: that he would trade it all for one more day with his late daughter.

Luz urged me over to a bank of seats that were surprisingly plush and comfortable. On the other side of the large waiting room, an extended family was watching something on the overhead TV, but here it was blessedly absent of people and of the incessant noise of the TV set.

Luz filled a paper cup from the watercooler and brought it to me. I took a long drink and tried to pull myself together. She sat beside me, her arm wrapped around my shoulders. Luz wasn't normally one for physical demonstration; this was a big deal for her.

"So, what happened?" she said softly.

I took a deep, shaky breath, then blew it out slowly. "I'm not exactly sure, but it's possible a ghost scared him so badly he fell and hit his head."

"A ghost?" Luz raised one eyebrow.

Ah, my old friend. Somehow it was more comforting when she looked at me as if I'd lost my mind than when she was uncharacteristically solicitous.

"The men on the crew were scared by something in the cloister. I went in to investigate and found a despondent knight. I mean, I guess he's a knight. A warrior of some sort. I'm not really up on my Scottish history."

"Okaaaaay. And he tried to kill you?"

"No. I think . . . I don't think he's the type to try to kill women."

"Well, at least there's that."

I nodded. "Kieran says he's part of a curse. . . . He carries a broadsword."

"Who's Kieran?"

"A Scottish guy."

"A Scottish ghost guy?"

"No. He's hoping to repatriate the building, or at least the treasure, to Scotland."

"There's a treasure now?" she said, her voice sardonic. "Any chance there are pirates involved?"

"I know it sounds crazy, Luz, but it may be true. I think this ghost may be guarding something."

"Wait a minute. Let's back up for a second. When you told me about taking this job a few days ago, you said the ghost was a woman in red."

"Yes, that's what I saw originally. But now there's a guy."

"A Highland warrior."

"I don't actually know that much about Scottish history. For instance, I have no way of knowing whether he was Highland or Lowland, because I don't even know what that refers to. But the warrior, I'm pretty sure we can go with that. He was covered in scars, and he was huge, and . . ."

"I'm envisioning Mel Gibson in *Braveheart*. Does he have a mullet, too?"

"I didn't notice. But this guy's a *lot* scarier."

"Okay. Let's come back to that. So the ghost went after Graham?"

I nodded. "Donnchadh and I—"

"Who's Donnchadh?"

"The ghost."

"You two are on a first-name basis?"

"We introduced ourselves."

"Well, of course. Death is no excuse for forgetting one's manners."

"We were talking, and then Graham came in looking for me. I can't tell you what it's like when Donnchadh goes after someone—it's a complete transformation. He turns so fierce and charges forward with his sword."

"And then what happened? I thought you always talk a big game about how ghosts can't actually hurt people."

"That's what I thought. What I still think, actually. Maybe . . . I think Donnchadh scared Graham and he lost his footing, and fell and hit his head on the cement floor."

Luz looked thoughtful. "I guess that's possible. It's hard to imagine a man like Graham tripping over his own shoelaces, though. He's gonna be pissed with himself when he wakes up."

I'd had the same thought. Nothing like adding insult to injury.

"The doctor's here," Luz said softly as Dr. Petralis walked in and headed for us. He wore a huge gold Rolex and had a fake tan and slicked-back hair. All in all, he looked like a self-described "swinger," the kind of man who tried to convince women many years younger than himself to be his lucky charm at the Vegas craps tables and then plied them with free drinks.

But I was going to have to trust Ellis on this; the doctor didn't have to be to my taste, just so long as he was the best in the business and could help.

Petralis gave us the lowdown on Graham's condition: As I had thought, this was a wait-and-see situation. So far, surgical intervention was not indicated. But it would take twenty-four to forty-eight hours to know if he was in the clear.

Afterward, we went in to visit Graham, now in a bed in the ICU.

I noticed his eye sockets were swelling and turning blue. "Is that normal?"

"Of course not. A fractured skull is not normal," said Dr. Petralis.

"No, I understand that. I mean, is that normal for a skull fracture?"

"Hard to say."

"I guess I was assuming it was your job for you to say, one way or the other," I said, feeling my ire rising.

Luz stepped in to rescue the situation. "What Mel is asking is: Is swelling around the eye sockets consistent with this sort of head trauma?"

Dr. Petralis looked at Luz with interest.

"Yes. It happens. They might turn blue, then black. We call it panda markings."

"And that means . . . ?"

"It's the result of internal bleeding. Could go either way. It's a bad sign because internal bleeding is never good, but it might mean the blood isn't staying on the brain, which is a good sign. In general, I think it's more positive than negative, in terms of brain injury."

"*Híjole,*" said Luz with a shake of her head. "I can't believe simply hitting your head on the floor could cause this sort of injury."

"On the floor?" asked the doctor.

"We think he was startled by something, tripped and hit his head on the floor," I said.

Petralis shook his head. "This injury isn't consistent with a fall."

"It isn't?"

"The angle of the blow indicates your friend was attacked from behind, by something heavy, which struck his skull at a downward angle. A blunt instrument of some kind. Looks to me like someone tried to kill him."

Dr. Petralis left after that pronouncement, murmuring something about checking in later, and Luz turned to me.

"Could someone have been hiding in the chapel, without your seeing anything?"

I thought back to those panicked moments. "I suppose so. I ran into the chapel after Donnchadh, but there was probably enough time for someone to run away, or hide. Under the circumstances, I doubt I would have noticed someone hunkering down behind a pile of stones."

"But why would anyone want to hurt Graham?"

"That's the ten-thousand-dollar question. Unless . . . Graham had just returned from talking to the widow of McCall, the building inspector who was killed. We were trying to figure out if Larry McCall might have known something, figured out something that would have led someone to murder him."

"Wait, wait, *wait*. I thought the police had his killer under arrest, that it was a crime of passion, a case of anger run amok."

"That's what they seem to think. They have Pete Nolan, the general contractor who was running the job, in custody. But whether Nolan's the killer . . . I guess I'm not convinced."

Luz looked at me with worried, angry eyes. "So, are you thinking maybe Graham learned something from the widow? Something incriminating, or . . . something about a treasure? And that's why he was hurt?"

I nodded.

"Don't take this the wrong way, Mel, but that seems rather far-fetched. I mean, if the building inspector knew about a treasure, why wouldn't he have done something about it? And if the killer is after the same treasure, why doesn't he just unearth it and run away? Why hang around attacking people, and in the process, risking exposure?"

"I have no idea. All I can think is that it's not that easy to get to."

"But you think maybe the widow knows something and told Graham?"

"That's all I can think of. And there's one way to find out."

"I'll go with you."

"No, Luz."

"Seriously, Mel, what makes you think you can go talk with her safely if Graham couldn't?"

"Because everyone knew Graham had gone to speak with her." I thought back to that crazy scene after the room collapse, with Ellis and his entourage looking over the site, plus Tony and Jacek and most of the men gathered around. Graham and I had spoken openly about where he was going, right there in front of everyone. "I'll be more discreet from now on. Surely, if the murderer's really out there, he'll assume I'm with Graham right now. In fact, come to think of it . . . I suppose that could be why he did it. To get me out of the way."

Luz looked at me, one eyebrow raised.

"Luz, do me a favor? Stay here with Graham? Just keep an eye on him?"

"The doctors said he's stable for now, Mel. I'm sure he's going to pull through, a big strapping man like him."

Like size has anything to do with his ability to survive a skull fracture, I thought, fear lancing through me. "He does have a hard head, it's true. But I can't leave him here, defenseless. If someone tried to finish the job . . ."

"Are you going to call the police?"

"Yes. But then I'm going to look into this myself. I don't trust the police to follow up. Will you stay here with him, just keep an eye on things?"

"On one condition: Don't go around talking to people alone. Bring someone big and strong, who you trust, with you. Maybe Zach?"

Zach Yablonksy had once kind of kidnapped me, but we'd moved on from that incident and had developed an odd friendship. But Zach wasn't close at hand.

"I promise, I'll take someone with me."

"Who?" Luz was a born skeptic.

"Kieran."

"The Scottish guy?"

"He's been trying to repatriate the monastery."

"The entire place?"

"Pretty much, or at least the treasure, if there is one. But he has no ties with Elrich or anybody else at the project. And he's a big, strong guy. Thanks, Luz."

"Keep your cell phone with you. I added Buzz's number to your contact list. He's waiting outside somewhere with the limo. But wait. . . . Do we know we can trust Buzz?"

"You mean, what if it turns out Elrich is a criminal mastermind responsible for all that's happened, and Buzz is one of his evil henchmen?"

"I wasn't going to use those exact words, but yes, that's what I meant."

"Good point. I'll figure out something else. But you have to promise to call me if there's any news about Graham. Anything at all."

"Roger that. I'm gonna go get the scoop from the

nurses, and then I'll see about getting access to the ICU
I'll tell them I'm his wife."

"His wife?"

She smiled. "I did a stint as a hospital social worker
remember? I know my way around this sort of thing
Leave it in my capable hands, *amiga*."

Luz had extremely capable hands, I thought, grateful
for my friend.

Kieran agreed to come pick me up. Then I called the
police and left a message for Detective Bernardino. Finally, I phoned Mrs. McCall, the widow of the building
inspector. I was loath to bother her while she was grieving, but I had to know what she had told Graham. And I
wanted to go in person, so I could study her body language. I told her that Graham had been attacked after
speaking to her, and she put the pieces together and
agreed to see us.

Twenty minutes later, Kieran pulled up in front of the
hospital in a silver Prius.

"How's our boy?"

"He's . . . We're watching and waiting now. He hasn't
woken up enough to say anything, but the doctor thinks
he was hit from behind."

"*Hit?* Someone attacked him? But . . . I thought it was
an accident."

"Apparently not. He was"—my voice wavered—"hit
over the head."

"Oh, *wow*." Kieran blanched but kept his eyes on the
road. His driving was precise, slow, and careful. In theory
I admired his prudence, but in reality, he was making me
crazy. I thought I might offer to drive on the way back
"So you're saying someone's already been killed on this
site, and now someone else is gravely injured—and you
still don't believe there's a curse?"

I didn't care for the term "gravely injured."

"It's not a *curse*; it's some maniac on the loose." Which, I thought to myself, was probably not much better than a curse. "Take a right at the corner." I gave him directions and decided to change the subject. "How did you score a Prius? Do you like it?"

"It's a rental. It was all they had available—costs more to rent, but I suppose I'm saving on gas. And, you know, less damage to the environment and all that. But do me a favor and give me a heads-up if I drive on the wrong side of the road, will you? It's been known to happen. I don't know why all you colonials insisting on driving on the other side, when the Brits have already figured all this out."

"I would think that as a proud Scotsman, you wouldn't be pro-British?"

He shrugged. "You know what they say: Choose your battles. Went to school in London; rather liked the place. So, where are we headed?"

"To talk with Mrs. McCall. She's the widow of the building inspector who was killed."

"What about?"

"Graham spoke with her right before he was attacked; it's possible she told him something someone didn't want him to know."

"Like what?"

"What if McCall wasn't killed by Nolan in a drunken fit of frustration? What if it was something else entirely, like the treasure you've been looking for? Maybe McCall knew something, found something, saw something . . . or something?"

"It's worth checking out, I suppose," said Kieran with a sigh. "Though if Graham had learned something vital, wouldn't he have called you?"

"Probably," I said with a sigh. "Unless he didn't realize he had learned it. Or, it could be something else entirely."

"Well, I'm happy to help, if I can. It's not like I was doing anything, anyway," he said in a wistful tone. "Elrich doesn't even come out those gates anymore, and the local press has moved on. The costumes aren't attracting attention like before. I'm going to have to think of something else."

"How's the lawsuit coming?" I asked, feeling as if I were playing both sides. Although I adored working on the building—Elrich was correct that I had fallen in love with the place—I was sympathetic to Kieran's cause. In general, I believed a nation's treasures should remain with the nation of origin.

He shrugged. "Ah, we'll see. Your legal system is a bit of a mystery, to be honest. I wish the government would step in, but they believe it's too petty. They're not even sure the treasure exists—they say it's based on nothing but old wives' tales."

"But you are sure?"

"As sure as I can be," he said. "Which isn't all that sure. I'll certainly feel embarrassed if, after all this, it turns out to be some ridiculous legend."

"I talked to Ellis about it," I said.

"Ellis, is it?"

"He's been nothing but inviting and friendly to me, so yes, I call him Ellis."

"He's a charmer, that one."

"I can't claim to be a great judge of character, but he strikes me as aboveboard. Anyway, he listened when I spoke to him about it."

"Did he make any promises?"

"No, but he said he would consider it if and when we

found something. Though I have to say, I can't think where they would have hidden things among the stones."

"There's that warehouse, though, right?"

"That's true. Do you know if Florian stores any items from the original monastery there?"

"I have no idea. I'd love to get access to them, though, check them out."

I nodded. "I'll see what I can do. Though I have to say, it really doesn't help having you out at the gate all the time. Especially since you've allied yourself with the striking workers, and they've broken into the compound more than once. As have you."

"I know. So, Florian Libole. How much do you know about him?"

"He's pretty well-known in renovation circles. Ellis brought him in from England to oversee the historical renovation."

He nodded.

"Why do you ask?"

"I was chatting with Alicia."

"Alicia? Alicia Withers?"

"I assume so. Not sure of her last name."

"When did you two chat? And where?"

"The other day, at the pub."

And here I thought I was the only one with secret assignations at the pub.

"And what did she say?"

"She thinks Libole is harboring secrets."

"She wouldn't have to be a mind reader to think that. But Alicia thinks everyone from Ellis's daughter Harper to Buzz-the-limo-driver is harboring secrets. Which, let's face it, I'm sure they are. Even *I* feel secretive around Alicia, because she always has her nose in everybody's business."

"Really? She seemed rather sweet to me. Except for calling the police on us at the gate. She's done that a few times. But then, that's her job, I suppose. I don't take it personal."

I smiled. Then I remembered Graham, and called Luz to check in. She told me Graham was still sleeping, no news yet, but the panda face was developing. She was planning on taking pictures.

We arrived at the McCall house, in San Rafael. It was a pleasant ranch-style home with a big yard. Someone was into gardening—besides neatly pruned flower beds, there were three small topiary trees snipped to look like animals: a lion, a rabbit, a turtle.

The woman who opened the door was plump with a pleasing, pretty face and a short graying, practical bob.

"Mrs. McCall? I'm Mel Turner. We spoke earlier? This is my associate, Kieran Lackey. . . ." I trailed off as I butchered his name.

"Lachaidh," Kieran put in.

"Yes, of course. Please call me Jeanine, and please come in," she said, and opened the door wide.

Chapter Fifteen

The house smelled of potatoes and roasting meat. Inside, an unsmiling young woman hovered in the kitchen doorway, a stained apron tied around her waist, eyes swollen and red from crying.

"This is my daughter Meghan. She's staying with me for a few days, because of . . . well, until after the funeral."

"I'm so sorry for your loss," I said, feeling like a heel. These women had lost a loved one, while my sole interaction with him had been watching as he'd had a hissy fit with Nolan. There was no denying I had entertained unkind thoughts about Larry McCall. Now I glanced around the foyer and saw old school photos of two girls and a boy—awkward middle school pictures, lovely young people graduating from high school. However petty McCall had seemed to me in our brief interaction, his was a life cut short, a family rent asunder.

But I reminded myself that Graham lay injured in the

hospital and steeled myself to intrude on the family's privacy.

"And I'm sorry to intrude."

"Thank you," said Jeanine. "Really, I don't mind. In fact, I enjoy telling people about Larry's work. Please come on in and make yourself at home. I was just having some tea."

We followed her and took seats in a comfortable, overcrowded living room. On the broad coffee table sat a plate of baked goods.

"Crumpets," she said. "Homemade. *Do* have some, or I'll wind up eating the whole plate myself."

Kieran didn't have to be asked twice. He jumped on them as though starving and served himself two, placing them on a napkin. Our hostess then poured three cups of tea and told us to help ourselves to cream and sugar. I took mine black; it was delicious.

"Mmm," said Kieran. "I don't believe I've had a proper cup of tea since I arrived in this country."

"I love your accent," said Jeanine. "Are you Scottish?"

"Aye. Guilty as charged, as they say."

"Is your family Scottish, too?" I asked. "McCall?"

"I'm a Velasquez by birth. But my husband's . . ." Her big brown eyes filled with tears. She took a deep breath and blew it out, seeming to regain her composure. "Larry's family came from Scotland, two generations ago. His grandparents on his father's side. He loved all things Scottish. He was an absolute nut when it came to genealogies. He traced both our family trees."

Kieran was studying the jumble of items on the wall. There were two reproductions of paintings: One I recognized as *Mary, Queen of Scots*. The other was a striking painting of a beautiful woman in a very severe palette of browns and blacks. The only bit of color was the touch of blush in her cheeks, on her lips, and the brilliant red of the jewel hanging around her neck. My eyes also lit upon a painting of a castle that reminded me a little of Wakefield. On the fireplace mantel was a collection of photographs of what I presumed were the Scottish Isles.

"Are those . . . ? Those aren't pictures of the monastery Elrich is building from Wakefield, are they?" I asked.

"Oh, no, of course not. Those photos are from our honeymoon. We went on a golfing and scotch-tasting trip in Scotland. I'll never forget it."

"I keep threatening to run off to Paris, myself," I said. "Do you still golf?"

"Not at all. And to tell you the truth, I don't much care for scotch, either. But I still enjoyed the trip," she said with an indulgent smile. "We stayed in darling bed-and-breakfasts and had haggis and eggs every morning. Such fun."

I didn't think haggis would ever edge out my fantasy of chocolate croissants and café au lait in a Parisian café, but to each their own.

"Those photos bring me great comfort. Larry and I used to sit here in front of the fire and recall those days," Jeanine said wistfully. "I keep meaning to light the fire, but it seems like too much effort. That was always Larry's job."

"I'd be happy to do it, if you like," said Kieran, jumping up.

"Oh! That would be delightful!" said Jeanine.

Kieran set about laying a fire with the newspapers, kindling, and firewood that had been laid out with care on the hearth. Soon a small but cheerful fire brightened the room.

In our part of California, fireplaces are rarely needed for heat, but they can serve as the emotional center of a home, the closest the modern family came to an altar. The mantel in my dad's house was crammed full of family photos, shells, rocks . . . mementos of happy times. I felt an unexpected surge of homesickness, making me realize how thrown off I'd been by what happened to Graham. I hadn't even had time to think about what my interactions with the ghost of Donnchadh might have meant.

"You said something happened to that nice man who came to see me?" asked Jeanine.

"Yes. When he returned to the jobsite, after talking with you, he was struck on the head. He's in the hospital. We hope he'll be fine." My voice wavered just a tad as I said this last bit. "But the timing of the attack, especially considering what happened to your husband, made me wonder if someone might have thought you told Graham something. Maybe something that someone else wanted to keep secret?"

"I confess I can't think what," said Jeanine. "We spoke about the business—you know Graham, so you must know he had been a building inspector as well, for Cal-OSHA."

I nodded. Graham had worked for the California Office of Safety and Health Administration for a few years before establishing his green-building consultancy.

"Larry just loved his job. He used to be in software sales, like everyone else in the world, right? But then he accepted a golden parachute. Retirement just didn't sit well with him. He's always been an active man, and he liked to be useful. I don't mind telling you that he was starting to drive me crazy, underfoot all the time. So he took a training course to get his certification and started doing home inspections, and that led to the job with the county. He loved his work."

"Did he ever say anything about this particular project? Could you try to tell me anything you told Graham?"

"Of course, I'll try." The smell of onions frying in the other room reminded me of my dad. "I knew he was working at Wakefield, of course. He was . . . bothered that Mr. Elrich was pushing his project past the regular channels, or so Larry believed. 'Shoving it down our throats' was how he put it."

I nodded and met Kieran's eyes, wishing she would spill the whole story. She was one of those people who seemed to pause and beg for encouragement every time they gave out a morsel of information. Given the circumstances, it made me feel ghoulish to push her.

"Did he think there was anything unsafe about the jobsite?" I asked. "Or that the building wasn't up to code?"

"There were problems with meeting code, because of all the new techniques being applied. I told Graham that, after he told me he was the one responsible for a lot of the green technology. Graham already knew my Larry, because of all the times he had been down at the permit office."

"So there were code issues because of new techniques, but not detrimental to health and safety per se?"

"Not that I know of. I think what bothered Larry more than anything was he felt Ellis Elrich thought of himself as above the law."

"Did he . . . ? Did Larry mention anything to you about finding anything on the site?" I asked. "Something that might have been valuable?"

She shook her head and nibbled on a crumpet. Crumbs fell onto her large bosom, and she brushed them off with a chagrined smile.

"Mom, we should start the casserole soon," called

Meghan from the kitchen. She clearly wasn't happy about us intruding on their sorrow, and I couldn't blame her. This little interview hadn't told me anything useful as far as I could tell, and we were taking up valuable energy the family needed for their own recovery.

"We've intruded on your privacy long enough," I said as I stood. "Thank you so much for speaking with us."

"Have I told you anything that might help figure out what happened to your friend . . . or to my Larry?"

There was such hope in her eyes that my heart went out to her. "I don't know, but I will try my darnedest to figure this out. That much, I can promise."

Jeanine reached out and squeezed my arm as she walked us to the door. "You do that, sweetheart. Don't let the bastard get away with this."

She seemed suddenly fierce for so accommodating a woman.

"Do you know something about this case?" demanded Meghan, finally emerging from the kitchen, wiping her hands on her stained apron. The bitterness in her eyes made her look older than her mother. "I thought the police had that Nolan guy in jail. Are you saying he didn't do it?"

"I don't know," I said with a shake of my head, afraid I was raising false hopes, or false doubts. "I think it's possible that whoever killed your father also went after my friend Graham, which would mean it couldn't have been Nolan. But I have no proof, or even a suspicion as to who that might be. Given my track record, I'm probably mistaken. I'm so sorry for your loss."

"That didn't tell us much," I said, in a gloomy mood as we drove back toward the hospital.

"I think it's interesting that McCall was such a Scot-phile."

"Interesting how? Did you know him?"

"I saw him go in and out the gates a few times, but that's about it. He stopped once and complimented my kilt. I thought he was making fun."

"He probably wished he had the guts to wear one, himself."

Kieran nodded. "Funny, out of all those photos and paintings in their home, there was only the one from his wife's side of the family."

"Which was that?"

"The Spanish painting. Didn't you notice? Very different style—those Spanish are all about the dark colors. They're a severe people, aren't they?"

"Right. Not peppy and lighthearted like the Scots."

Kieran smiled.

"When Jeanine said her maiden name was Velasquez, I just assumed she was Mexican-American. Mexican art is usually anything but dark and somber."

"I don't know the first thing about Mexico. But I'd like to go, sit on a beach, sip a margarita. Wouldn't that be lovely?" Kieran sighed. He sounded so plaintive, he reminded me of my depressed ghost. I guessed standing outside the gates wasn't all it was cracked up to be. But if he was staying at the Pelican Inn, Kieran must have some resources. That place wasn't cheap.

"I wish I could invite you to Ellis's place to use the pool. But it might be awkward, given the circumstances."

Kieran shrugged and kept his grip tight on the wheel, as though keeping himself on the right side of the road through sheer concentration. I wished I had remembered to offer to drive.

"Maybe you should declare a truce with Elrich," I said. "I can give you my word that if I learn anything about a treasure, I'll let you know. Then you could get the Scottish authorities involved, or whoever would be the agency to deal with this. Interpol, maybe?"

"Bringing that place over is technically legal. It's not like he's involved in international smuggling or engaged in espionage."

"Really, Kieran, I don't think Ellis wants to cheat anyone out of their national heritage. I really don't."

"How about Florian Libole? I wouldn't put it past him—that's for sure. Look what happened in Strasbourg."

"What happened in Strasbourg?"

He gave me a significant look. "Ask Libole. But make sure you have some time on your hands—he'll talk your ear off trying to convince you it wasn't his fault."

I filed that away for future reference. "Hey, I've been meaning to ask: Do you know anything about a woman who was present at the monastery at some point?" I kept wondering about the weeping woman: Who was she, where had she come from, and why would she be haunting the monastery?

"A woman? No," he said with a shake of his head. "I can't imagine such a thing, to be honest. I mean, a woman among all those desperate men?"

"The men were desperate?"

"I'm just guessing. I mean, after all, they were a whole bunch of men living together, supposedly celibate. I don't mean to be hard on my sex, but I don't think it's particularly healthy for men to live without women."

He looked at me rather soulfully. It made me realize just how immune I was to his charm. Harper seemed quite taken with him, but I'd had a few more years to develop skepticism.

My phone rang. It was Raul, calling with a couple of questions about a stone countertop that was being installed at the Art Nouveau house. After answering his questions, I filled him in on what had happened to Graham. I hung up and was about to call Luz, only to find a text message from her that all signs were still normal and I should concentrate on finding out the identity of the culprit rather than wasting her time and mine by calling every half hour. Her text made me smile.

"Where to now?" Kieran asked.

"Back to the hospital, I guess. I can't think of anything else. Do you mind if I make a few more phone calls while you drive?"

"Not at all."

I called Dad and filled him in on what had happened. Graham's father had died young, which was one reason he looked to my dad as a father figure of sorts, which made our relationship just a little too incestuous for comfort. Dad said he'd come up tomorrow and sit with Graham; he also told me he'd call Graham's mother, who lived in Florida, and let her know what was going on.

Then I dialed the number for SFPD homicide inspector Annette Crawford.

"Please tell me you're not standing over a body," she answered without preamble.

"The way you talk, a person would think you weren't happy to hear from her."

"You're not calling about a murder?"

"Only tangentially."

"Can't wait to hear this."

"Here's the deal: I'm on a job in Marin County, and yes, a body was discovered several days ago."

"I like you, Mel, but I'm not putting my reputation on the line to spring you from the county jail."

"Did I say I was calling you from lockup?" *Sheesh.* Yes, Inspector Crawford and I had been through a few murders together. But I had never actually been *guilty* of anything. And on our last case, *she* had asked for *my* help, so you'd think she would cut me a little slack. "I have a question, that's all."

"Shoot."

"How certain of a person's guilt would police have to be in order to hold someone as a murder suspect? And once they make an arrest, do they continue investigating, or is that the end of it?"

"That's a complicated question, I'm afraid. If they have a person of interest, they'll keep him around to talk with him, see if they can build a case. Normally, they would still follow up any other leads, unless they are completely convinced they've got the guilty party. It depends on a lot of factors."

I gave her the rundown of what had happened to Larry McCall, why Pete Nolan was being held, and how I came to be running the job at Wakefield for Ellis Elrich. Then I added: "Graham's been hurt."

"I'm sorry to hear that. What happened?"

"He was hit over the head. Skull fracture. We're hoping he'll be all right, but . . ." My voice caught in my throat.

"And you think the murderer was responsible?" she asked, her voice gentle.

"It's possible. As usual, I'm not sure what's going on. And I'll say one thing: The Marin police aren't nearly as sweet and accommodating as you are."

I heard a chuckle.

"Tell you what," said Annette. "I'll make a couple of phone calls and see what I can find out. Will that help?"

"It would, yes. The detective on the murder case is named Bernardino. Also, could you ask them if they recovered a clipboard at the scene of McCall's death?"

"A clipboard? Holding what?"

"I don't actually know, but it might have had something to do with his murder. The construction workers called it his Clipboard of Doom. If the police didn't pick it up, I think it's possible that the killer took it. And that the killer isn't the man they have in custody, Pete Nolan."

"All righty. You realize I can now follow your thought process with ease? Do you know how much that thought terrifies me?"

"Think of it as wind sprints for your brain."

"Anything else?"

"Could you . . . ?" I glanced over at Kieran, who appeared to be concentrating on the road. I lowered my voice, though it was obvious he could still hear me. "Could you also check on one Alicia Withers? She's Elrich's assistant, and someone mentioned that she might not be who she says she is."

"I'll see what I can do."

"Thanks, Annette. I really appreciate it." I hung up and pondered a bit more. I couldn't think what my next step should be.

"I don't suppose . . . Maybe we should stop by the warehouse where Libole keeps the other items he's collected," suggested Kieran.

"Just how is it you know about things like the warehouse?" I asked him.

"People tell things to me." He shrugged. "I think it's the accent."

"If I knew where the warehouse was and how to get in, I'd be happy to oblige. But I don't."

"You could use that magic talking device you're holding in your hand and call someone," Kieran suggested.

"Good point." When Florian didn't answer, I tried Alicia, who suggested I take it up with Mr. Elrich. He had an opening tomorrow at three, she said, and she'd be happy to pencil me in. I made the appointment, though I was willing to bet I could corner Ellis at the breakfast bar or out on the terrace with a glass of cognac or building his cairns before then.

"No luck," I said to Kieran after I hung up. "Maybe later. Unless . . ."

"Unless what?"

"We could break in," I mused aloud. "If we could find someone to tell us where it is."

Kieran looked at me, startled. "Break in?"

"I'm pretty sure you're familiar with the concept, Mr. Gee I Just Had to Look Around the Ruins Even Though I'm Not Permitted on the Property."

He appeared to be blushing, his gaze still fixed on the road ahead. He mumbled something.

"What was that?"

"I said, it's one thing to wander onto an unsecured piece of land looking for a national treasure, quite another to break in to a locked building. Besides, I didn't break *in*, exactly. Technically, I was invited."

"By Harper? Don't play with her emotions, Kieran. You're too good a guy to do that. She's young and vulnerable and ripe to get her heart broken."

"Who said I was playing with her emotions? We're friends; I like her. She's actually quite knowledgeable about plants, and is sympathetic to my case for repatriation. She said she'd talk to her father about it. Anyway, about breaking in to the warehouse . . . I can't be a party to something like that. What if we get caught?"

"I'm pretty sure we'd be able to talk ourselves out of it, what with the connection with Elrich and all."

Kieran seemed unconvinced.

"What, did you overstay your visa or something?"

Now he looked guilty.

"Kieran—I'm sorry—I was just joking. That can be erious, though, can't it? Overstaying your visa these lays could bring the wrath of Homeland Security down on your head."

He shrugged again. "I'm working on it."

I nodded and hoped part of his plan didn't include marrying a gullible American citizen. But it really wasn't any of my business.

"You know what? I happen to know a few scofflaws who don't have visa issues." I placed another call.

"Mel! How are you?" my friend Zach asked when he picked up.

"I've been better. I was wondering if you're free tomorow or the next day to help me break in to a warehouse."

"I swear, Mel, it pains me that you have such a sketchy opinion of me. One little incident of breaking and entering and I'm forever a marked man in your mind."

"It wasn't the breaking and entering so much as the involvement in murder, and you know, the kidnapping."

"Again with the kidnapping," he said with a put-upon sigh, as though kidnapping were the moral equivalent of denting a fender.

I ran through what had happened to Graham, what I knew, and why I wanted to get into the warehouse. "So, can I count on you?"

"Maybe."

"What do you mean, maybe?"

"I might get a better offer."

"Yeah, right. I'll call you when I have the location."

"Oh, goodie."

I hung up.

"You're off the hook," I told Kieran. "I found a bona ide US citizen to help me bend the law."

"You're not bending the law; you're breaking it."

"Semantics."

"Will you let me know what you find?"

"Of course. We're looking for a chalice, right?"

"Could be."

"You really don't know, do you?"

"The legends say the ghost is protecting a priceless vessel, so I assume . . ."

He trailed off as we pulled up to the hospital.

"All right. I'll keep my eyes open, and if we find anything that looks like a national treasure, I'll let you know."

Chapter Sixteen

Back at the hospital, there had been a shift change, so the nurses on duty didn't recognize me. I was stopped when I tried to access the ICU.

"I'm here to see Graham Donovan."

"Who is he to you, exactly?"

"My boyfriend."

She looked a little surprised and turned to gaze at Luz, who smiled gamely.

"It's the twenty-first century, after all," Luz said. "As long as everyone behaves themselves . . ."

When the nurse turned away, Luz whispered: "I'm supposed to be his wife, remember?"

"Oh, right. I forgot."

Luz flung her arm over my shoulder and led me to Graham's cubby in the ICU.

"I bet we'll be the talk of the hospital for a few days. Intensive care ménage à trois and all that. But hey, you're into all things French, right, *ma chérie*?"

I glared at her. She just grinned and gave me another squeeze.

I stood for a moment by Graham's bed. He looked even worse than he had before; the panda markings were becoming more pronounced, he had a pallid complexion, and his stillness was unnerving.

"So give me the lowdown: What did McCall's widow say?"

"Nothing much. Unless there's something there that I'm just not seeing. Graham announced he was going to speak with her in front of a whole bunch of people, but it could just as easily have been someone following him, or watching the widow's house, I suppose. But she really didn't seem to have anything useful to tell us."

The sour-faced nurse returned. "You can't stay here."

"Excuse me?"

"No visitors in the ICU after eleven p.m. Hospital rules."

Great. I had a Mrs. Danvers to contend with at the Elrich mansion and a Nurse Ratched here at the hospital. Good thing I knew so many cool women, or I might start to become pessimistic about our sex.

"I suppose I could call Elrich and have him raise a stink, or sweet-talk folks, or however it is he manages to get impossible things done . . . ," I said, thinking aloud.

"Graham's not going to be waking up and needing you anytime soon, Mel," said Luz gently. "The nurses assure me they have pretty tight security here—he'll be looked after. The best thing for you to do at this point would be to get some rest and come back tomorrow."

"I guess I really should get back to Dog. . . ."

"Right, back to Dog, as well. Want me to come stay with you?"

"Don't you have classes?"

"Papers are due this week; my graduate teaching assistants can handle it."

"Thanks, *amiga*. I appreciate your willingness to exploit your students on my behalf. But you've done enough. I'm okay, really."

"Really?"

"Really."

Luz dropped me off at the Elrich house a little before midnight.

"Watch out for Mrs. Danvers," she said with a smile. "Get some sleep, and call me in the morning to let me know how you are."

"Sure thing."

"And, Mel? Watch your back."

"Thanks. I'm on it."

Dog was especially excited to see me, and though I was sure he had probably dined on steak that evening, I fed him dinner anyway, and afterward sat on the floor and rubbed his belly for a while. I didn't feel a bit sleepy. And I could hear that mournful flute music again, wafting up from the Wakefield building site. *I think my ghost needs Prozac.* I smiled, thinking what Luz's reaction would have been if I'd asked her about it.

My eyes came to rest on my toolbox. It reminded me of home, of family. Caleb had written my name on it in Magic Markers back when he was a boy and still thought I was cool. I had inherited many of my tools from my father, and though there were newer, fancier versions out on the market, I enjoyed the familiar feel of the old metals in the palm of my hand.

I set my toolbox on the fireplace hearth, opened it, and brought out a small chisel and a strong putty knife, then started scraping at the mess left behind when I had taken the tiles off the hood. The old plaster was disinte-grating, and the tiles hadn't been put on properly in the first place, which was why they had fallen off so easily. I wondered whether I should check the rest of the tiles throughout the house—there were a lot of them. The ones used for decoration weren't as much of a worry, though it would be a shame if the glazed squares started to fall and break. But tiles in wet locales—showers, backsplashes, the Jacuzzi—would pose a serious problem if they hadn't been properly cemented into place and then grouted.

Brendan had started completing tasks on the fix-it list in the Elrich house yesterday. I'd gotten the sense he was happy to be working here rather than on the monastery—he'd been one of the men chased out of the building by Donnchadh on his first day on-site. I made a mental note to check in with him and see how the work was coming along.

I kept scraping, and of course the other tiles had to come off, as well. Even a small job like this one created a huge mess of plaster dust and chunks of the old glue; but in order to reapply the tiles properly, the underlay-ment had to be thoroughly clean. I feared Alicia was not going to be pleased with me.

Thinking of Alicia, I realized that it was the middle of the night and I was scraping plaster off walls. The house was exceedingly well insulated, but I wondered whether the noise I was making might be disturbing the peace. Specifically, I wondered whether my neighbor, Florian Libole, was back, and whether I was driving him nuts with my scratching, tapping, and grinding.

And thinking of Libole, where had he disappeared to?

I blew away the last bits of dust and debris from the fireplace hood and then set my tools carefully back into the toolbox. I used a small brush and pan I'd found under the sink to clean up the biggest part of the mess. Tomorrow I could reapply the tiles with proper mastic, and when the plasterers were here for the other small jobs around the house—there were many—they could patch this area at the same time.

Walking out my French doors and across the terrace to Florian's bedroom, I put my ear to the door and listened. Nothing. I knocked softly at first, then louder.

Still no answer.

Glancing around to make sure no one was watching, I tried the door handle.

Locked. Of course. *Darn it.*

I went into my bedroom and out to the hall to Florian's other door. I tried the handle, just in case, but it was locked as well.

Then I heard something.

A muffled sound, like people talking. The television was on. Probably the sullen Harper was watching music videos or some comedy I wouldn't understand starring actors I wouldn't recognize. But at the moment I was in need of a distraction.

I snuck into the television room only to find none other than Alicia slouched on the down-filled cushions of a large sectional. She looked less like Mrs. Danvers and more like one of Caleb's teenage friends.

Potato chips went flying when she saw me and jumped, letting out a little squeak.

"Sorry I startled you," I said, stifling a smile.

Alicia's face flamed, and she picked up a few errant chips that had escaped the beautifully glazed handmade bowl. "I hope the television didn't disturb you. I thought everybody was asleep."

I glanced at the massive flat-screen, where a big truck

was pulling away, revealing to a large family their newly remodeled home.

"It's . . . uh . . ." Alicia stood and hit a button on the remote, turning the TV off. "Sorry. Is there something I can help you with?"

"Please don't turn it off on my account. What were you watching?"

I wouldn't have believed her face could grow a deeper red, but it did. "HGTV."

"What's that?"

She gaped at me. "Home and Garden TV network. You don't know it?"

"I'm not a TV person. And even if I were, my dad maintains control of the remote at all times. He's like a dog with a bone."

"I would have thought . . . I would have thought someone in your business would watch this channel."

"Turn it back on," I said as I plopped down on an overstuffed armchair. It felt like heaven. Maybe I was more tired than I thought. "Let's give it a go."

"Are you sure?"

I nodded.

She clicked the remote and sat back down but seemed uneasy. She kept sneaking glances over at me. "Mr. El-rich says that Graham is going to be all right. Is that true?"

"It's too early to tell for sure, but they think so. It's sort of wait and see, but it looks like he'll be okay. We hope."

She nodded, awkward, then turned to the TV, where the show was wrapping up. I asked questions, and she filled me in on the setup: A couple bought a house and needed help renovating it. They brought in some gorgeous guy in a tool belt, and the subcontractors showed up when they said they would, and if there were disasters, they were funny, and then the job was completed on time and on budget.

I could hear my father's voice in my head: *They should call this channel* Fantasy *TV.* Still, it took my mind off Graham.

Then a show came on featuring a perky blond woman who was a fanatic for historical renovation and recycling. She drove her crew and coworkers nuts with her zealous insistence upon historical accuracy and original materials. At one point she crawled into a Dumpster behind of a house that had just been cleaned out in order to salvage a cupboard and a bunch of old moldings.

"That woman's like my twin," I said. By now I was sitting next to Alicia on the couch, my hand in the chip bowl. "Except she's cute and blond. And perky. And she looks a hell of a lot better in jeans than I do. But other than that, we're like this." I held up one hand with two fingers crossed.

Alicia laughed. Just the tiniest little chuckle. She seemed almost embarrassed about it, and kept sneaking looks at me when she thought I was absorbed in watching the TV show.

"How's Brendan working out?" I asked.

"Well. He's very nice."

"Good. I was noticing a small problem in my room, with the tiles. It's really mostly cosmetic stuff—I could teach you how to check them, and to take them off and then put them back properly, if you like. It's not difficult."

"Really? You think I could do it?"

"Sure. I mean, only if you're interested. I'm sure Ellis has more than enough money to foot the bill for repairs, and you're probably busy with work already."

"Oh, but I enjoy working with my hands."

"I had a feeling."

We shared a smile.

"So, Florian's still out of town?" I said, real casual-like, during a commercial.

She nodded.

"What's he doing? Do you know?" I know I sounded snoopy, but I was hoping Alicia would recognize a kindred spirit.

"I believe it was personal business."

Or not. I tried again.

"I'm only asking because I understand Florian has a warehouse full of relics that will eventually be incorporated into Wakefield. I'd love to take a look at them, so I can have a better sense of what all we've got."

Her attention remained fixed on the TV. Okay, one more try.

"Also, according to the paperwork I was looking at, several industrial-sized kitchen appliances will be arriving any day now. Wakefield's kitchen space isn't ready, not by any stretch of the imagination, so I was thinking maybe we could store them in the warehouse. But that's okay. . . . I'll just have them delivered here at the house."

That got her.

"Here? Here where? There's no room for kitchen appliances here!"

"Yeah, and these are industrial-sized suckers, too. Huge."

She let out a dismayed gasp.

"I suppose we could stash them in the garage . . . ," I suggested.

"Oh, no. That wouldn't work at all," Alicia said, sitting up straight. "We wouldn't be able to park inside! Mr. Elrich has a Lexus LFA Nürburgring."

"The weather around here isn't that bad. That Lexus-
urger would be okay sleeping outdoors, don't you think?"

Alicia looked shocked.

"It would only be for a couple of months, tops."

"No, no, no, that won't do at all," she said, collapsing
ack against the soft cushions. "This is terrible."

"Mmm." I nodded, pretending to be riveted by the TV
now, where one of the hosts was trying to teach a hap-
ess homeowner how to use a jigsaw to shorten newel
osts. It wasn't going well, but they were all good-natured
bout it.

Agitated, Alicia appeared to be running through op-
ons in her head. She nodded.

"You're right; there must be room in that warehouse.
nd Mr. Elrich is footing the bill, after all."

"That's true. It's not really Florian's warehouse, is it?
really belongs to Elrich Enterprises."

She slumped. "But I don't have the address."

"You don't?"

"No, but I could probably track it down. Also, I don't
now where Florian keeps the key. Perhaps he has it
ith him."

"Could be. Unless he left it in his room. I know when
travel I leave nonessential keys at home. We could take
look. . . ."

"I imagine his room is locked."

I nodded, my eyes still fixed on the screen, trying to
retend I didn't care one way or the other and that I
adn't already tried both doors.

"Then again, the truth is he left without informing me
r Mr. Elrich of his plans," she said, her pursed lips con-
eying just how she felt about Florian going AWOL. "I
ppose it would be all right if I took a quick peek to see
the key is on his desk."

"Yes!" Forgetting to play it cool, I hopped up from th[e] couch. Then I remembered not to overplay my hand. "[I] mean, I think that makes sense. It wouldn't be like w[e] were tossing the place."

Alicia looked a little uncertain, but took her heav[y] key ring from her purse on the coffee table and starte[d] down the hallway. Other than the muted clanking of he[r] keys, the house had the almost otherworldly hush th[at] came from excellent soundproofing.

We reached Florian's door, where Alicia looked bot[h] ways, then knocked softly. "Mr. Libole?"

I looked at her questioningly.

"Just in case he came back, maybe slipped in witho[ut] my noticing. Since he left so precipitously, maybe he['ll] come back the same way."

"Makes sense," I said with a nod.

"It's just . . . Florian once mentioned that he sleeps [in] the nude. I'm simply not prepared for such an encounter[."]

The thought of Florian Libole in all his naked glor[y] made me giggle. I clapped a hand over my mouth, b[ut] that made it worse. I started snorting.

And wonder of wonders, Alicia started smiling, the[n] shaking with silent laughter.

"Shhhh!" she scolded, but giggled some more.

I was suddenly transported back to the night in mi[d]dle school when I had led a pack of kids on a successf[ul] raid to toilet-paper the principal's house. I had bee[n] grounded for a month after my sister Cookie tattled o[n] me, but nothing took the edge off my night of glory. I wa[s] a legend at school for a full week, until my peers remem[]bered what a geek I was.

"I don't hear anything," Alicia whispered. "Do you[?]"

I shook my head. Alicia slowly inserted the key int[o] the lock and turned it with a muted *click*.

She pushed in the door.

As she did so, it occurred to me that there was something worse than finding Florian Libole in bed naked. Finding Florian Libole in bed naked and *dead*. Given the way events were unfolding lately, one couldn't be too sure. . . .

We peeked in.

I let out the breath I held. The bed was made, the room as neat as a pin.

"I'm impressed," said Alicia with an approving nod. "He's refused maid service since he arrived, so I wasn't sure what to expect."

"He refused maid service? Why would anyone refuse maid service?" As far as I was concerned, maid service was just about the best thing about staying here at Club Elrich. Well, that and the snack bar. And the pool. Although the pool was still pure theory—it sparkled outside my doors, aqua waters glittery and inviting. One of these days soon . . .

Alicia was inspecting the desk, which had nothing at all on its gleaming wood surface except the empty green blotter. I was hoping she'd start rifling through the drawers, but I took a moment myself to peek under the bed—no dust bunnies, no romance novels—and in the bedside table drawers, hoping I might come across the Clipboard of Doom, or at least whatever papers had been on it. I found a few books, including one about Hearst Castle. Funny how often that Hearst came to mind lately. Maybe Florian Libole and Ellis Elrich had set out to imitate Hearst's legacy, for the sake of the Elrich Method.

"I don't see it here," said Alicia.

"Maybe the pockets of his pants? Isn't that where most men keep their keys?" I asked, and went to the

closet. It held three sleek suits, several loose white shirts
jeans, and a row of shined shoes and boots. Also athletic
gear, which surprised me—Libole didn't seem like any
one's portrait of health. Perhaps he was like me with the
swimming pool: full of good intentions.

A suitcase on the overhead shelf was empty. There
were several cardboard blueprint tubes in one corner—
checked each one, but found only construction drawings
There weren't any other obvious hiding places in the
neat-as-a-pin bedroom, besides the desk.

Alicia was sitting at it, hands flat upon the blotter, a
though debating.

When I met her eyes, she shrugged. "I hate to com
promise his privacy."

"It's like we were saying, though," I said, surprised
and a little dismayed at how easily the lies came to me
these days—but then the visual of Graham on the floor
of the chapel, blood seeping out onto the new concrete
floor, eased my conscience and strengthened my resolve
"That warehouse really belongs to Elrich Enterprises
and you don't want to be crawling over industrial-sized
kitchen appliances for the next several months, do you?"

"True."

"Check the main drawer," I suggested. Alicia pulled i
open and found a key ring with almost as many keys as
Alicia had on hers. "Well, would you look at that? It'
got to be one of these, right?"

"Unless these are entirely unrelated," she said. Ever
the optimist.

"Okay . . ." That gave me the justification to hun
through the rest of his drawers. I found old-fashioned ink
pens, extra ink cartridges, and letter-writing supplies, in
cluding heavy cream-colored linen paper, matching en

velopes, and a stick of sealing wax and a signet with a capital "FSL." He was a classy guy.

"Now that we have the keys, I think we should go," said Alicia, clearly nervous.

"Check this out," I said, holding up the sealing wax and signet. "No wonder poor Florian feels surrounded by cretins all the time."

She chuckled. Every time I made Alicia smile, it felt like a small victory; it reminded me of being with Caleb.

"Let's go."

As soon as we turned around, I could see that someone lurked in the doorway.

Chapter Seventeen

Backlit by the lamps in the hallway, the face was shrouded in darkness. But I would recognize that frizzy halo anywhere.

Harper.

"What are you guys *doing* in here?" she demanded.

"We're worried about Florian," I said, stepping in front of Alicia, who looked as though she was hoping the floor would open up and swallow her. "No one's heard from him for a couple of days. Have you?"

"No. But it's not as if anyone checks in with *me*. He's probably just off on one of his jaunts. Good riddance, I say. Guy's a creep. It's freakin' two o'clock in the morning. I thought everyone around here was an early riser."

Aha, I thought. She was hoping to have the place to herself, maybe watch a little HGTV. Or whatever it was that her ilk liked to gorge on.

"You are absolutely right, Harper. It's well past our

bedtime. Boy, I'm beat. Aren't you?" I directed this last to Alicia, who was still cowering behind me.

She nodded.

"All righty, then," I chirped. "We're off to bed. Don't stay up all night, young lady. See you in the morning!"

Harper glared at me.

Alicia and I scooted out of Florian's room. Alicia locked the door behind us and said good night to Harper, who rolled her eyes and made a beeline for the TV room.

"Do you think she'll say anything to Mr. Elrich?" Alicia whispered as we halted outside my bedroom door.

"There's nothing to say," I said. "We were worried about Florian and peeked in to make sure he was okay. That's all."

Alicia nodded. "Yes, you're right. That's all."

"Just . . . don't mention the keys," I said. "That would probably be best. We can put them back where we found them after I get into the warehouse. You'll get me the address?"

"Yes. I'll have to go back through a stack of invoices, but I'm pretty sure I'll be able to find it."

"Great. We'll take care of things before Florian returns, and he'll never know the difference."

"Won't he notice you've put huge appliances in his warehouse?"

Oops. I'd forgotten that little lie. "I'll just tell him I picked the lock, or something. You know how we contractors are. Nefarious characters."

"So I'm learning," she said with a smile. "I'll see you in the morning, Mel. And this may sound silly . . . I don't know if you believe in the power of prayer, but I do. I'll pray for Graham tonight."

I was left at my door with a lump in my throat. I wasn't

sure what I believed, but right about now I would take all the prayers I could get.

As I watched Alicia walk down the hall, I thought perhaps I had misjudged her.

I sure hoped it didn't turn out that she was McCall's killer.

Only a few short hours later, I was fumbling with the lid on my coffee mug and thinking about calling the hospital when Ellis walked into the breakfast bar.

"Mel, glad I caught you," he said. "I spoke with Dr. Petralis a few minutes ago, and there's good news: It seems the swelling has gone down, so they won't have to operate. They're keeping Graham in a medically induced coma for the moment, but he anticipates there won't be any more complications."

"Thank you so much," I said, and then lost it. I collapsed onto a blue wooden bench, landing with a thump.

"Are you all right?" Ellis asked, sitting beside me.

I nodded and then blew out a long breath. "I've been . . . I guess I didn't really realize how worried I was. I was going to call the hospital right after I got my coffee—I wasn't sure I could face it without caffeine."

Ellis gave me an understanding smile. "I'm sorry you weren't able to sleep in. I sent all the men home for the day."

"Thank you. That's very thoughtful. Though, truth to tell, if we want to keep on schedule, we can't afford to lose much time."

"One day," said Ellis. "With the collapse and now this . . . Give yourself a break, regroup. I can see how hard you work. Go visit Graham; then come back and enjoy the pool. Maybe take a hike or go for a horseback ride—there's a stable not far from here. This is a beautiful place, which I have to remind myself of from time to time. It's too easy to get caught up in the work and ignore the amazing locale around us."

I smiled and nodded my thanks.

I would go visit Graham, all right. But after that . . . ? I wanted to try talking with Donnchadh one more time. Maybe with an empty jobsite, I'd have a shot at getting through a conversation with the ghost without being interrupted by his need to run every Y chromosome out of the building.

Whoever had killed Larry McCall had gone after Graham. I felt sure of it. Maybe my old pal Donnchadh could help me figure out the guilty party.

What is it about hospitals that makes spending time in them so anxiety-producing yet deadly dull? I had forgotten to bring a book, and the folks in the ICU frowned on the use of cell phones. I flipped through a couple of very dated *People* magazines, checked out a two-day-old *San Francisco Chronicle*, and tried not to worry about Graham, which was impossible. Watching him breathe, hooked up to machines . . . the way he lay there, so still, was petrifying.

A couple hours later, Dad showed up. It was good to see him, and after a short visit he shooed me away, saying he'd keep Graham company for a while and reminding me I had a business to run. I allowed myself to be convinced and headed back to Wakefield to have a little chat with my depressed ghost. Still, I knew better than to expect the encounter to turn out the way I wanted. Ghosts never seemed able to tell me what was going on, who had killed whom, or anything useful, really.

But it was all I could think of to do at the moment.

I stopped off at the house, took Dog out for a walk,

returned him to our room for his afternoon nap, and slipped my dad's Glock in the pocket of my sweatshirt before heading down to the ancient stones.

I entered the chapel and crept as quietly as possible through the chambers that led toward the refectory.

Footsteps.

Someone was in the cloister.

Ghost or human? Which would be scarier? I put my hand on the hilt of the gun and crept around the corner.

"What?" demanded Harper, hiding something behind her back.

For a heart-stopping moment, I thought she might be holding a gun, herself. But then I heard the crinkle of paper.

"What are you doing here?" she said. "I thought you were . . . You scared the *crap* out of me! I thought maybe you were that ghost, or whatever."

"Just me. What do you have behind your back?"

"None of your beeswax."

I smiled. It was such a little-kid thing to say.

"Do you have some of the original plans to this place, by any chance?"

"No. It's nothing like that."

"Then what is it?"

She shrugged, but finally showed me a sheaf of papers.

They were full-color landscape drawings. I took a few and held them out in front of me to get the full effect.

"These are really lovely," I said. "Did you do these?"

She nodded.

"You're very talented."

She shrugged, but a blush stained her cheeks.

"So." I gestured to a graph on one side of the drawing. "Is this the key to the plants?"

"Yeah. They're all native plantings. It doesn't make sense to landscape with imported species. They're more expensive. Plus a lot will die anyway because they're not suited for the conditions. Native plants can adapt to the local climate, and they're better for the environment and everything. It's called, like, habitat planting because, like, it provides a habitat for things."

I nodded.

"So anyway, I included things like goldenrod, and Douglas iris, and California fuchsia." She leaned over my arm and started pointing out features of the drawing. "Here's yarrow—you can get that either white or yellow, so I like to mix them—and instead of regular grass, I stipulate Siskiyou blue grass, 'cause it's, like, tufted? Deergrass is good that way, too. And Bee's bliss sage, and this yellow part, right here? That's sticky monkey flower."

"That's a thing?" I laughed. "Sticky monkey flower?"

A smile lit up her face. "Right? So funny. I don't know how they get these names, though it *is* sticky. But it doesn't look much like a monkey."

"This is really beautiful work. I guess Florian has talked to you about designing the garth, or the herb garden, to be planted within the cloister?"

"He mentioned it, yeah. But he wants it to be all perfect, historically accurate and everything."

"I'm sure he has some sources you could use to re-create a historically accurate garden. I don't agree with Florian on everything, but I think he's right in this case. We can't very well work so hard at making this place a showcase of historical renovation and then fall down on the garden design. And those medicinal plants are really cool. Plus, I read they used a lot of spices in their beer— that would be kind of fun to play with as well."

"Why's he such a stickler about the historic character of some parts of the building but not others?"

"How do you mean?"

"I mean, he had the original key for the stones, but then he altered it."

"He did? Have you seen the originals?"

"He had a couple of sets. I was in here once when he dropped them. He tried to cover it up, but I saw before he could gather them all up. But when I asked him about it, he just treated me like a child, said I wouldn't understand. Like I was stupid or something. But I understand this: He had altered those historic drawings to make it look like they were original."

"Why would he do that?"

She shrugged. "I think he's, like, cheating? Or trying to take credit for someone else, or something."

But that didn't make sense—everyone knew he was changing the original schema, such as it was, in order to update the building. Why would he try to cover it up?

"Anyway, I gotta go. Um, good luck with the building and everything. And I hope Graham is okay. He's a nice guy."

"Thanks. Nice talking with you."

I watched her walk out by the side gate from the soon-to-be garth. Then I returned through the building.

As always, the sound of my work boots rang out in the echoey space. Even in the areas that still had no real roof, the stone walls created phenomenal acoustics. It must have been hard to sneak up on people in the medieval era.

I stood in the antechamber for a moment, gathering my resolve. It didn't take much today: All I had to do was think about Graham and I felt focused.

Donnchadh and I went through our now-familiar

greeting ritual: He pulled his sword and began to charge, I stood stock-still, and then he realized I was a woman and stood down.

As far as friendships go, I suppose it left a lot to be desired, but at least I always knew where to find him. And, like those people in the cartoon about the bottomless pit, I was getting used to it.

Once he'd relaxed, I asked him: "Do you remember last time I was here? You ran after someone you heard in the sacristy?"

He tilted his head, a quizzical look on his face.

"Is that a no?"

"I dinnae recall."

"You don't remember running out through the sacristy and into the chapel? I'm wondering if you maybe saw something?"

He shrugged and slumped back down onto the step.

"What's wrong?" I asked.

"I cannae . . . I cannae remember things."

I was disappointed but not surprised. I'd heard this before from ghosts. It would be nice if the specters could simply tell me who was guilty and what had happened. But apparently the spirit world had different rules and parameters from our earth-bound existence.

"Can't remember things such as . . . ?"

"What I'm guarding. You asked me about it last time you were here. . . ." Apparently, he remembered me asking, which was interesting. "I cannae stop thinking about it. I dinnae even know exactly what it is I'm protecting. I simply . . . I know I must keep the men away."

He looked at me with anguish in his eyes. He must be so confused, I thought. Bound by duty to protect something he couldn't even remember.

"How about this?" I decided to change the subject

entirely, just to see what would happen. "Do you happen
to know what went into the original mortar used with
these stones?"

"What went into it?"

"Yes," I said, sitting on the stone step beside him.
"The recipe for the mortar."

This, Donnchadh could remember. Though he hadn't
been a builder per se, apparently back then everyone
knew a little about such things. I started pumping him
for architectural information, and we talked for some
time.

I hit another ghost-buster milestone: I spent a perfectly pleasant afternoon with a ghost. He was still depressed, but he perked up a bit as we talked.

Suddenly, he sat up straight and put a finger to his lips
to shush me.

"Have you seen her?" he whispered.

"Her who?" But I knew whom he meant as soon as a
frigid cold engulfed me.

"Ssshhh." He hushed me again and got up to creep
over to the doorway. I joined him.

I couldn't see anything at first, just a flash of red in my
peripheral vision. But then I heard the whispering and
weeping as she walked by.

"Isn't she beautiful?" Donnchadh whispered, rapt.

"I . . ." Were Donnchadh and I seeing the same thing?
How did ghosts appear to one another? This was a whole
new ball game for me. "Sure, yes, she really is lovely."

This time I was prepared for the sadness and hunger,
but they still made me feel weak. Donnchadh, for his
part, had an enthralled, amazed expression on his face,
and there was a hint of a smile.

"Have you spoken to her?"

If it was possible for a ghost to blush, I do believe

Donnchadh MacPhaidein would have done so. He started sputtering. "I dinnae . . . I . . ."

"Surely she would be happy to meet—" I was about to say "one of her kind," but stopped myself. What was I, ghost matchmaker? And *were* they the same kind? "Someone like you."

"She's a lady. Can't you see? Gold brocade on her dress . . . She's like a dream. Wouldn't be seemly. I'm nae of her class."

"Oh." If I thought I was at a loss with the whole ghost thing, now I was dealing with ancient forms of what was proper and not. I wasn't all that good with twenty-first-century social conventions, forget those from centuries ago. Still, given the circumstances, it seemed like a little New World informality might help things along.

"Have you at least spoken to her?"

He shrugged, looking depressed again. "I've tried, but I cannae understand her."

"You can't?"

"I believe she's from the far-off lands."

"She speaks another language?"

"Aye, I believe so."

She passed by us, and I shivered from the cold. This was not the chill from the stones; it was a bone-deep freeze, causing my breath to come out in little white puffs. Donnchadh, of course, was impervious. I wondered why he didn't have the same effect on me.

"She is verra frail, verra hungry."

"Are you the one who's been stealing food? And you put it out for her?"

Again, if only a ghost could blush. He shrugged and ducked his head. "There is nourishment. She is verra hungry."

"Do you know her name, anything else about her?" I

asked. I was going to have to figure out who this woman was and what she had to do with Donnchadh or this monastery.

He shook his head. "But I shall keep her safe. I stake my life upon it."

I wasn't convinced the poor guy had a life to put to the stake for anyone anymore, but I got the gist.

Alicia was waiting for me when I walked into the foyer of the main house.

"Did you find the address of the warehouse?" I asked.

"No. I'm sorry. It seems Mr. Libole removed the address on each invoice. I didn't notice at the time, which was incredibly sloppy of me. I just had no reason to suspect he'd be keeping such secrets. Now I'm making phone calls—I'll track it down, one way or another," she said with determination. "I feel terrible that it's taken me this long."

"I appreciate your looking," I said, disappointed but trying not to show it. Alicia was so hard on herself there was no need to heap on more punishment.

"But I was thinking about that other thing you asked me about. The security tapes from that night."

"Do they show anything?"

"Nothing visual. But like I said, it has that strange voice on it. . . . Anyway, I thought you might want to listen." She gave me a significant look. "Maybe you'd be able to understand something."

Our eyes held for a long moment, and she continued. "Brendan told me about your . . . abilities. With spirits. I'm . . . It's amazing. What an incredible thing to be able to contact people from the other side."

"I don't . . ." I was about to deny it, to decry my rotten luck. But then I decided that Alicia was right. I had just

nt much of the afternoon chatting with a man from
 fifteenth century, or thereabouts. It hadn't been the
st scintillating conversation I'd ever taken part in, but
en I thought about it, it was nothing short of miracu-
s.

I nodded. "Thanks, Alicia. I'd love to listen to that
e."

She led me to a small, windowless cubicle in the base-
nt not far from the Discovery Room. It was full of
ctronic equipment, from computers to surveillance
nitors displaying several sections of the monastery,
 surrounding woods, and portions of the perimeter
ce.

Alicia cued something up on one of the computers
I hit play.

The voice was ghostly; no doubt about it. Covered in
tic and fading in and out, it was a strange, ethereal
ispering that rose to weeping and wailing. The same
iling I'd heard when I first found Larry McCall. I
n't have to understand the words to feel the chills go-
 up and down my spine.

"Is that . . . ? She's speaking Spanish, isn't she?"

Alicia's eyes were huge. "I think so. Or Portuguese, or
ybe Italian. It's really hard to make out."

"I keep intending to learn Spanish," I said. "But so far
 a restricted to construction-site vocabulary. Which is
ite limited. And somehow I doubt a centuries-old
ost would be speaking about circular saws, which for
ur information is *sierra circular*."

Alicia smiled. "She . . . The poor woman sounds like
 needs help. Do you . . . do you think we have to help
r, somehow?"

I couldn't help but note that Alicia was now using the
onoun "we." It felt nice to think that now we were in

this together, that I had an ally here at Elrich's eccen‹
estate.

"I think you may be right," I said. "She needs so›
thing. The first step would be to get someone to lister
this and interpret it for us."

"I'll copy it to a thumb drive for you."

There were plenty of guys in my employ whose 1
language was Spanish. But I didn't want to ask any
them for help. They were already freaked-out enou
what with the goings-on at the project. Besides, I kr
another native Spanish speaker who might be able
help.

Luz. She was the perfect person. Unfortunately,
hated ghosts. The woman wasn't scared of anything
this life except ghosts. And clowns. But I was despera

Time for her to face one of her fears.

"You want me to do *what*?"

After promising Alicia I'd let her know what I fo›
out, I hopped in my car and zoomed across the Gol‹
Gate Bridge to San Francisco State University, whe›
cornered Luz in her office.

"Just listen to the recording and see if you can m;
anything out."

"Who's on the recording, Mel?"

"It could be stray radio waves."

"Uh-huh. What's behind door number two?"

"It could be a woman saying something in Span
Or Portuguese. Or maybe Italian."

"Is this a ghost?"

"It's a recording."

"Of a ghost?"

"Maybe. They're the security tapes that are suppo
to run all the time—there was no visual at all, but so

dio, at the time Larry McCall was killed. Probably the
ler erased them on purpose, but it's just possible it's
nething else."

"Like what?"

"Every time this one ghost comes by, the temperature
immets. Sometimes ghosts drain energy sources, like
shlight batteries and that sort of thing. It's possible the
ost came by during the murder, or perhaps was even
racted by the violence, somehow, and her energy ru-
ed the recording. Maybe."

Luz gave me her one-eyebrow-raised stare.

"Just listen and tell me if you can make anything out.
 Graham's sake."

She glared at me, but settled down to listen.

"She's praying," said Luz after a few moments. "I
nk she's saying the rosary."

"That makes sense—I saw her carrying beads."

"And . . . she's looking for her room."

"What room?"

"The presidential suite, of course." Luz gave me a
k. "She doesn't say."

"Anything else?"

"She's . . . hungry. Very hungry. She keeps repeating
it: *"Tengo hambre, mucho hambre."*

"Is *that* what she's saying? This makes a lot more
ise. . . . I thought she was saying she had a man."

"*Hambre*, not *hombre*," lectured Luz. "This is why
onunciation matters."

"Yes, Professor." I actually *had* been confused, but
ostly I said it to annoy Luz and keep her tethered to
 usual snide sense of humor.

"Wait . . . ," said Luz. "Play that part again."

The recording was scratchy and faded in and out. A
tener had to be pretty creative to figure out what was

being said; a lot of words could have gone a number
different ways.

"I think . . . she's a prisoner. Was there a prisoner b
ing kept here?"

"At a monastery? I don't think a woman would ha
been kept there."

"Is there a way to find out for sure? How much
you know about the building?"

"I've been reading up, but it was an old building,
habited for a very long time. Plus there are huge gaps
the records. But I would be surprised to hear of a wom
prisoner being kept at a monastery. Wouldn't you?"

"Seems odd, but what do I know?" she said with
shrug.

"Does she say anything about a man being killed w
a bag of mortar? No names or descriptions? Or anythi
about a treasure?"

She shook her head. "Not that I can make out, but
take it home and listen to the recordings again, see i
can hear anything else."

"You don't have to, Luz. You've done a lot alrea
and I know how this freaks you out."

She shrugged, but seemed agitated, almost ang
"She . . . she's obviously in need of something. I'll ta
them home and listen again, just in case."

"Thank you."

She just nodded. Yep, agitated for sure.

All this time, when Luz said she was afraid of ghos
I thought it was in an abstract "ghosts are profound
disturbing" kind of way.

Now I wondered: Had Luz experienced somethi
she didn't want to tell me about? If so, why wouldn't s
have confided in me? But looking at her now, the stu
born tilt of her chin, the determined look in her eye

alized: Luz Cabrera did things on her own time, in her
wn way. It was that determination that had helped her
aw her way out of her working-class neighborhood and
rough graduate school, that had given her the fortitude
ith which she approached the vicissitudes of life and all
e difficulties that the world of social work threw at her.

I supposed we all had to come to the spirit world in
ur own fashion.

s I drove back over the Golden Gate Bridge toward
arin, appreciating the picture-perfect late-afternoon
n glinting off the ocean and the almost comically fluffy
hite clouds over the Marin Headlands, I realized that
though Donnchadh's revelations about his love for the
panish-speaking Lady in Red were fascinating, they
ought me not one step closer to figuring out what was
oing on. So I stopped by the house, filled Alicia in on
e little the recordings had revealed, grabbed the paper-
ork on the job to go over one more time, and snagged
eper of the Castle.

Then Dog and I headed back to the hospital.

Graham was in that strange, vacant sleep. His eyes
ere encircled by patches of solid black—not blue like a
ack eye, but true deep purple-black. It was disconcert-
g.

I sat by his side and thumbed through all the paper-
ork associated with the job, but found nothing perti-
ent. So I brought out the novel. *Keeper of the Castle*
ally was a darned good read. I was completely ab-
rbed in the travails of the star-crossed couple when my
one rang.

Nurse Ratched glared at me. I apologized and jumped
o take the call out in the corridor.

My stomach fell when I saw the readout: Valerie. My

ex-husband's wife and my stepson Caleb's current step
mother. And one of my least favorite people.

Of course, I was also one of *her* less than favorite peo
ple, so if she was calling me, it was probably important.
swore under my breath and then answered the phon
with all the sincerity I could muster.

"Valerie, what a surprise. How are you?"

"Oh, I'm *exhausted*." If the woman on the other en
of the line had been anyone else, I might have taken thi
more seriously. After all, Valerie was now pregnant. Bu
since she had always claimed to be exhausted *pre*preg
nancy as well, despite having no job and employing bot
a maid and a gardener, I wasn't all that sympathetic. Lik
that of a lot of underemployed wealthy people I'd met i
my line of work, Valerie's exhaustion seemed to expan
to fill her vast number of hours of having nothing to d
but gaze at her well-massaged navel and complain.

"And I just got a call from the police," she continued
"Caleb was picked up in Golden Gate Park."

Chapter Eighteen

"*What?*" Now she had my attention. "Where? What happened? Is he okay?"

"He and his little hoodlum friends were picked up for vandalism."

"You're kidding me."

"I wish. And Daniel's out of town, and Caleb's mother AWOL, as *usual*."

Angelica was a caring mother, though she was a big-wig financial type and did travel a lot for business. But unless I missed my guess, she had arranged for Caleb to stay with Daniel and Valerie while she was gone. Daniel, no doubt, had interpreted this as Caleb staying at the house, not as Caleb needing any active parenting. But Caleb was at an age ripe for screwing up.

"I'm a little busy, Valerie. I'm actually up in Marin on a job, in the hospital, and . . ."

"You're in the hospital?"

"No, a friend of mine was hurt."

"Oh. Sorry to hear that. Anyway, if we don't get Caleb by six, he'll have to spend the whole night in jail."

Valerie was fond of using the royal "we." We both knew she meant if *I* didn't get Caleb out, he'd be there all night. And she probably wasn't all that worried about him staying the night with the cops. She was simply stating a fact. Picking up the phone to call and tell me about Caleb's situation was as far as Valerie was willing to commit herself.

Why did I even try to fight this sort of thing? I wondered.

I sighed and gave in to the inevitable. I quizzed Valerie until she coughed up all the pertinent information and she accused me of being mean only once. Then I made a couple of phone calls and learned where to go and how to go about getting Caleb released into my custody. That led to the next question: What did I do with him once I got him? I called Dad to see if he'd be willing to have Caleb at the house for a bit, until his parents returned and came up with a plan.

When I got back to the ICU, I surprised Nurse Ratched standing by my chair, immersed in *Keeper of the Castle*. Probably the sexy bits.

She let it fall onto the chair, and blushed.

"I'm almost done with it—why don't I leave it for you when I'm finished?"

"Oh, I don't . . . Oh," she stammered.

"You won't believe how it ends," I said. "It really is a darned good book."

"Vandalism? Seriously?" I shook my head. *"Vandalism?"*

"Why do you keep repeating the word?" asked the sullen teenager in the passenger's seat, nursing a black eye.

"Because I really can't believe you. I mean, at least with shoplifting, maybe you get a candy bar or something out of the deal. But what possible motive could you have to *vandalize* Golden Gate Park?"

Caleb just shrugged. He would be listening to his iPod except that I had confiscated it, so I knew he could hear me. Whether he was actually listening was another matter. The arresting officer at the station had been kind enough to pull me aside and suggest Caleb had gotten in over his head with a few guys who were known to be punks. They had spray-painted on some of the walls of the park, but when a couple of the guys started snapping off newly planted saplings, Caleb had intervened and received a black eye for his trouble.

Helping fuel my anger was the realization that I had driven straight to Oakland without stopping to pick up Dog. I had called Alicia, and she'd agreed to take him for a walk and feed him, but I still felt guilty.

"Did you tell Bill?" Caleb asked.

"Of course."

"What did he say?" Caleb's voice caught on the last word.

I glanced at him and caught the glint of tears in his eyes. My bluster left me just as soon as his left him.

"Well, you know my dad. He wanted to know how you intended to clean up the mess you made."

Caleb looked out the window at the dark park and wiped at his eyes surreptitiously.

"Let's swing by and see how bad it is. That way we can come up with a plan."

"It's a washable kind."

"Washable spray paint?"

"I heard about it at the Garfield Lumber barbecue. It was my idea."

"Defacing public property was your idea?"

"No, using the washable kind of paint."

I couldn't help but smile. The cop also told me that Caleb had apologized and offered to clean up the damage, which made the other punks he was with hoot in derision.

"Anyway, for now, Dad's cooking dinner, and you're staying with him," I said. "I'll bring you back tomorrow so you can start cleaning the place up."

"And after that?"

"I don't know yet. I imagine Dad will have some suggestions. It's a good bet the phrase 'elbow grease' will be mentioned."

"Hey, I heard about Graham. Is he going to be okay?"

"Yes, I think so. He has a very hard head. And he looks like a panda—check this out." I showed him the photo on my phone.

He smiled for a moment; then his face fell.

"Mel, I'm . . ." His voice wavered again.

I reached over and tousled his rich brown hair. "I know. You screwed up. We all screw up from time to time. But you just used up your Get Out of Jail Free card. Next time, I'm telling them to go ahead and throw away the key."

It felt great to be home, in the embrace of family. Dad was making chicken soup, and the scents of sage and marjoram wafted through the house, reminiscent of countless Thanksgiving Day aftermaths. The actual day of Thanksgiving celebration was always fun, what with the traditional roast turkey and as many friends as could crowd around the dining table. My mother had never believed in turning anyone away, so Thanksgiving Chez Turner was always an event. Half the workers of Turner

Construction joined us, bringing contributions of home-made tamales and guacamole and pies, many experiencing their first Thanksgiving since arriving in this country.

But it was the day *after* Thanksgiving I'd really cherished as a kid. My dad would get up early and fix some sort of elaborate breakfast of leftovers, then start the soup from the turkey carcass. The aromas would wake me up and wrap themselves around me like a warm hand-knitted shawl. The day would be spent hiking in the redwoods, or going to a matinee, or playing Monopoly. The Turners weren't Black Friday shoppers, more like Black Friday hangers-out. My parents almost never just did nothing, so this was a magic day.

Today Dad was making beef stew for dinner; the chicken soup was merely an afterthought from last night's leftovers. Dad liked to keep busy in the kitchen, multitasking while he listened to the radio.

Watching Caleb as he clumsily chopped carrots for a salad, I felt sad that he had no such memories. In many ways, he was incredibly lucky. His well-to-do parents could afford to give him the best of everything, including a first-rate education. He was healthy and had more than enough to eat. But he had never known the kind of consistent emotional warmth and support that I had enjoyed, the rock-solid certainty that I belonged and was wanted. Growing up, I had found it stifling at times and had to be out on my own for a while before I fully appreciated how good I had it, but still.

Vandalism?

I had a hard time accepting that Caleb had gone along with something as stupid and pointless as vandalism, washable spray paint or not. I didn't need Luz's social work expertise to tell me this was a cry for help, for attention, for guidance. Not for the first time, I wondered how much to intervene. It wasn't my place to tell Caleb's parents what they should be doing, much less to suggest that he move in here with Dad and Stan and me. But unless something changed, and soon, Caleb could get himself into real trouble.

Conversation was a bit stilted as Stan, Dad, Caleb, and I studiously avoided a number of subjects: Graham's injury, the state of my ghost-ridden job, and Caleb's arrest. There were moments of long silence—a rare commodity in the Turner household—and while I was enjoying being back home, it was a little awkward.

"Your new client mentioned the Chapel of the Chimes the other day, didn't he?" Dad said. "I see they're playing jazz over there on the weekends."

"We should go. Have you ever been?" I asked Caleb. "It's an amazing place, not so much a columbarium as a work of art. Full of mosaics and fountains and concrete tracery . . . It was designed by Julia Morgan."

Caleb barely refrained from rolling his eyes. He may have heard me go on about the underappreciated local architect and builder a time or two.

Dad met Caleb's eyes and smiled as he peeled a bowl of pearl onions. "Mel may be a little obsessed with Julia Morgan. But with good reason. Morgan was talented, and smart, and kicked ass at a time when most women didn't see a lot of options other than getting married and having babies. Not that there's anything wrong with *that*," he added with a significant glance at me. "Mel's mother did pretty well for herself on that score. And they probably made their families very happy."

I ignored that last bit. And, of course, because it was coming from Dad instead of from me, Caleb actually listened. The teenager nodded.

"You know what would really blow you away is Hearst Castle," said Dad. "Down the coast. You ever been?"

Caleb shook his head.

"My wife and I took the girls there once, when you were, what, Mel? Eleven or twelve?"

"Something like that." I nodded. It had been a memorable family vacation. A framed snapshot of the five of us on that trip still stood on the mantel in the living room. We had camped at a state park near the beach, then taken a guided tour of Hearst Castle, which wasn't a castle so much as a grand estate atop a hill overlooking the ocean. My memories of the interior were vague, but I recalled sumptuous tapestries, Gothic archways, and of course the incredible cobalt-blue-and-gold underground pool, which fed into any number of childhood fantasies.

My sisters and I had played a game we called "Rosebud" for months afterward, in which one of our Barbie dolls always wound up being asked by a mysterious wealthy stranger to come stay as a guest in a castle suspiciously Hearst-like in nature, lounging by the pool. . . .

Wow. I realized I was living out one of my childhood Barbie dreams, living as a guest at Ellis Elrich's beautiful estate. But like so many dreams fulfilled, the experience was rather different in the adult world from what I had imagined as a child. I didn't recall anyone dying in our Barbie scenario. And while the Ken doll had endured his share of abuse, he had never wound up in the hospital with panda eyes and a head injury.

"Hearst Castle is an example of what happens when you give a talented woman an unlimited checkbook," continued Dad. "Like Mel here, on that Marin job."

"Funny, I've been thinking about Hearst a lot lately, too," I said. "I guess the comparison is inevitable. How many filthy-rich people import entire buildings from Europe?"

"Speaking of Chapel of the Chimes," said Stan, "did you know Morgan was doing that project around the same time as she was working with Hearst? She used some leftover pieces at the Chapel of the Chimes. I remember the docent saying that one of the staircases was originally intended for Hearst Castle."

"Just imagine having 'leftovers' from a job like that," I said.

Dad looked thoughtful as he stirred burgundy wine into the stew. Finally, he asked: "You suppose those ghosts would get mixed up?"

I nearly choked on my wine. "Excuse me?"

"Say you had two buildings, each with a resident ghost," said Dad. "They each hitch a ride on over to America on the steamer, or whatever Hearst used to bring the buildings here. And then Morgan's crew mixes and matches the buildings to create Hearst Castle, and before you know it, the ghosts don't know where the heck they are, or who those *other* ghosts are. Can ghosts from different times and places even see one another?"

Well, color me impressed. This was more than my father had ever deigned to say on the subject of ghosts. He had been aware of my mother's ability to see spirits but had kept mum—and seemingly embarrassed—about it my entire childhood. When I started showing signs of having inherited her special sight, he had been just as uncomfortable, which he demonstrated by being generally annoyed and cantankerous whenever the subject arose.

Adding to my amazement, Dad had put his finger on something I had been wondering about with regards to Wakefield. Could my ghosts, Donnchadh and the Lady in Red, have separate and distinct origins? Might this be why one group of stones, the ones with the bits of plaster still adhering to them, seemed so different from both the stones from Scotland and the newly quarried pieces from Texas?

"Well, Mel?" asked Caleb.

":Those are all great questions, Dad, to which I have absolutely no answers. I never really thought about it before. I'll ask Olivier what he thinks when I take Caleb to the city tomorrow."

Caleb assumed a hangdog expression, and I flashed him a *Don't Even Start with Me* look. Dragging my almost-but-not-quite stepson to Golden Gate Park to repair his damage was not high on my list of good times. It wasn't like I had anything else to do, like check in on Graham or build Wakefield or talk to ghosts or catch a killer. . . .

"Speaking of French fruitcakes," Dad said, noting the tension, "how's his shop doing?"

"He seems to be doing well. I'd say he's not a 'fruit-cake' as much as a good businessman. There's a lot of interest in ghost busting and spirits and whatnot in San Francisco."

Dad snorted.

I took a sip of wine, then excused myself to do some paperwork in the office and to call the hospital to check up on Graham.

I also spent some time on the Internet, but I'm not great with technology. While I found some boring histories of monasteries in Scotland, I couldn't find anything about the people who actually lived there, much less if any of them were Spanish women, which was seeming less likely all the time.

I did, however, track down a scandal that Kieran had mentioned to me, which revolved around Libole's renovation of a castle in Strasbourg. There was fierce public debate over whether all the bones Libole had claimed belonged in the ancestral family catacombs were genuine, or whether they had been pilfered from a village cemetery. It was a fascinating glimpse into Libole's character, I supposed, but I didn't see how the kerfuffle was relevant to the Wakefield Retreat Center, much less the death of Larry McCall.

"Do you know any Scottish people?" I asked Stan when he came in to join me.

"I know a lot of folks with Scots blood in them, myself included," Stan said. "But not Scots as in from Scotland. Why?"

"I'm trying to figure out some of the history behind this monastery I'm working on."

"I thought you were working with Florian Libole up there? I expected he would know everything and everyone there was to know."

"Yeah, well, he's pulled something of a disappearing act."

"He's gone missing?"

"I don't think he's *missing* missing," I said, though I realized there was no way to know. Maybe Libole had stumbled onto the same thing as McCall and had suffered McCall's fate. But this time the killer got smart and hid the body. What a terrible thought. "I think he's probably just off somewhere for a few days."

"Okay," said Stan after a brief pause. "So you can't find what you need on the Internet?"

"Some stuff, sure. But I get confused. Everything's got two spellings—the Gaelic and the English, and they're both confusing. And there are about a million results here, and my eyes are losing focus."

"You do look tired."

"Gee, thanks."

Stan smiled. "You know I think you're gorgeous. I'm just sayin', seems like maybe you're burning the candle at both ends these days. Caleb's walk on the wild side isn't helping, I'm sure, not to mention Graham landing in the hospital in addition to working all the hours God gives you. It's no wonder you'd be a little tired. How 'bout you go on to bed right after dinner, and let me do a little research on the place for you?"

"Really? You wouldn't mind?"

"I'd be happy to. Nothing but reruns on TV tonight anyway."

"Thanks, Stan. You're a peach."

Just as I was falling asleep, my phone rang: Annette Crawford.

"So, about the clipboard: There's no record of a clipboard or papers being gathered as evidence at the scene. Could be nothing; could be something. Right?"

"Right. And what about Bernardino? Anything on him?"

"He says you're a pain in the ass."

"He said that?"

"No, actually I did. He just agreed."

"Seriously?"

"Just kidding. Just because you dealt with a shady police inspector once doesn't mean we should all be tarred with the same brush," Annette said.

"I don't think *you're* shady."

A soft chuckle. "Well, there you go. Not sure I can return the compliment, but be that as it may, I asked around, and Bernardino seems okay. Maybe not the swiftest guy, and he might be a little starstruck by Elrich. What's he like, anyway?"

"Elrich? Impressive. Charming. Capable of makin otherwise rational people starstruck."

"Including you?"

"Me? Nah. You know me. I'm bitter and twisted. cynic of the highest order, that's me."

"Sure you are. That's why you're trying to save som poor schmuck from taking the fall for a murder he didn commit."

"It's complicated."

"Right. Oh, here's one interesting tidbit. You're righ Alicia Withers didn't exist six years ago. No sign of criminal record, but . . ."

"If she didn't exist, there's no real way to know."

"Right. Also, I thought you might be interested t learn that Pete Nolan has been released on bail."

"Oh, okay."

"Mel, be careful. If you're wrong, and Nolan really di kill McCall, and he killed to keep something a secret in stead of just in a fit of pique over building permits, h might be someone to worry about."

"Hey, speaking of that . . . Florian Libole is a designe involved in the historical re-creation. He seems to hav disappeared. Maybe."

"Are you thinking he was involved in the murder? O that he's in danger of being murdered?"

"I really don't know. Maybe neither. It just seem strange."

"You should report it to Detective Bernardino."

"Okay. I suppose you're right. Just in case."

After a short pause, Annette said: "I take it there ar ghosts on this building site?"

"Mmm."

"I don't know how you do it."

"Neither do I, believe me."

"Mel, do me a favor and watch your back. Find out what those ghosts want, what they have to do with this murder, and then move on."

"Yeah, thanks. That's the general idea."

"And buy yourself a can of wasp spray."

"I'm sorry?"

"Shoots twenty feet, capable of taking down bad guys in their tracks. As effective as mace."

"Oh, um . . ." I decided she wouldn't want to know about my father's Glock, which I was carrying. Without a license, of course. "Good safety tip. Hey, Annette? When things settle down a bit, you should come see Wakefield. It's really something. We could have lunch. Maybe even lounge by the pool."

"I'd like that. Keep me posted. And buy some wasp spray."

Chapter Nineteen

The night in my bedroom was surprisingly restful. N
flute music, no mysterious lights shining in far-off ru
ins. I slept like the dead.

In the morning I called Tony on the jobsite and e:
plained that I would be late. He and I went over th
schedule for the day, and I asked him to set up a perim
eter around the round room and not to allow any of th
men to go near it. As long as they weren't getting chase
out of the monastery by Donnchadh, they had plenty t
keep them busy without me there.

I then called to check on Graham. I knew the nurse
voices by now and was happy when I got one of the nic
ones. She told me there was no change, which was good
and that Dr. Petralis was considering bringing Graham ou
of the medically induced coma within the next day or two

Caleb was due at the Park Police substation at eleve
I planned to drop him off, then go by Olivier's place an
have a little ghost chat.

As I was having my morning coffee and fending off Dad's offers of breakfast—which Caleb was shoveling down with gusto, even while grumbling at the early hour—Stan came into the kitchen.

"I printed out a few articles for you," he said, handing them to me as he poured himself coffee.

I glanced through them: a few general histories of the area, a long history of the monastery and its rulers, the Scottish Reformation. A lot of information, a lot of names and dates.

"Anything particularly interesting?" I asked.

"Not really, sad to say. No fun ghost stories, gruesome murders, anything like that. But as you said, there were a lot of potential references. I only made it through a few. Here's one thing I found, though: There's a Scottish paraphernalia shop right here in Jack London Square."

"What's a Scottish paraphernalia shop?"

"Isn't it obvious?" Dad said. "It's a shop that sells paraphernalia." He glanced at Caleb, and the two of them said in unison: "From Scotland!" and started laughing.

Good Lord, what have I done? I thought to myself. They weren't even related. How could they be so much alike?

Stan grinned. "Makes a person wonder, right? I'm imagining a lot of plaid, but what do I know? But I thought maybe the owner would be Scottish, and indeed she is. So I called her. She seemed to have a lot of information about folklore, that sort of thing. Said she'd heard of the monastery in question, that there might be a ghost story associated with it, and she was going to look it up."

"Stan, you're amazing. It's like you've been hiding your snoopy light under a bushel. I'm using you on all my murder investigations from now on."

Dad and Caleb gave me the same scathing look.

"Not that I'm getting involved in any more murder investigations," I clarified. "Nope, not me. Ghosts or no ghosts. Maybe I should start building new tract houses—what do you think?"

"You'd probably build it on an ancient burial ground," said Caleb, "like in that old movie *Poltergeist*."

He and my dad exchanged glances, grunted, and returned to their respective breakfasts, hunkering down over their plates.

"So this Scottish store?" I asked. "Hard to imagine there's a whole lot of demand for plaid in downtown Oakland."

Stan shrugged. "You know how hard it's been to get merchants into those spaces. Maybe they gave her a good deal. Anyway, she opens at ten, but she said she'd be there a little after nine, if you wanted to stop by."

"What's this article about Hearst?" I asked, flipping through the pages.

"We were talking about him last night, so I thought I'd see what I could find about him importing buildings. Turns out Hearst bought a whole Spanish monastery in 1925, dismantled it, and had it shipped over and put in storage in Brooklyn, where it remained essentially abandoned. In 1952 two wealthy historians bought it and rebuilt it in North Miami Beach. Now they say it's the oldest building in the western hemisphere, originally built in Segovia in the twelfth century."

"That story sounds fishy to me," said Dad. "Since when have historians been wealthy?"

"My point was that Hearst brought over other buildings and then abandoned them. So maybe there are other such stones floating around, or even entire buildings."

I was staring at one of the photos that went with the

article about the Hearst monastery. It was a pile of lichen-covered golden gray stones, with bright blue numbers and letters marked on them. They were from Spain.

"Those look a lot like the stones behind the Japanese Tea Garden," said Dad, peering over my shoulder. "Remember those? That's when I had to go pick *you* up in disgrace from Golden Gate Park. Guess it runs in the family."

The Japanese Tea Garden in Golden Gate Park was the hub of many a school field trip. When I was a kid, I had adored running around koi ponds and scamming almond cookies, but I had been banished after Chris Marriott and I split off from the rest of the class and clambered around a pile of old stones that sat in a clearing behind the garden.

That was what had been bothering me since the first time I saw those stones in a pile at Wakefield: They reminded me of the stones in the park.

"Now I have to go to a Scottish store? Seriously?" whined Caleb. Apparently, his chagrin had worn off overnight.

"Yep. I'm your ride to Golden Gate Park, so you're stuck with me. You can stay in the car and read if you want. There are some architectural magazines behind the seat, plus the latest *Haunted Home Quarterly* featuring yours truly."

Since I had confiscated his iPod and his cell phone, Caleb's entertainment options were limited. Apparently, *Haunted Home Quarterly* wasn't enough of a draw, so he trailed behind me as I headed into the World of Scotland.

There was a lot of paraphernalia crammed onto the store shelves. Tams, wool fisherman sweaters, aprons referencing scotch, golf, and the Loch Ness monster. There were hankies, bagpipes, bumper stickers, sporrans, golf balls, and shortbread cookies. And overriding everything was plaid: plaid scarves, plaid wall hangings and pillows, and plaid doggy raincoats. Behind the register hung a sign advertising genealogical research services. I couldn't help thinking a shop with a focus on all things Scottish was a long shot in this town, but then I tended toward the pessimistic.

My knock was met by a pretty sixtyish woman with long gray hair worn in a braid pinned on top of her head. She asked us to call her Amy, and before we got past the first rack of plaid shawls, she told me how much she had enjoyed her talk with Stan and asked me if he was single.

"As a matter of fact, he is," I said. "He's a great guy."

"He sounded like it," Amy said with a sweet smile. "He mentioned that you're working on a re-creation of a monastery in Marin?"

"It's a re-creation in the sense that we're putting the old place back together, but it's the original building."

"Oh, my. How about that?" She brought out several books and laid them on the counter. "Stan gave me the name, so I looked it up last night."

"This is great," I said, anxious to see if any of the volumes could answer my questions. There were a couple of old photos of the Wakefield monastery, mostly black-and-white, not nearly as clear as the ones Florian Libole had shown me. There was a brief paragraph that didn't say much beyond what Libole had already told me.

After I had exhausted all the references to the monastery, I looked up, deflated. Caleb was poking around at the back of the store, perusing a collection of decorative knives and daggers. Leave it to him to find the one dangerous thing in such a wholesome shop.

"You look disappointed," said Amy. "The information isn't helpful? What were you looking for, exactly?"

"If only I knew. I guess I was hoping for something more personal, maybe about the monks who lived there, that sort of thing. I mean, this is probably a really stupid question," I began, thinking I should find an expert on Scottish history at a university and wondering if Luz might be able to point me in the right direction. "But, for instance, did knights live in monasteries?"

"No, of course not," said Amy. "However, this particular monastery served as a kind of inn for passersby of importance, the aristocracy, that sort of thing."

I nodded. "And there are no . . . ghost stories, nothing like that?"

"No. But there is a wonderful ghost story associated with another monastery, not far from Wakefield." She pulled a well-read copy of Scottish lore out from a desk drawer. "This book's not for sale, I'm afraid. But it tells the legend of the curse of Eochaidh and Sidheag."

"Now we're talking." I wasn't even going to *try* to repeat what she'd just said.

"There was a noble lady who had taken refuge at Eochaidh Monastery. Her family was trying to hide her from a powerful laird—that's Scottish for "lord"—who wanted her hand in marriage."

Amy turned the book toward me; it was splayed to show woodcuts of a lady in a procession, medieval structures behind her. The noblewoman was dressed in finery, with a dozen horses, and a man with a broadsword was standing nearby. She tapped on his picture.

"She was protected by a great warrior, named Donnchadh MacPhaidein." She continued, reading aloud: "'He was a man of uncommon height and strength, whose loyalty knew no bounds. He vowed to protect his ward even unto death.'"

Well, Donnchadh MacPhaidein, we meet again. "And what happened to him?"

"He died defending her. He held off a small army 'with the strength of ten men.' They say he was in love with her, which is why he fought so bravely."

"Until he was killed."

"I'm afraid so. And ever since then, the place was cursed. MacPhaidein's ghost would attack any man who ventured in—though he spared the women. The villagers started tearing it down over time, hoping to get rid of the spirit, but still he roamed the ruins."

"Was the noblewoman Spanish, by any chance?"

"No. No, of course not."

"And was she killed as well?"

"No. She was abducted and forced to marry the laird."

"How sad."

"It is, yes," said Amy with a shrug. "Of course, she went on to live a noble life and gave birth to several sons. So . . . I don't know. It's hard to see those days with modern eyes, I think. Everything was so different then; you were pretty lucky not to starve to death as a peasant, or die in war or plague, or be starved out in a siege."

"I suppose that's true."

"This is interesting," said Amy. "The lady was referred to as *cuach*, which translates, roughly, as 'the vessel.'"

"Excuse me?"

"The 'vessel.' Which shows how women were thought of back then. She was considered to be the vessel for the next generation, her bloodline associated with greatness."

"So, just to recap: Donnchadh MacPhaidein, a large man with a broadsword, was killed while defending a woman known as the vessel, and ever since has been said to haunt the ruins of the monastery?"

"After putting up a heck of a fight, yes."

So maybe the vessel wasn't an actual treasure at all. Maybe it was a woman who had lived, and died, centuries ago. The one Donnchadh had died defending.

It would break Donnchadh's heart to know he had failed. Perhaps this was what kept him around, knowing somehow that he had failed in his duty; he couldn't let go of his charge. I wondered if it would help him to move on if I told him what had happened. How could a poor, despondent knight be made to understand he no longer had a duty to protect anyone?

And who the heck was the sad, hungry ghost, then?

"But . . . you say this tale refers to another monastery, *not* Wakefield?"

"Yes. It was a place on another island, not too far away—by modern standards, of course. The Isle of Inchcolm, in the Firth of Forth. But those isles are full of similar ruins."

"You're saying the monastery on the Isle of Inchcolm in the Firth of Forth isn't Wakefield?"

"That's correct." Amy perused the photos in the book and shook her head. "Compared to others of their time and place, neither of these monasteries was operational for very long. And the isles were too out of the way to be critical for nation building, or anything historically significant like that. I imagine that's why the state allowed Wakefield to be hauled away to Marin County, of all places."

"I suppose you're right."

"Could I . . . ? Would it be possible to take a tour sometime? I would love to see it."

"I don't see why not," I said, and handed her my card. Dad and Stan were asking about it as well—maybe I could have them all come by on the same day. Who knows? Maybe Amy and Stan would hit it off in person as well as they did on the phone. Just call me Mel Turner, Matchmaker. But . . . it would be better to rid the place of ghosts first. "I'm working on a few urgent projects right now. But maybe in a week or two, when things settle down a bit?"

"Perfect," Amy said, looking around the store. It was now officially opening time, and the store wasn't exactly jammed with eager customers clamoring for Scottish paraphernalia. "I can come anytime, really."

Before leaving, I bought a tin of shortbread, some tea, a plaid scarf for Graham, and some little decorative golf balls.

"Who are the golf balls for?" Caleb asked as we walked back to the car.

"Elrich must like golf, right? I mean, don't all rich people like golf?"

"My *dad* doesn't like golf."

"He's wealthy, but he's not stinking rich like Ellis Elrich is rich, if you know what I'm saying."

"Don't mention that to Valerie," Caleb grumbled. "She'd freak out. She's already talking about a debutante ball for the baby."

"What if it's a boy?"

"I know, right? So why are you buying presents for Ellis Elrich, anyway?"

"I'm not, really. I just wanted to buy something from Amy. She was so nice to do all that research for me, and I felt bad. I get the sense she doesn't make a lot of sales."

He nodded. "So your ghost was killed trying to protect some lady?"

"How did you know there was a ghost on my site?"

He gave me an incredulous look. "Seriously?"

"Yeah, you're right. There's a ghost."

"He's a real knight?"

"I guess so. Or a guardian, anyway. He carries a huge broadsword; that much is true."

"Is he . . . friendly?"

"I wouldn't say *friendly*, exactly," I said as we climbed into my Scion. "It's more like he doesn't see me as a threat, 'cause I'm a girl."

Caleb started laughing, and as I pointed the car toward the freeway entrance, I joined him.

I dropped Caleb off at the Golden Gate Park police station, forcing myself not to walk him in as though he were a toddler.

After leaving the kitchen last night, I'd overheard Dad's stern voice giving Caleb a *talking-to*. And this morning Dad informed me at breakfast that he would pick Caleb up this afternoon, and Caleb was going to spend the next few days with him and Stan at the house. He would make sure he got to community service until things were put right in Golden Gate Park. Caleb had called his dad and worked it out.

I felt guilty for handing off the responsibility to my father, but Dad would be much more effective than I in this situation. Besides, he was retired and had the time and attention to spend on a boy who needed help. Whereas my current to-do list was a little long.

Before heading to Olivier's shop, I wanted to follow up on those stones behind the Japanese Tea Garden. True, it had been many, many years since I had last seen them, but ever since I'd spied that pile of stones at Wakefield, the memory of them had been niggling at the back of my mind. And since I was already in Golden Gate Park, it would be a quick detour. As if the fates were smiling on me, I found a free parking spot on the street not far from the de Young Museum.

I located the clearing behind the fence, but the area was now cleared out. No surprise there; it had been a few years. But the ground seemed freshly trampled, with no saplings and just a few young weeds. Small stones and gravel in the same golden gray hue as the stones littered the ground.

An impossibly old man was raking the sand in the Tea Garden.

"Excuse me, sir?" I said, speaking to him through the cyclone fence. "Do you remember a pile of stones that used to be here?"

He nodded.

"Really? Do you know what happened to them?"

"They cleared them out a year or so ago."

"Who did? Do you know?"

He shrugged.

"Do you happen to know where they came from originally?"

He shook his head and continued with his meticulous task. The tines of the rake left parallel lines in the smooth sand, the lines drawn in careful swirls and shapes that suggested the flow of water. Or so it seemed to me—I supposed it was open to interpretation. The man was methodical, meticulous, raking over his own footsteps, ensuring that each sweep of the tines overlapped so that the individual strokes were indistinguishable. I wondered how long it took him and how often he did it . . . and whether some rogue squirrel would come by and ruin in two seconds what had taken him all morning to accomplish.

The man's calm absorption in his task reminded me of Ellis Elrich stacking his smooth round stones. I would never be able to live my life with a Zen approach—I was more the carefully choreographed chaos type—but I was starting to appreciate how mesmerizing this sort of thing could be.

The man looked up from his raking, mistaking my silence for expectation of more information.

"You could probably ask the Parks Department. I imagine they keep records."

"Okay, thanks. The, um, raking is really beautiful," I said, and turned to leave.

"Thank you. And good luck. Those were beautiful stones."

Two people sat behind the counter at the Parks Department: One looked like the stereotype of a sweet grandma, complete with white bun and mother-of-pearl half-glasses on a gold chain; the other a young man with pearl stud earrings in both ears, a buzz cut on the sides with his hair longer on top, and heavy black spectacles. He wore skintight black jeans and tennis shoes with no socks. He was adorable in an androgynous way, which, I supposed, was the point. His name tag read CUR.

"Your name's 'Cur'?" I asked. Grandma would have been my first choice for information, but she was already helping someone.

"Yeah."

"Oh. Cool. So, I'm wondering about the old stones that used to be behind the Japanese Garden."

"They weren't of any use to anyone," Cur said, glancing over at Grandma.

"I imagine they weren't. What happened to them?"

"City sold them."

"Who bought them?"

"We can't go around giving out that kind of information."

"You can't?"

He shook his head, glancing at his coworker once again.

"Do you have any pictures of the stones, by any chance?"

"I don't think so. It might be in the file."

"And would you have this file here somewhere . . . ?"

Another glance over at Grandma. Cur shook his head. "No."

After years of dealing with bureaucrats, I had learned that nine times out of ten "no" didn't mean "no." Sometimes it meant I wasn't asking the right question and needed to rephrase. Sometimes it meant they didn't know the right answer and couldn't be bothered to find out. Sometimes it meant what I was asking would take time and effort, and they didn't feel like doing it. Patience was required to figure out what "no" really meant.

"So, if a person needed this information, how would she go about getting it?"

"Well, if you insisted, you could fill out a request-for-information form."

"I would love to do that."

"They're really long."

"I don't mind."

He let out a long breath of exasperation but opened a huge file cabinet and started rifling through the hanging folders within the drawer.

"No one was using those stones," he grumbled. "A few were used for landscaping, but then someone got uptight about that 'cause they were historic and everything. But it was well within the rights of the city to sell them."

"I'm not arguing that," I said. "I'd just like to know who bought them."

"Why?" he asked as he finally pulled out a manila der, put it atop the file cabinet, and extracted a three-ge form, which he handed to me.

It really wasn't any of his business. But I doubted Cur s any sort of threat, and as Inspector Annette Craw-d always liked to remind me, sometimes witnesses n't realize that tiny little details are important. He ght not know what he knew.

"I'm researching the history of such things. Do you ppen to know where the stones came from origi-lly?"

He shook his head.

"Do you know anything more about them? Anything all?"

"Nah."

I took a seat in a beige plastic chair and filled in the m, though much of the information didn't pertain to at I was asking. But bureaucracies followed their own ernal logic; no sense in fighting the Parks Department.

When I brought the form up to the counter, along th a five-dollar check for processing, Cur took them d told me someone would be in touch.

"So, like, why's everyone so interested in these stones? ey're there, like, for decades and no one cares, and w everyone's interested all of a sudden."

"Who else has asked about them?"

He shrugged. "Some old guy in a suit, just last week, ybe the week before."

"Did he leave his name?"

"I guess it's on the form. But I remember he tried to t out of paying the processing fee, 'cause he was with e Marin County Building Department."

Chapter Twenty

As I drove across town to Olivier Galopin's gho
busting store in Jackson Square, I kept turning thin
over in my head. If Amy was right about the legend
then was Wakefield even Wakefield, or had Libc
bought some other monastery he was trying to pass
as Wakefield? Had he then used some of the old stor
from Golden Gate Park to fill in missing parts of
pseudo-Wakefield? And if so, why was he keeping it su
a secret?

And was Dad right to wonder? Could each source
stones have its own ghost attached? That would expl:
why they couldn't understand each other. And . . . if t
"vessel" was a woman and not a precious goblet as K
ran assumed, then there was no treasure to be fou
And yet people had been attacked over it. Unless th
had been assaulted for another reason entirely?

It was a good thing I'd slept well last night, beca:
this was making my brain hurt.

And it made me want to get into that warehouse
re than ever. I hoped Alicia was able to locate the
dress soon.

Olivier Galopin's Ghost-Busting Shoppe had made a
splash when it opened not long ago, and business was
booming. Olivier supplemented his storefront sales
giving classes on detecting spirits, and interest in the
ost world was strong in a town like San Francisco. No
ed to import spirits from Scotland—there were plenty
locally sourced specters right here.

After swapping hellos and getting caught up—I told
ivier about Graham—we got down to the nitty-gritty.

"Do you think a spirit could have done that kind of
mage?"

"As I believe you know, there is still considerable de-
te as to how much physical harm ghosts are capable of
icting. They seem to specialize in terrorizing people,
en when they're not trying to, rather than causing
ysical harm. Though there have been numerous in-
nces of touching, even a quick shove at the top of the
irs, that sort of thing. But striking someone over the
ad with a tool of some kind, hard enough to kill or
und . . . ? I've never heard of a documented example
that. That happens in the movies, not real life."

"That's what I thought."

"How is Graham?"

"Healing, we hope. I still haven't been able to talk to
n about what he might have discovered that would
ve prompted someone to hurt him."

"Perhaps it was enough that he was asking questions.
ver discount the danger posed by being curious."

"Maybe. Anyway, here's what I wanted to ask you:
ppose the Wakefield stones were mixed with elements
m other buildings. Would it be possible for ghosts to

cling to the stones from separate sources and then become confused . . . ?"

"Very much so. The reason ghosts are so often associated with buildings is that their energy has seeped into the very walls of the structure. If those walls are dismantled and moved . . . well, often a ghost will dissipate. Particularly strong visions may follow the bits and pieces but they will feel . . . disjointed. Scattered. Sort of like ghostly multitasking."

"And if stones from different buildings were mixed together in a new construct, will the ghosts with different origins be aware of each other?"

"Perhaps. Nothing I have read suggests that could happen."

"And could they interact?"

"That's another matter entirely. . . . To tell you the truth, this doesn't come up much. I'm really not sure. You know, it would be fascinating to try to record the ghosts of yours and listen to see whether they communicate. If you bring the recording to the lab, we can use the computer to alter the frequency and edit out the ambient noise. Often it is only *after* a ghost hunt that we see evidence of spirits—though I know this has not been your experience!"

"Actually, I think we might already have a recording of one of the ghosts."

Olivier did a double take. "Are you serious?"

"Dead serious. Do you speak Spanish, by any chance?"

"I speak French and English."

"I realize that. But I thought all you European types spoke, like, five languages."

"With French, why learn another language?"

"Oh, I don't know . . . in case of vacation, or invasion during a world war, or . . . ?"

"How many languages do *you* speak?"

"I know how to say 'circular saw' in Spanish."

He smiled. "But seriously, Mel, if you have recorded evidence of a ghost, that would be amazing. I would love to analyze it."

"A friend of mine is listening to it right now—she's going to try to translate it. But you can take a crack at it next."

One more quick stop before heading back to Marin was to see my faux finisher, Yuri Andropov. Yuri ran popular decorative-painting classes on the weekends for rich people, which allowed him to remain in his studio in the China Basin area of San Francisco. Most of his artist neighbors had been pushed out over the past few years by high rents. San Francisco's loss was Oakland's gain; our East Bay nightlife, café and restaurant scene were flourishing with the influx of creative types.

Yuri was a generally cranky, but quite talented, fifty-ish man who as a child had immigrated to Madison, Wisconsin, with his family from the Ukraine; as soon as he'd turned eighteen, he had come to San Francisco and had never looked back.

"What do you know about traditional fresco methods?" I asked, watching as he painted foliage on a massive canvas that was destined for a hotel in Singapore. The decidedly Renaissance-inspired scene featured frolicking water nymphs and leering satyrs.

He frowned as he dredged his brush through a bit more sap green paint. "I know everything. You know that."

"Right. I forgot," I said. "So, give me a crash course."

"The *faux* fresco method we use today is simply watered-down paint, to which we add chalk to mimic the

patina of true fresco. But genuine fresco isn't a layer o
paint on top of the wall; instead, dry paint pigments ar
placed in wet plaster so that the colors become *part o
the wall. This was sometimes supplemented with pai
on top, called secco painting. But over time the seco
painting flakes off, whereas the fresco will never be de
stroyed unless the plaster itself falls off the wall."

"That's fascinating."

"Often the plaster was used to strengthen the wall, s
it wasn't just decorative but structural."

"Huh. I'm assuming this was long before Portland co
ment was developed; what was plaster made of, back i
the day?"

"Bits of straw and clay and sand were in the main pa
but the fine plaster on top was made of ash. Pigments we
made from ground stone—which is why there's a prepor
derance of so-called earth colors, such as terra-cotta an
ocher—as well as from flowers and saps and vegetables. I
addition, all sorts of things used to be burned: vegetatio
even bones, then ground into a powder used in patinas."

"How can you tell what a plaster was made of?"

"These days it's easy. Micro X-ray diffraction, infrare
spectroscopy, gas chromatography coupled with ma
spectrometry and carbon-14 dating."

"That's *easy*?"

Yuri smiled. The knit cap he wore because his studi
had no heat was covered in paint stains, like everythin
else on his body. He was unshaven and probably hadn
done laundry in a while. Because he was often mistake
for a homeless man, people tended to underestimat
him. He was a fine artist.

"I thought you told me you used to be an anthropo
ogist. These are common archaeological techniques."

"Yeah, I wasn't that kind of anthropologist."

"What kind were you?"

"The kind without skills or useful knowledge. The kind likely to go off about theories of cultural relativism. Interesting at cocktail parties but generally useless when it comes to anything practical."

"Ah."

"So, I don't suppose you have one of these diffraction dealies lying around?"

He dabbed a few highlights on some leaves that were starting to look three-dimensional under his skilled hands, and then fixed me with a quizzical look.

"You have some old plaster you're interested in learning more about? I thought you were here to hire me to create new murals that are meant to look old."

"Right—for Elrich's *house*, I want you to paint some traditional Spanish Revival murals. You're going to get a kick out of this place: It's a Victorian mansion with a Spanish interior. Don't ask. By the way, I showed the clients the drawings you sent, and they loved them. Especially the market scenes. We'll want them to look faded, as though they've been there forever. How soon can you start?"

"As soon as tomorrow. The project I was set to begin tomorrow has been rescheduled due to construction delays. So I can fit you in."

"Great. We're ready for you. Anyway, the plaster I'm interested in investigating pertains to another project. I'd love to figure out more about it."

"Take the machine if you want. It's not large."

"Seriously?"

He set his brushes and palette down on a sheet-draped table and started climbing a rickety-looking ladder to a little storage loft. I hurried over to steady the ladder; it squeaked loudly in protest as he climbed.

"You need a better ladder," I couldn't help but point out.

"It's on my shopping list. Let's see . . ." He scrounged around for a minute. "*Here* it is," he said as he held up a device that looked like a large hair dryer. "One micro X-ray diffraction doohickey."

"Do all artists have these close at hand?"

"I shouldn't think so. I bought it used off the Internet, believe it or not." He shrugged. "I put in a bid to restore the Coit Tower murals, so I thought it would come in handy, let me know exactly what I was dealing with."

"You worked on Coit Tower? The Diego Rivera murals?"

"Nah, lost the bid. That would have been something though, right?"

"So, what will this thingy show me?"

"It's going to give you a picture, like this. . . ."

Step by step, Yuri walked me through how to use the device.

"It won't give you, in itself, a breakdown of what the plaster is composed of, but it will give you a spatial mineral cartography that would then have to be analyzed. You'll have a starting point for figuring out exactly what you're dealing with."

"Okay . . ." This seemed like a little more detail than what I needed. "I guess I was hoping I could hold it up to the wall and get a readout."

"This isn't *Star Trek*. It's chemistry. You should check out that old plaster, though. It could tell you a lot."

"Thanks. I will."

Back in Marin, the worksite was humming along. I answered several payroll questions, ordered some more supplies, and inspected the progress in the chapel and

he reinforcement projects. As long as the men stayed
away from the round room, there didn't seem to be fur-
her problems with the fierce guardian ghost.

Then I checked out the suspect blocks of stone.

I put the diffraction device up to one of the stones
hat retained its plaster. Yuri had said that plaster strengthened walls, but I was guessing that it also provided a
mooth, even surface to camouflage the rough-hewn
tone. Back then, when everything was handmade, peo-
ole valued the perfection of form. Now that everything
s churned out by machines, we value the slight imperfec-
ions and flaws of handmade items. The grass is always
greener.

"What are you doing?" came Tony's voice from be-
ind me.

"I'm checking out these stones with this fancy con-
raption, here. It's supposed to tell me something about
he composition of the plaster."

"Libole said that stuff didn't matter, that we were go-
ng to go over it with new plaster anyway."

"We probably will. But I'd like to know what we're
lealing with so we can replicate it properly," I said. "Do
you have any idea where Libole is, by any chance?"

He shook his head.

"Hey, Tony, I've been meaning to ask. . . . You said this
s the second time that round room has imploded, yet
Libole didn't suggest devising any sort of external support, any sort of reinforcement?"

"No, and . . ." He let off with a shrug.

"What?"

"Well, it's supposed to be a tower, not a single story.
That's what all these extra stones are for. But we can't
even get it to stand up like it is. It's strange, like Libole's
rying to shove this thing in there, but it doesn't fit. He

showed me how it was on the drawings, which are supposedly the original schema, but . . . I don't know what
he's smoking, or what sort of Scottish history he's been
reading, but it doesn't make any sense."

"I agree with you. It seems odd."

I stepped back and looked again at the lines that indicated there had been a painting, or fresco, here on
these stones. Traditionally, murals were used to tell stories or recount historical events. Medieval monks were
among the few literate people of their day, but none-
theless art was used to reinforce stories of redemption
and risk, or heaven and hell, as Florian Libole had
pointed out.

So what story might the pictures on these stones have
told?

"Could you help me stack these stones together? I
think this one goes with that one. See how the line of red
in the plaster carries through?"

Tony looked decidedly uncomfortable. "I don't know.
Libole was pretty adamant that we don't mess around
with those stones."

"I'm not suggesting we mess around with them, just
restack them, like this." I tried to move one near another.
It took all my strength, and I managed to move it about
six inches.

I left off, panting. "I see now why the men have been
using the heavy equipment with these things. Can you
operate the crane?"

"Sorry, Mel. Count me out," Tony said, shaking his
head as he backed toward the little office trailer. "Those
things are nothing but trouble."

I considered calling one of my guys over to help me
with the crane, but then I realized there was no need.
Instead, I used my phone to take a picture of each sepa-

rate piece, then ventured into the building to do the same with whichever stones I could access from the demolished section. I had a vague notion that I could transfer the photos to the computer and then mix and match to re-create the original mural picture. Unfortunately, I had no idea how to use any computer graphics programs.

My phone rang: It was Luz. The hospital, assuming she was the wife, had called to let her know the doctors were ready to bring Graham out of the coma. I dashed to the house to grab Dog.

I saw Alicia in the hall and told her the happy news.

"That's wonderful!" She gave me an awkward hug.

That did it. I was just going to come out and ask her. "Alicia, could I ask you . . . ? Why don't you have a past?"

"Pardon?"

"Someone pointed out to me that Alicia Withers didn't exist a few years ago."

She froze.

"I'm sorry. It's really none of my business—"

"I had to get out of a situation," she said suddenly. "Mr. Elrich helped me."

"I understand."

"No, I'm not sure you do," she said, now fixing me with a straightforward look. Serious as ever but filled with a sudden passion. "Ellis Elrich saved my life."

"What happened?"

"We used to be neighbors when we were kids. There were a bunch of us back then, in a working-class neighborhood in Columbus, Ohio. My father was an alcoholic. Ellis's dad used to beat him up. Anyway, we had a few things in common.

"Over the years, our lives went in different directions and we lost touch, as people do. But . . . I was damaged, by my childhood. I learned later through therapy that sometimes people try to 'solve' childhood trauma by marrying people who remind them of their abusive parents. As though, as adults, they can relive the whole thing, but change things for the better. I wound up marrying a charming alcholic who was a lot like my dad. He . . . um . . ." Her carefully sculpted affect seemed to crack just a little. "He was violent."

I thought of the scar near her eye and on her lip. The ones I thought gave her character.

"Like a lot of people in that situation, I was afraid to leave, afraid to find help. I always found an excuse for his behavior, and each time he cried and came back, I convinced myself that he really loved me and it would never happen again. One day I saw a poster for the Elrich Method, and I called Ellis. Do you know that until recently, he answered his own phone?"

"You mean, instead of having a secretary do it?"

"Exactly. If you looked up Elrich Enterprises on the Internet, there was a company directory, and Ellis Elrich's number was listed right there. When I finally got the courage to call him, of course I expected an assistant to answer. I about fell off the bed when I heard Ellis answer it himself." At this a tiny half smile lit up her face.

"Did he remember you?"

"Yes. Can you believe it? He said he recognized my voice, even after all those years. I wound up telling him my whole sordid, ugly story. He said: 'I will give you the means to leave. After that, it is up to you to do so. If you decide to stay where you are, I will mourn for you, but I won't help you again.'"

Her eyes had an almost fanatical gleam, as if she were a member of a cult. But I could imagine what Ellis's offer must have meant to a woman in need of a lifeline.

"He offered me a job, a place to stay. He had his lawyers help me change my name, and we covered my tracks so my ex-husband couldn't find me. Ellis Elrich gave me my life back. More importantly, he gave me myself back. I would do anything for him."

Once again I was reminded of how some people drew the short straw in life. I sensed Alicia didn't want my sympathy, though, so I simply thanked her for telling me and told her I was going to the hospital to visit Graham.

As I was about to walk through the front door, she called out, "Mel?"

I stopped and turned.

"I would do anything for Ellis, but I didn't kill Larry McCall."

Chapter Twenty-one

According to the doctors, Graham was out of the danger zone. But he still fought extreme nausea every time he so much as moved his head. There wasn't much modern medicine could do except wait and allow Graham's body to heal.

Unfortunately, Graham wasn't what one might call an accommodating patient.

"I think it's interesting that people in here are called 'patients' when a lot of them aren't particularly patient. Don't you?" I asked.

He glared at me.

After a little while had passed, he was able to maintain a conversation. Unfortunately, he had no memory of what had happened in the chapel, or who might have attacked him. Neither could he suggest anything he might have learned from McCall's widow that had prompted the assault.

I told him that I suspected Libole had purchased the

stones from Golden Gate Park, that the Wakefield monastery was not the original Wakefield but another building entirely, and that Florian Libole was hiding the truth from everyone and had disappeared. And that maybe Larry McCall had found out about the stones and had been killed because of it. I just couldn't figure out why.

"Big deal, right?" I said. "So Florian mixed and matched some stones. Julia Morgan did the same thing at Hearst Castle and elsewhere, and everyone lauded her as a genius."

"Not the same thing," Graham said. "Morgan told Hearst what she was doing. But Libole hasn't said anything to anybody. Wakefield is supposed to be original, the actual building Ellis knew, a place with special significance to him. If Libole's changing it, using other stones . . ."

"But Ellis knows some of the original stones were missing. Libole told me himself he had some new stones quarried in Texas."

"Good point. I don't know. Maybe the pressure got to him. There's been a lot going wrong on this project, and as you may have noticed, people hate to disappoint Ellis Elrich."

"He's hard to figure out, isn't he?" I said. "I didn't want to like him, but I may be falling under his spell."

"That's how cult leaders are: charming, apparently caring, and utterly sure their way is the right way. I think it's the confidence that attracts people. Just look at Hitler."

"I hardly think it's fair to compare Ellis Elrich with Hitler."

Graham shrugged, then winced at the movement.

"Oh, hey, I do have some good news," I said as Graham closed his eyes. I noticed that he surreptitiously gave himself another little squeeze of morphine. "I think I've got the key to the authentic mortar mix."

"What would that be?" he asked, though he seemed not at all interested.

"Horse manure."

"Bull."

"No, horse. My source was pretty specific."

"And how do you know this? Or should I even ask?"

"The warrior ghost and I have become pretty good friends. I mean, he still threatens to kill me whenever he sees me, but then he sheaths his sword 'cause, you know, I'm a girl."

Graham closed his eyes, and I wondered if he had drifted off. But just in case he was still listening, I kept talking.

"Yep. I have been consulting on traditional building practices with a centuries-old ghost who was shipped over the ocean with those mossy stones. Just call me the contractoress with the mostess."

Graham grunted.

"You don't believe me?" I asked.

"I think you just want to see if I'll actually put horse manure in the mortar."

"And here I thought all good relationships were built on trust."

"Mel?"

"Yes?"

"Shut up."

"Sure thing," I whispered, and placed the gentlest kiss I could manage on his whiskery cheek, then tiptoed out to let him sleep.

I tried to fight the tears that sprang to my eyes every time I left Graham's hospital room. There was something so upsetting, so wrong, about seeing a man like that as helpless as a baby.

I looked up as my father and Caleb walked into the ICU. We hugged.

"Sorry. I think he just fell asleep," I said. "He's grumpy and feels terrible, but it looks like he's officially on the mend. They're planning on moving him to a regular room today."

"That's good news," said Dad. "Well, Caleb, what do you say we find a hamburger somewhere, and come back after and see if he's awake? Unless you need something from us, Mel?"

"Caleb, you've always been good with puzzles. Do you think you could help me with something?"

I took out my phone and showed Caleb the pictures I'd taken of the stones with the bits of mural on them. "I think these can be arranged to form a larger image, though some pieces may be missing."

"Sure," Caleb said. "I'll use Photoshop, see what I can come up with."

"I still need my phone, though," I pointed out.

"You are such a computerphobe," Caleb said as he e-mailed the photos to himself, then handed the phone back to me.

"Yeah, Mel," my dad chimed in. "Join the 'now' generation."

"The *what* generation?" Caleb asked.

"You're a groovy dude, Dad," I said.

"Don't I know it."

"Oh, one other thing: Could you guys take Dog for a bit? He's in the car. I'm going to be running around a lot, and it would be easier if I didn't have to worry about him."

"Happy to," said Dad.

They escorted me to the parking lot, where Dog was overjoyed to see them.

"Thanks for this," I said as we made the transfer. "I things settle down, I'll come back and get him soon. He's good company."

"Be careful, babe," said my dad as I climbed into my car and took off. I glanced at myself in the rearview mirror as I pulled out of the parking garage. Stan was right I hardly recognized myself. I never had been what one might call a particularly "well put-together" person, but now my eyes had a shadowed, harried look.

I imagined Luz would tell me that seeing one's boyfriend in the hospital, bailing one's stepson out of police custody, and stumbling across a murder victim all in one week wasn't good for one's mental health.

I glanced at my watch. I had a million things to do, but I could sneak away for a little while. It would be nice to be free of everything: my worries about Caleb and Graham and ghosts and Elrich and all his minions. The constant requests and questions on the jobsite. The strange living situation and the sparkling pool that was beginning to feel like a reproach, since I still hadn't managed to swim in it, much less lounge by it.

I headed toward nearby Highway One, one of the most beautiful roads in the United States. Car commercials love depicting their shiny new cars negotiating its hairpin twists and turns, the road so challenging in spots that you can't go much faster than fifteen miles per hour Careening off the highway into the forest would be bad enough; the real danger was flying off one of the sheer cliffs overlooking the ocean.

The Northern California coast is often shrouded in fog, but not today. The sun shone in a crystal clear blue sky; the water churned a deep blue-gray. A few fluffy clouds hung on the horizon. Waves crashed over jagged rock outcroppings, seagulls perched on massive boulders, and a half dozen big-billed pelicans flew right along the cliff, so close I felt as though I could touch them.

I slowed to negotiate a curve and noted in the rearview mirror a gleaming black SUV not far behind. It seemed to be picking up speed. I wasn't sure what the driver's hurry was; I was already going five miles an hour over the speed limit, and there was only one lane in each direction. It is impossible to pass on Highway One, so whoever was driving would just have to slow down anyway when he or she caught up to me.

The first time I drove the coast was on my sixteenth birthday, the day I got my driver's license. It was a rite of passage where I grew up, a coming-of-age ritual, the sort of thrilling, dangerous challenge teenagers loved. Every so often, someone drove off the cliffs, plunging to their death on the steep rocks below, or drowning in the rough ocean. Ours was a wild, savage coast. It was one reason we Northern California types held ourselves above our southern neighbors; if you swam in these waters, you were lucky if you weren't dashed to the rocks or eaten by sharks—assuming you didn't die of hypothermia first. Surfers around here were about as fit and fearless as Navy SEALs, basically.

It struck me as I drove that it felt good to think about nothing for a while, to just concentrate on the road, the ocean, the forest. It was hard to take in these ocean vistas without pondering the beauty of life. Ellis Elrich no doubt would have a quote at the ready to encapsulate these emotions. I smiled to myself, breathed deeply of the air blowing in off the sea, and felt myself start to relax.

Until I glanced in my mirror. The SUV had caught up

with me and was now edging up to my rear bumper. I didn't recall there being so many tailgaters in my younger days, and wondered whether the Bay Area was growing so crowded that it encouraged road rage, or whether people today simply hadn't learned to share.

I sounded exactly like my father. *Sheesh.*

My phone rang. Even though it connected to a Bluetooth, I didn't answer. The tricky highway demanded every bit of my attention. A few seconds later, the phone beeped. We were on a straight stretch of road, so I risked a glance, in case the text was about Graham.

The second my attention was diverted, I felt a jolt. Confused, I looked up, fearing I'd hit something.

Then I saw it: the SUV, looming in the rearview mirror.

It clipped me again.

Chapter Twenty-two

Another bump, and I had to brake to stay in my lane. I sped up, trying to think. The SUV had been nosing me from behind. Could it have been accidental? The vehicle fell back, and I breathed a sigh of relief . . . but then it started gaining on me again.

The road took a brief jog inland, and I was coming up to a 180-degree turn in the thick of the forest. I went as fast as I dared, but the SUV was still on my tail. I'm no slouch driving on winding highways—Dad taught all his girls to drive in the mountains, figuring if we could manage a stick on twisty mountain roads, our odds of negotiating city streets were that much better. So I did as I'd been taught, braking before entering the turn, then accelerating out of it. I didn't understand the physics of it, but somehow the acceleration in the middle of a turn helped the driver maintain control.

Unfortunately, the SUV driver appeared to have some training, himself. I was assuming it was a *him*—I suppose it could have been a woman, for all I could see. The windows were tinted, in the way of drug dealers and the sort of people who intended to run a person off the road.

As I careened through the next turn, it hit me: This person wanted to kill me.

Adrenaline pumped through me. My heart pounded. While I willed myself to stay focused on the road, I was also trying to think ahead. Where was the nearest town? How could I turn off the highway, or at the very least get away from the deadly coastal cliffs?

The occasional turnoffs were just dirt pathways. I was going to have to assume that if the SUV's driver was willing to push me off a cliff, she or he might also be carrying a gun and wouldn't hesitate to blow me away if I got stuck up a dirt road. My gun—Dad's Glock—was in the farthest reaches of the closet in my room back at the Elrich mansion, of course, where it would be of no use whatsoever, unless I was threatened while hiding in the closet. This wasn't the time to examine my actions, but it occurred to me that if I wanted a gun for protection, I really should get used to carrying it.

I sped through a series of sharp curves, and then another, the SUV on my tail. Up ahead was a bad one: a 180-degree curve on a narrow stretch of road right above the ocean, with only a yard or so leeway on the edge of the road.

Tires screeched and I fought to retain control. The big vehicle raced up behind me again, but this time I was ready and accelerated just as it started to tap my bumper, causing the SUV to fishtail. I felt a moment of fierce joy at the thought of my tormentor flying off the cliff and smashing against the rocks below, but the driver regained control. The vehicle spun and sprayed gravel, but came to rest pointing in the right direction.

But at least I had gained a few seconds of breathing space.

Finally a sight I thought I'd never be happy to see: traffic. A long line of cars ahead was crawling behind a slow-moving flatbed tow truck carrying a bulldozer.

This could be my salvation, I thought. That, or it would be a disaster.

I didn't know what to do if the SUV was ruthless enough to try to take out a whole line of cars. But when I glanced in the mirror, I saw the menacing vehicle falling back, before finally disappearing from my sight behind a curve in the road.

I was trembling and felt nauseated, but before stopping, I wanted to put some space between me and that homicidal SUV. And I wanted to find someplace crowded with people, who could either help me if needed or at least testify at the trial of my murderer. Ten minutes later, I pulled into the parking lot of the Pelican Inn. I was shaking but relieved at the beautiful sight of folks lolling on the grass, bicyclists and hikers and just plain folks out enjoying a sunny Bay Area day.

The parking lot attendant pointed me to an empty space at the back of the building, out of sight of the road. As I pulled in, I scanned the parking lot, irrationally fearful that the SUV somehow had gotten here first.

I got out and checked my bumper: There were several new scrapes and dings, scrapings of black paint.

As I made my way toward the inn, I asked the attendant if he knew whether Kieran was here.

He checked his clipboard.

"Lessee, he's in room six," he said, then looked to the empty spot marked with a 6. "Nope."

I walked straight past the front desk and into the bathroom. The nausea had passed, but I was still shaking.

I splashed water on my face and checked myself out in the mirror: I was pale, my eyes wide and dazed.

"You okay, honey?" asked a woman who was flipping her bountiful blond hair to give it more body.

"Thanks, yes. I . . . had a close call in the car."

"Poor thing. You should sit for a while, have something to drink. They have great fish and chips here."

"Thanks. That's not a bad idea."

It was the adrenaline crash. I didn't think I could drive safely at the moment. Maybe she was right. I needed a drink. Or food. Or both.

The tiny pub area was as crowded as ever. A long line at the bar dashed my hopes for food and drink; I didn't think I could stand that long. But I was able to snag a seat on the window bench next to a burly man with a motorcycle helmet.

"You all right?" he asked solicitously. "You look like you saw a ghost."

Despite myself, I had to smile. "Yes, thank you . . . I um . . . almost hit a deer, almost ran off the road."

He nodded. "That'll shake you up, all right. Lot of deer 'round here; my wife and I ride Highway One all the time. I'm Roger, go by Rog. Delia's in the restroom trying to fix her helmet hair."

I nodded. "I think we met."

"You want me to order something for you?"

His solicitousness surprised me, and for a crazy moment I wondered if old Rog here might be trying to kill me. But the bench where we were sitting was right next to the bar, so I could watch to be sure he wasn't slipping something into my drink.

Relax, Mel, I told myself. *The man is just being kind.*

"Thank you. I would really appreciate it." I asked for a hard cider and some fish and chips. It dawned on me I

adn't eaten in a while—another rarity for me and a
lear example that I wasn't coping all that well.

Then I caught something out of the corner of my eye,
nd this time it wasn't a ghost.

It was Buzz. In the front hall.

Buzz, the professional driver. One of Elrich's devoted
minions. His hazel eyes, which I'd once thought of as
easygoing and friendly, now appeared flat and emotion-
ss as a snake's.

My already addled mind flailed around, trying to think
what to do. Enlist the help of Rog and Delia? Would Buzz
e willing to hurt innocent bystanders just to get to me?

I remembered there was a hard-to-see door next to
he dartboard that led to a room called "the Snuggery."
ust beyond that was a back door that opened onto the
parking lot.

Could I get to it in time? Did Buzz have an accom-
lice waiting at the exit? I'd have to chance it.

I started to stand, but got only about halfway up when
Ellis walked in, flanked by his ever-present bodyguards.

"You sure she's okay?" I heard Delia ask Rog be-
ind me.

Ellis took in the room, his face brightening when he
aw me.

"Mel?" he asked, coming over to where I sat. "What
pleasant surprise. What are you doing here?"

I sank back down onto the bench. "I was . . . just hav-
ng a bite."

"I hear the fish and chips are excellent," he said with
his signature smile and a duck of the head.

"Best in Northern California," Delia said, and Rog
nodded.

"What are . . . ?" I had to clear my throat. "What are
ou doing here?"

"I took your advice and agreed to meet with Kieran Lachaidh."

"Oh." I was having a very hard time breathing.

"Are you all right?" he asked, sounding concerned. "You look pale."

"She had a run-in with a deer on the road," said Rog. "Bad scare."

"Well, no wonder, then," Ellis said. Turning to Rog, he held out his hand. "I'm Ellis Elrich."

"No kidding? I *thought* that was you!"

"We took one of your seminars!" exclaimed Delia.

"I gotta tell you, Mr. Elrich," said Rog, "I wouldn't own my own garage today if it wasn't for you and your program."

"It's true," said Delia. "You changed our lives."

The fandom went on for several minutes, with Ellis graciously accepting the compliments while assuring Delia and Rog that they had done the hard work of changing their lives themselves and that they should always remember that. The bodyguards, Andrew and Omar, subtly but effectively placed themselves in the way of any further adoration from the crowd. Meanwhile Buzz, far from trying to kill me, had ordered a round of beers and was vying for the prime table, the corner bench.

I used these few minutes to pull myself together. Escaping a near-death experience on the road, then nearly scaring myself to bits, had taken the starch out of me. I started wondering if I hadn't exaggerated the whole terrifying episode, then remembered the fresh scratches on my rear bumper.

It really had happened. Someone had tried to push me off the road. And they'd damned near succeeded.

Just then Kieran came down the stairs.

"Mel? You came with Ellis to negotiate? That's really lovely of you."

"I thought you weren't here," I said.

"Got here a few minutes ago. Is everything all right? You don't look well."

"Bad deer encounter," Rog explained.

"Just needs a bit of a pick-me-up," Delia added.

"She'll be fine," Ellis said.

I smiled weakly, by now sure everyone in the pub knew I'd had a run-in with a deer and no doubt thought I was milking it for all it was worth.

"I'm glad you're speaking with Ellis," I said. "I hope it goes well."

My food was up. I sat on the window bench, ate the delicious fish and chips, and listened to Delia and Rog extol the virtues of the Elrich Method. From time to time I cast a glance at the men in the corner huddled over the barrel that doubled as their table. Their discussion seemed heated but civilized.

After a little food and rest, I felt almost like myself again. I thanked Rog and Delia and wished them well. Not wanting to interrupt the negotiations between Kieran and Ellis, I slipped out without saying good-bye and checked the parking lot. Kieran's Prius was in slot number six, and the stretch limo at the rear of the lot, I assumed, belonged to Ellis Elrich. The parking lot was jammed with cars, but nary a black SUV in sight.

Back at Elrich's house, Alicia met me at the door with the address of Libole's warehouse.

"There's good news and bad news," I said on the phone to Zach. I was waiting outside a Safeway supermarket near the warehouse. "We might not have to break in. It's possible I have the warehouse key."

"You're not sure if you have a key or not? Is this key somehow caught in an eddy in the time-space continuum?"

"I have a very large key ring, on which I presume is a key to the warehouse, but I can't be sure until I try them."

"Dare I ask what the bad news is?"

"Someone is trying to kill me."

"When's the last time someone *wasn't* trying to kill you?"

"That's not true. I mean . . . Okay, it's a little true. But it's not like someone's trying to kill me all the time. It's more sporadic, like every once in a while. And this is one of those times."

"Are you okay?"

"In a manner of speaking. I have made the transition from terrified to royally pissed. But I thought I should give you fair warning."

"Backing out now would make me look unmanly, wouldn't it?"

"It surely would."

"Okay, fine. I'll gird my loins and risk life and limb in a patently transparent attempt to prove my masculinity."

"I knew I could count on you."

"Where and when?"

"Meet me at the Mill Valley Safeway, across from Mount Tam High School, soon as you can get here."

"Just for the record: This is the reason I don't hang out with you more, Mel. You aren't good for a person's health."

I snorted. "The reason you don't hang out with me more is spelled G-r-a-h-a-m."

Silence.

"Seriously, Zach. I have a gun, but I really do need backup."

"Wait—you're carrying a *gun*?"

"And bullets, even."

"Okay," Zach said with a long-suffering sigh. "Safeway parking lot. Give me half an hour."

While I waited, I bought Zach his very own can of wasp spray.

We caught up while we drove in my car to the warehouse. I asked him to talk about anything but murder and ancient stones. Zach had been trying hard to make a living as a photographer, which was no easy gig in the days of smartphones with their built-in cameras.

"These days everyone and his brother thinks he can take photos, or even make videos. It's a crying shame, is what it is."

I could relate. That was how I felt in do-it-yourself hardware stores, with those cheery signs that made people think they *could* do it themselves. My one ace in the hole, however, was that most people got themselves in over their heads, and as the renovations dragged on and on and costs mounted, the torn-up kitchen and nonfunctioning bathroom became too much to bear, and I'd field the call. Whereas the worst that could happen with photography was taking crappy pictures.

Speaking of which, I wondered if Caleb had made any headway with the photos I'd taken of the mural.

We found the warehouse down by the water, near the estuary. On one side was an unmarked building, and on the other, a wine-storage facility. The sun was setting, and I was glad to be here with backup, and a gun.

"How come we can't break in to *that* one?" Zach asked, eyeing the warehouse with the wine, as I tried the tenth key on the key ring.

"We're not breaking in. I have a key. Remember?"

"At the risk of quibbling, I must point out that if we

were here legitimately, I wouldn't be standing guard while you fiddled with the damn door lock. You would know which one of those purloined keys might fit this padlock."

"Did I ask your opinion? You're the hired muscle."

"You're paying me?" Zach perked up.

"It's an expression."

He deflated again. "One of these days I'm going to get smart and not answer the phone when you call."

"But then you'd miss out on all the good stuff. Anyone coming?"

He shook his head. "Neither man nor beast roams this foul desert. It's deserted out here. Silent as the proverbial grave. Quiet as a tomb. Hushed as a baby's—"

"Aha!" I exclaimed as the padlock finally fell open. "Success!"

I pushed the door open with care, hanging back a little. I wasn't expecting a guard dog or anything, but I wasn't so sure about ghosts. If haunted stones were stored in here, I wanted to be ready for anything.

"Could I hold the gun?" Zach asked in a whisper.

"I gave you a can of wasp spray."

"Yeah, that was my point. I'm a spritzer of the highest degree, but I'd rather hold the gun."

"Why are you asking me this *now*?" I demanded as we ventured inside. The warehouse smelled musty and dank, as though fresh air had not circulated in there for a very long time. I was whispering, not for fear of anyone in particular, but because the large space was so echoey that speaking made me feel self-conscious. It was full of wooden shipping crates, their contents stenciled on one side. Some crates had been pried opened to reveal carved stone pieces.

"I didn't really get weirded out until right now," said

Zach. "And frankly, the whole wasp-spray-can thing doesn't suit my tough-guy image."

"I hate to break it to you, but you don't really *have* a tough-guy image."

"Well, now, that's rather mean-spirited of you, especially since you begged me to be your backup. And besides, that was sort of my point. How am I supposed to be a tough guy carrying a can of wasp spray? The only bad guys who would be impressed by that are wasps."

"It sprays twenty feet and disarms a bad guy just that fast," I said. "Inspector Crawford recommended it. I used to carry hair spray, but this is even better because it shoots farther. And you don't need a license for it like you do with mace or pepper spray."

"Maybe if I got a can-shaped leather holster . . ."

He trailed off as we passed by a line of tombstones leaning against the metal wall of the warehouse.

Zach glanced at me. "Is that normal? Shouldn't tombstones be in a graveyard?"

I removed the top of a nearby crate and found an ornately carved wooden credenza. I put the lid back on. "Ancient tombstones are considered works of art. I mean, it's not like the immediate family is going to object."

"I do like the gargoyles," said Zach.

"Those aren't gargoyles so much as hunky punks."

"Hunky punks? That's an architectural term, is it?"

"Oh, we've got some doozies. Listen, we should be systematic about this search. You start at that end of the line of crates, and I'll start at this end. We'll work toward the middle."

"I thought you told me the supposed treasure wasn't a treasure at all, but a woman."

"True. But if people have been killed over this . . . I

don't know. I keep thinking there's more to this story
And this seems like a pretty good place to hide a treasure, doesn't it?"

There was a loud bang.

I dove behind a crate.

Zach whirled around and let his wasp spray fly. It
landed with a splat on the hunky punk, drenching it in
foam.

"All clear," said Zach. "It was the lid from the first
crate you opened. It fell."

I sagged in relief. "Gotta say, I'm impressed. Way to
show that hunky punk who's boss."

"Sorry. I'm a little jumpy."

"So am I, believe me. If I'd been quicker on the draw
I probably would have *shot* the poor little guy. At least
the wasp spray washes off."

We shared a smile and resumed our search.

"Um, Mel? What do you suppose is in here?"

He was standing with his hands on a crate stenciled
BONES.

"I'm gonna guess bones."

"Yes, okay, but . . . you really think there are *bones* in
here?"

"Probably they don't mean bones as in . . . bones
Maybe it's animal skeletons, or . . ."

I trailed off as Zach opened the lid, peered within
and made a face.

"Mel, this wouldn't be a serial killer's warehouse, by
any chance, would it?"

I came over to stand next to him, and we both studied
the open crate. I'm not the kind of anthropologist that
studies bones, but I knew enough to recognize that these
were human. But they weren't part of a skeleton; instead
they appeared to be arranged in some sort of design. It

s hard to make it out with the packing peanuts sur-
unding them.

"Let's—"

The lights went out. We were plunged into darkness.

"Um, Mel?" whispered Zach.

"Shhhh." I pulled Zach down behind the crate with
e. I have a tiny flashlight on my key chain, but in case
meone had turned off the lights, I didn't want to reveal
ir exact location.

"The lights are probably on a timer or motion sen-
r," I whispered. "They probably turn the lights off au-
matically after a while. Just an energy-saving device,"
vhispered. "Probably."

"Want to know my opinion of environmentalists right
out now?"

We crouched in silence for another moment. Finally,
eeked over the edge of the crate.

The warehouse door flew open, and the lights flicked on.

Florian Libole was standing in the doorway with a
n.

Chapter Twenty-three

Florian pointed his gun in our direction, I stood w
my pistol aimed in his direction, and Zach popped
holding up his wasp spray in a shooter's stance.

"Don't even think about it, pal," Zach growled.

When Florian recognized me, he made an exasp
ated grunt and put the gun in his bag. "Oh, it's you
thought someone had broken into my warehouse."

"I thought you were dead."

"What *are* you going on about? And what are y
doing in here? And why are you carrying a gun?"

"Why are *you* carrying a gun?"

"I'm not. It's not an actual gun. . . . It's a water pis
spray-painted silver."

"That's illegal," I said.

"Not to mention stupid," said Zach.

"I could have shot you," I added.

"After what happened to McCall . . ." Florian shrugg
"I know how you Yanks are with your guns. Which bri

back to the pertinent question: What the hell are you doing in my warehouse, with a gun?"

"I'm, uh . . . was checking to see if there was room to have those kitchen appliances delivered here, since we're far from being ready for them on-site," I said. "And I'm happy to confirm that there is, indeed, plenty of space."

Florian gave me the stink-eye. The fact that Zach and I were ankle-deep in packing peanuts, next to an open shipping crate, might have undercut my story.

There was nothing to do but confess.

"We were snooping," I said. "I apologize. It wasn't right, but I knew you had some objects in here for the building site, and you haven't been around lately. . . ."

"And you thought I was dead?"

I nodded. "Hey, I was worried. I reported you missing to the police."

"You called the *police*? I was hiking the Dipsea Trail."

"You didn't say anything. And it's been three days— that trail's only eight miles long."

He shrugged. "I took my time. You had the day-to-day operations well in hand, and I needed a little time to myself. We British are great walkers, you know."

A great walker could have gotten a little farther than eight miles in three days, I thought to myself.

"You want to explain what you're doing with a bunch of human bones in crates?" demanded Zach, taking up the offensive.

"And who might *you* be?" asked Florian.

"This is my . . . personal assistant," I said. "Zachary Jablonsky."

Florian was shaking his head. "Cretins," I heard him mumble.

"Are the bones some of the remains that were found in the building upon dismantling?"

"No. They're from Eastern Europe, primarily. They'r
decorations to increase the authenticity of the buildin
although Ellis now tells me he finds them rather too ma
cabre for today's sensibilities. But I assure you, it's hi
torically accurate. There's a long and honorable traditio
of incorporating bones into historic buildings."

Zach was staring at me as though I should either bac
up Libole's story or call him out as a liar. I had heard o
human bones being used as architectural decorations b
was fuzzy on the details; besides, I couldn't help b
think of what had happened in Strasbourg. Had Libo
been digging up unauthorized bones again?

"Doesn't anyone go to college anymore?" asked Li
bole, sounding exasperated. "Haven't you heard of oss
aries, great collections of bones?"

"Like in the catacombs in Paris?"

"Yes. But more so. One famous one is the Capela d
Ossos, in Évora, Portugal. It was built by a sixteenth-centu
Franciscan monk to encourage the contemplation of ter
porality. In other words, that life is fleeting, transitory."

"He did this by putting up bones?"

"Ossuaries served an important purpose. People wante
to be buried on consecrated or sacred grounds, or i
places of historical significance. But there's only so mu
land. It was a common practice to bury people, let the
be for a number of years, then exhume their skeletal r
mains and place the bones in ossuaries."

"I get that part. It's making the bones into decor
tions that leaves me a little flat."

"I don't see why, really. I mean, what else are you go
ing to do with them? There have been a lot of people o
this earth, and their remains have to go somewhere. Th
skulls and skeletons of about five thousand monks wer

xhumed from a variety of cemeteries. Upon entering
ie Capela dos Ossos, visitors are greeted with the say-
ig: *Nós ossos que aqui estamos pelos vossos esperamos.*
llis isn't allowing me to display the bones, but he has
sked that the phrase be carved into stone at the Wake-
eld refectory."

"And that means what, exactly?"

"'We, the bones that are here, await yours.'"

"Um, okay . . ."

"In other words, life is fleeting."

I suppose I should know that better than a lot of peo-
le, given how often I had witnessed it snatched away
rom people in the last year. Still, I wasn't sure a phrase
a Portuguese was going to change anyone's attitude.

I met Zach's eyes. He looked as queasy as I felt.

It was fascinating, and macabre. Now that I saw ghosts
rom time to time, and those ghosts were often—though
ot always—attached to the remains of the person, I
ould only imagine what it might be like for me to walk
hrough that Portuguese chapel. Confused spirits would
robably glom on to me before I passed the first pew:
emanding, yearning, begging for help. I made a mental
ote not to go anywhere near Évora when I finally man-
ged to move to Europe.

"Well, then, it's all good news. You're not dead, and
here's plenty of space for the kitchen appliances. Here's
our key ring."

"Where did you get my key ring?"

"Like I said, I was worried about you."

"So you went into my room and rifled through my
esk?"

"There was no rifling. I gently opened a drawer to see
there might be a key, and voilà, there was an entire key

ring. By the way, hardly anyone maintains the old letter
writing traditions. Sealing wax? I'm impressed."

"Cretins," Florian mumbled, shaking his head.

"I don't get it . . . ," said Zach as we climbed into m
Scion, feeling a bit deflated. "You thought this guy wa
dead?"

"I thought it was a possibility. Either that, or that he'
killed the building inspector on the job and had fled th
country."

"But now you don't think he's the killer?"

"I can't be sure. . . . I mean, as you know, I've bee
wrong before. Apparently, I'm not a great judge of char
acter." I started driving us across town. "But although
think Libole's sneaky and underhanded, he doesn't strik
me as a murderer. For instance, if he was a ruthless kille
why would he carry a water pistol?"

"We don't actually *know* it was a water pistol," Zac
pointed out. "He just said it was. It could have been real.

"True, but then why would he hesitate to shoot us
We were in an isolated warehouse full of shipping crate
Pretty good place to kill somebody."

"You're frightening."

"Or even easier, why wouldn't he just stay missing?"
Zach helped himself to a piece of gum from the glov
box, tossed the wasp spray into the backseat, and nodde
thoughtfully.

"What I *do* believe is that Florian Libole has bee
perpetrating a fraud against Ellis Elrich by replacing th
Wakefield monastery—the one Elrich wanted him t
bring over from Europe—with a different one."

"Which one?"

"It's from the Isle of Inchcolm, in the Firth of Forth
above the Cairn of the Kerr."

"If you don't want to tell me, you could just say so."

"I'm not kidding. That's where it's from. The one Elich wanted was from an island I can't pronounce. Gaelic isn't for sissies."

"Gotcha. How did you figure this out?"

"A very nice woman in a Scottish paraphernalia shop."

"What do they sell in a Scottish paraphernalia shop? The mind reels."

"A lot of plaid. But I mean, think about it: They're tumbled ruins of dark gray stones. There's a key that's supposed to help reassemble the portions of the building that were still intact, but much of it is just conjecture. By the time those stones arrived, how was Ellis going to notice these weren't the stones he thought he'd paid for?"

"A stone's a stone."

"Exactly. Except it's not, because these stones carry their very own curse with them. And on top of that, Libole supplemented them with stones originally from Spain via Golden Gate Park, again without telling Elrich."

"Why be so secretive? Why not just tell Elrich the truth?"

"Apparently, people have a hard time letting Ellis Elrich down."

"But you don't think he wanted to keep the secret enough to kill over it?"

"He could have. . . . I really don't know."

Could he have dispatched someone to get rid of Larry McCall when the building inspector found out about the stones from Golden Gate Park? I couldn't be sure, but I was finally getting smart. It wasn't wise to make possibly career-ending accusations at someone when they were armed and in an isolated warehouse. Even if Libole's weapon was only a toy, and Zach and I had real weapons . . . I wasn't prepared to start shooting people, either

This was a job for the police. So when I dropped Zach back at his car in the Safeway parking lot, I called Detective Bernardino. We had a very uncomfortable chat during which he informed me that the police had their person of interest in Pete Nolan, thank you very much and Ellis Elrich would surely deal with any fraud perpetrated by Florian Libole if and when he was ready. Bernardino also told me to stop insinuating to the McCall family that someone besides Pete Nolan might have killed their loved one and to ask the SFPD to stay out of his case and off his back. And, finally, he said not to call him again at this hour of the night.

I would never again complain about Annette Crawford.

I limped back to Ellis Elrich's house, exhausted. I was happy to see that the protesters had dispersed for the day; I wasn't up for running the gauntlet at the main gates. This had been one hell of a day . . . and I still hadn't figured things out.

All I wanted to do was go to my room, take a very hot shower for a very long time, and put on some clean clothes. I crossed my fingers that I wouldn't run into the sour Vernon Dunn, or even Alicia. Maybe I could grab something in the snack bar and slip into my room without being spotted, flick on the fire in the fireplace and . . .

But Ellis was in the foyer when I walked in.

"Mel, how are you? I was sorry you slipped out at the Pelican Inn—I was going to offer to spare you the drive back. One of the men could have driven your car."

"Thanks. That's thoughtful of you. But I was fine, just needed to pull myself together. Do you have a few minutes to talk? In private?"

"Of course." He led the way down to the Discovery Room.

"I don't quite know how to say this," I said as we settled ourselves under the watchful eyes of Madame Curie. "And I'm tired, so I might fumble it a little. But . . . I think Florian Libole may have imported the wrong monastery."

Ellis took the news pretty well, considering he had spent a fortune on—and garnered a great deal of press over—a mistaken monastery.

I showed him pictures of the original Wakefield in Scotland, with its half-tumbled tower, then compared them to the ruins on the Isle of Inchcolm in the Firth of Forth. The pictures helped to illustrate my point, but even to my own ears the story sounded far-fetched. Ellis listened attentively, thanked me for the information, and then went out to the terrace.

Last I saw, he was picking up smooth river stones and building his little cairns by the silvery light of a nearly full moon. If only everyone could deal with frustration so calmly.

I felt like I was tattling on Libole, but I wasn't brave enough to accuse him in person. The funny thing was that despite everything—the fraud, the pomposity—I sort of liked Florian. He was a font of knowledge about obscure architectural history. And the plan he had invented for the monastery we were rebuilding was genius, mixing and matching his resources to create a historic building from several sources, just like Julia Morgan at

Hearst Castle. Too bad he hadn't figured out a way to embrace the situation with full disclosure.

After my shower, I crawled into bed and finished *Keeper of the Castle*, which had a very satisfying ending. I missed Dog's company but was lulled to sleep by the odd, lilting notes of Donnchadh's flute.

Chapter Twenty-four

I woke up half expecting to find some proclamation from Ellis about the Wakefield project being halted. But since there was nothing untoward on today's schedule slipped under my door, I grabbed some coffee and headed down to the jobsite, to continue on with the job.

At lunchtime I headed to the hospital. Dr. Petralis had declared Graham to be out of imminent danger, and he had been moved to a regular room. If Graham continued to improve this quickly, the nurse said, he would be able to go home tomorrow or the next day.

I did my best to make him laugh, but my best wasn't good enough, and even with a head injury, Graham was too perceptive not to pick up on my questionable mental state. I insisted I was fine, but he didn't believe me.

I left after an hour, telling him to hurry up reknitting his skull, because I needed him back on the job.

"Whatever you say, boss lady," he said quietly, his eyes already closed, as I slipped out.

This experience had brought one thing home with full force: I was an *idiot*. Graham had been offering me his heart for some time, and I had been hesitating, too caught up in my own trust issues to recognize what was right in front of me. But no more dinking around. If Graham still wanted me when his head was unscrambled, I would act like a grown-up and dive into this relationship, once and for all.

Now that I had come so close to losing him, I realized just how much Graham meant to me.

Happy with my decision, I strode down the hospital corridor, where I ran into Jeanine McCall, carrying a cellophane-wrapped paper plate full of cookies.

"Jeanine," I said. "What are you doing here?"

"I just . . . When I'm unhappy, I bake." She shrugged. "I've been baking a lot lately. And then I thought about your poor friend in the hospital, so I thought I'd drop these by and wish him well."

"That's so thoughtful of you. Unfortunately, he just fell asleep. Also, he's not eating yet—in fact, I imagine the nurses would appreciate the cookies more than he would at the moment."

"Oh, that's a good idea. I'll leave them at the nurses' station."

"Could I ask you something? Your husband went to Golden Gate Park not long before he was . . . attacked. Do you know what he found there?"

"He brought home a copy of a schema, a map of old stones that belonged to William Randolph Hearst. They were once part of a castle on the coast of Spain."

"Is that so?"

"He thought I would be interested because my family's from Spain, though my people come from a small town at the foot of the Pyrenees. Still, it's all so interesting, isn't it?"

"Yes, it certainly is."

"I can't remember the name of the castle, but it was on the coast of Valencia. The sad part is that a woman was held prisoner there, kept in a tower, and during a siege meant to secure her rescue, the poor thing starved to death."

"That's terrible."

She nodded. "There's so much sadness in the world, isn't there?"

I had to agree with that. "Still, the men in the permit office mentioned your daughter is getting married. That's exciting, isn't it?"

"Oh, it is. She wanted to delay the celebration, but her father wouldn't have wanted that. Life goes on, as they say. Here. Have a cookie."

I took one, and she left the rest with a grateful nursing staff.

On my way out of the hospital, I stopped by the ICU, where I was happy to find Nurse Ratched on duty.

"I wanted to thank you—and everyone—for taking such good care of my friend while he was here," I said, pulling *Keeper of the Castle* from my bag. "I brought this for you."

She avoided my eyes. "Oh, I couldn't . . ."

"I think you'll enjoy it. It's very entertaining. With a tough job like yours, I'm sure you could use an occasional distraction."

We shared a smile.

This junior ghost buster was confused. So I took the little I knew to Olivier and begged for his counsel. I told him what I had learned about Donnchadh and the Lady in Red and their origins. But I still didn't know what they were after.

"It's possible the Lady in Red is searching for her room."

"The one in the tower, where she was trapped and died?"

"The very one."

"What if it isn't built yet?"

"Build it, and she will come."

"But I don't understand. If she was being held there as a hostage, a prisoner, why would she be searching for it?"

"Because she is very confused right now. She is looking for something familiar, and as strange as it seems, that room was her environment for the last months of her life. It sounds to me as though she's searching for some semblance of normal amid her decidedly abnormal current existence."

"So we build her tower, and then what? Find some way to put her to rest?"

"As you know, none of this is hard science. But yes. I believe that would be a good place to start. You might also want to leave food out for her, as an offering."

"Do ghosts eat?"

He gave me a smile and a Gallic shrug. "Donnchadh seems to think so. It couldn't hurt. Leave food out— whether she eats it or not, she should find it soothing to know it's there. And your warrior ghost could protect her."

I tried to imagine what Alicia would say if I asked her for food for a ghost. *Vegan? Gluten-free? Any religious concerns?*

"But the spirits appear to have made the tower fall

twice now. It imploded, with no known cause. Why would they do that, if she's searching for her room?"

"You are not building it right."

I blew out a breath. I was willing to bet that Larry McCall had had a copy of the original schema on his Clipboard of Doom and that the murderer had absconded with it.

I should follow up with my old pal Cur at the Parks Department. Perhaps they had processed my paperwork, and I could get a copy of that original plan for the tower stones.

But I might have a way around that. Caleb had told me last night that he and Dad and Stan had been working with the photos of the mural, piecing it together. If we could reconstruct the painting, we would have a leg up on understanding how the stone blocks fit together.

"One more thing," added Olivier. "The strength of her appearance makes me think her remains might be present somewhere. It would be helpful to gather them, too, of course, and perhaps place them in her tower."

"I don't know where they could be. I've searched these stones high and low. There are few chambers or openings, nothing like a spot where remains might have been stashed. We found a couple of tombstones, but that was it."

Unless hers were among the bones in the warehouse. But if so, why would her ghost be haunting the ruins? Wouldn't she be wandering around the warehouse, more confused than ever? Besides, those "decorative" bones had come from Eastern Europe, according to Libole, and the origin stamps on the crates seemed to back him up.

But thinking about Florian Libole's macabre collection of bones made me wonder. . . .

*   *   *

Yuri had arrived at Elrich's house this morning. He had set up and was working in the entryway under Alicia's excited, watchful eyes.

After Elrich signed off on the drawings for a mural that featured life on a hacienda in the eighteenth century—heavy on bright flowers, colorful produce, and beautiful women; light on livestock and sweat—the artist had worked out the dimensions and composition on paper before transferring the outlines onto the wall. This "cartoon" would guide his painting.

"You mentioned the other day that plaster was sometimes made of ground bones?" I said, watching as a few flicks of Yuri's skilled hand created the illusion of a horse's leg in motion.

"That's true. Usually they were burned first, in very hot fires. Calcination of the bones occurs at a little less than one thousand degrees Celsius."

"When you say 'bones,' whose bones are we talking about?"

"Not 'whose' bones—at least I should hope not. I meant animal bones, probably deer and, I don't know, other large animals with bones big enough to make it count."

"And that's not . . . unusual?"

"You know, back then they used everything they had. Think about it: no plastics or synthetic glues or binders."

"True. I've stripped a lot of wallpaper put up with dried milk or oatmeal—that stuff stays stuck for generations."

"It's the enzymes in milk. Don't know what it is about oatmeal, but it's powerful stuff."

"So, back to bones: Were human remains ever used?"

There was a long pause. Yuri started shading large areas of the mural with hatch marks.

"Or am I being creepy?" I asked when he still didn't answer.

"Did you find hydroxyapatite?"

"Excuse me?"

"In the plaster. The results from the diffraction spectrometer should tell you. Hydroxyapatite comes from bones. There was evidence of ground bone plaster all over Europe in the Middle Ages. The bone was used as black and white pigment, as well as to strengthen the walls."

"So it is possible they used *human* bones?"

"I wouldn't be surprised. Those people used everything they had, back in the day."

I went back to work with the crew for the rest of the afternoon.

When the men started to pack up and leave at the end of the day, I decided I would try talking to Donnchadh once more. At the very least, I could inform him of my plan. And if the Lady in Red happened by, perhaps I could speak a little Spanish to her, see if she and I could communicate somehow. I wondered how far my construction-site Spanish would take me. I was betting she didn't particularly care that a circular saw was called a *sierra circular*.

If the broken fresco on the tower blocks truly contained the ashes of bones of the Lady in Red, then perhaps she would feel more restful when I gathered things together properly and reconstructed her tower. She would be able to inhabit her familiar room, with her remains close at hand.

There was no way I could move those stones by myself, even with heavy equipment. And I shouldn't rush into it, in any case. I would wait to see whether Caleb,

Dad, and Stan could work out the order for the reassembled painting, and I would get a copy of the origina
schema from Cur or Libole. If Florian Libole was sti
employed by Elrich and deigned to work with me,
would enlist his help in coming up with a working set c
drawings to rebuild the Lady in Red's tower and to mel
it gracefully with the rest of the monastery.

It was worth a shot.

When all the workers had left the site, I took time t
center myself before entering the chapel, running throug
my mental body scan, reminding myself that I was a
tached to the earth and drawing up compassion not onl
for the eternally vigilant Donnchadh, but also for the poo
tortured soul who had been imprisoned and starved t
death. She scared the hell out of me, but the ferocity c
her feelings was no doubt a reaction to the brutality c
her existence.

I stepped through the chapel, into the sacristy, throug
the series of low chambers, to the vestibule outside c
what used to be the round room but was now nothin
but felled stones and bags of mortar that had broke
open in the collapse, spewing their dusty gray conten
everywhere.

No sign of Donnchadh.

No food, either. And no sensation of hunger. I wor
dered where all the ghosties were. . . .

But then I glanced out the side entrance and spotte
someone in the fenced garth outside.

Alicia.

She was on the ground, her hands tied behind he
back. Alicia was breathing like she was about to hype
ventilate, her eyes huge with terror, duct tape coverin
her mouth. A man held a gun to her head.

"Kieran?" I said quietly. "What's going on?"

"I'm going to watch you from here," he said. He was breathing hard, as well. That made three of us. "Go on in and get that chalice. Bring it back to me, and I'll let her go."

My mind raced. My cell phone didn't work within the walls of the cloister. I could run out the other side and try to call for help, but from his vantage point in the garth, Kieran would see me escape, and there was no telling how he would react.

"Go on, now," Kieran continued. "That *thing* told you where it was, didn't he?"

"I don't know anything," I said with a shake of my head. "But I'm really disappointed. Somehow I thought . . . I don't know. Scottish people just seem so civilized. Do you even know how to use that weapon? Do they have guns in Scotland?"

He wasn't holding it the way an experienced marksman would. But at this range, lack of skill didn't make a gun any less lethal.

"Have you forgotten about the fierceness of the Highland warrior?" Kieran said, perking up. "They scared the pants off the rest of Europe."

"Is that why they wore kilts?" I asked, hoping a little levity would put Kieran at ease and reassure Alicia. "So you see yourself as a Highland warrior, do you? I'm not sure it was a warrior move to seduce the boss's daughter into letting you onto the property."

"This ghost . . . It was always bad, but once McCall had his accident, I couldn't go back into the cloister."

"McCall's death was an accident?"

"Of course it was. I didn't mean to kill him. I was hiding on that stack of mortar bags, and I thought I'd just push one over on top of him. Warn him off. I didn't think it would *kill* him."

"Those are sixty-pound bags," I pointed out. "Wha did you think it would do?"

He shrugged. Alicia whimpered, and I thought abou what she'd been through with her violent ex-husband. wondered if she was reliving the panic and fear of tha time in her life.

I tried to convey with a look that she would be a right, but I wasn't sure my meaning was getting throug

"You said you can't go back in the cloister. Why not?

"I just told you. The ghost, or whatever she is. Sh seems to *know* me now, after what happened with M Call. She's horrifying. She makes me feel . . . terrible."

"Me too," I said, thinking of Donnchadh's reaction t the Lady in Red. He didn't seem to feel her sadness hunger, only her fragility and loveliness.

"And then, as if she wasn't bad enough, that warri chases any men out with his sword. He was the one knew on the isle, but he's much worse here than he w back home."

In the past few years, I have become very good at u ing my peripheral vision, since I often see ghosts th way. So without looking at her and cluing Kieran in what she was doing, I could tell Alicia was working freeing her hands.

I had to keep Kieran talking, to give her time.

"So you were the one who tried to run me off th road? You've got some mad driving skills, after all."

"Brilliant, if I do say so myself. Harper exchange cars with me—I told her I needed to drive a group protesters to a function. We switched them back at th Pelican Inn parking lot, and when I came downstairs ar saw you there, I about collapsed. I thought the gig w up—I swear I did. But you didn't put it together."

"No, I didn't. I guess I'm pretty slow. So why did you attack Graham?"

"Okay, now, that was another accident. I was hiding in the chapel, and I could hear you talking about the sacred vessel—I guess you really can talk to the ghost? And then Graham came in and I was afraid he was going to ruin everything. I wanted to hear what the ghost told you. And I didn't think I hit Graham all that hard. Guess I don't know my own strength."

"But I don't understand. . . . I get that you were using Harper for access to the site. But why befriend me?"

"You say that like I had a *plan*. I came here searching for the vessel—when they were packing up the stones and shipping everything out, I started listening to the stories from the old-timers. I used to think they were just tall tales, the ramblings of old drunks, but my uncle, his friends, they started telling me about the precious vessel, and I realized I had missed my chance. I wanted access to the site so I could find the stupid thing, but the spirits kept chasing me out."

"Thing is, Kieran, there was never a priceless vessel, not in the way you're thinking. The warrior ghost was guarding a *woman*. A noblewoman who was considered the vessel holding noble genes, I guess."

"You're lying. Why would he still be here, then? What's he guarding now? A woman would be long dead."

"He seems to be confused. There's a lot of that going around."

Kieran shook his head and said again, "You're lying."

"I'm not, and what's more, I think you know I'm not. You killed Larry McCall because you thought he knew something about the treasure, right? You thought he had some kind of treasure map on his clipboard?"

"It was nothing but a copy of a schema for stones, not even *these* stones, but *other* stones."

"Right. The plan went with a bunch of stones William Randolph Hearst brought over from Spain."

"What are you talking about?"

"You said yourself not to trust Libole. And for good reason. Libole pulled a fast one on Elrich. Elrich never wanted the monastery from the Isle of Inchcolm. He was after a different one, called Wakefield. Didn't you ever wonder why he called it that?"

"I thought it was just what he called his retreat."

"It isn't. The name Wakefield comes from some ruins he had seen while in Scotland—an old monastery with a tower, on an island whose name I can't pronounce. Libole couldn't get that one for Elrich, and rather than lose the job, he bought this one, gambling that Elrich would never know the difference."

"That's crazy. Who would do something like that?" This from a man holding a woman hostage.

"But the tower would have given it away," I continued, "so when Libole learned about the ancient stones in Golden Gate Park, he folded them into the design without telling anyone. McCall figured it out; he was a big Hearst fan, and he knew about the leftover stones from Hearst Castle."

"So McCall wasn't after the treasure?"

I shook my head. "I keep telling you, there *is* no treasure."

"Then why was McCall so pleased with himself that day?"

"I imagine he was happy to have uncovered Libole's scheme. I'm not sure why it mattered so much to him, but he seemed to be a real stickler for this sort of thing."

"I can't believe it. . . ." Kieran started to deflate. "If you're telling the truth, then it was all for nothing."

I nodded. Not much to respond to that.

Kieran's eyes went flat. He squinted at me and stood straighter. "Nice try. Go get the chalice, or ciborium, or whatever the treasure is, and bring it out. Otherwise, this nosy bitch is gonna get it. I'm not kidding, Mel. I'm losing my patience."

"But—"

Alicia broke free, grabbed a large rock, and brought it down, hard, on Kieran's instep. He cried out and started hopping around on his good foot. Alicia leaped up and kicked Kieran in the kneecap. His leg buckled and he crashed to the ground like a sack of potatoes.

I ran toward them, launching myself at Kieran when I saw him trying to point his gun. He grunted as I landed on him full force and grabbed for the hand that held the gun. I jammed it into the hard-packed ground, and then Alicia, standing over us, stomped on his wrist.

He cried out again and let go of the weapon.

I went for the gun. Alicia went for Kieran.

She started yelling, swearing, roaring in rage as she kicked him, landing blow after blow. Blood poured from a broken nose, and a kick to his gut made him double over in pain.

"Help!" Kieran yelped, his voice panicky and high-pitched. "Get her *off* me!"

"Alicia," I said. "Enough. I have the gun."

She continued, landing another blow on his already injured knee. He screamed.

"Alicia." I took her by the shoulders and physically drew her away from him. "That's enough."

"But he . . . he was going to . . ."

"I know. But look at him now, helpless and whimpering. He's no match for you."

Alicia's eyes met mine, huge and solemn, as always. But then she smiled.

"He's no match for *us*. We make a good team."

I laughed in relief. "Yes. I think you're right. Let's tie him up and call the police."

"They're already on their way," said Alicia. "I called them before I came down—I saw Kieran sneaking around, and I thought you were here, and I was afraid he was up to no good."

"So you put it together, that he was the one who killed McCall?"

"Not really. But I've been trying to keep an eye out for you. I didn't want anyone else to get hurt. Hey, I have an idea! Let's drag him into the cloister and let the ghosts terrorize him until the police come!"

"*No!*" Kieran sobbed. "No, please . . ."

"Just until the police come," said Alicia.

"It's not that I don't see the karmic justice in that, Alicia," I said. "But we should let the police handle things from here on out."

Chapter Twenty-five

Two days later, the jobsite was humming along, Graham had been released from the hospital, and Luz was visiting for the weekend.

Ellis, Alicia, and I were in the Discovery Room. I was trying to explain the Lady in Red and her overzealous protector.

"She's been searching for her place for centuries now. And Donnchadh has been trying to protect someone who hasn't been there for centuries. Let's let them rest for a while. We'll build her tower, give her plenty of food, and let Donnchadh protect her."

Ellis looked a little discomfited. I rather enjoyed watching him squirm—he always seemed so sure of himself that it was sort of gratifying to see he was as human as the rest of us.

I continued on with my plan. "With your permission, I'd like to build the tower and piece together the mural. I've had some folks working on it, and they've come up with this." I showed them the picture Caleb, my father, and Stan had pieced together. The mural seemed to be a scene of a bucolic paradise, trees full of fruit, a splashing fountain, and frolicking birds. There was no way to know whether it was some sort of homage to the poor woman who had died there, or if it was a simple decoration. But the fresco contained her fired bones and covered the walls she knew as her final resting place.

"But after we build it, I propose we wall up the access to the tower so no one comes near. Otherwise I'm afraid people will get curious and sneak up there, and one of these days Donnchadh is bound to scare someone enough that they fall down the stairs."

"And this way he can feel as though he's keeping her safe?" asked Ellis.

"I think so," I said.

"And that's it? They stay like that forever?"

"I'm not sure, exactly. I was thinking that once things are built, I should try communicating with the ghosts again. Maybe I can help them to understand where they are and help them cross over to wherever they should be going. But for now they've been through a lot. They need a little time, I think, to rest."

"Is that how it works?" asked Alicia.

"To tell you the truth, I'm no expert. But this is the gist I'm getting, and Olivier Galopin, an official ghost guy, agrees with me. In fact, if you're amenable to the idea, I'd love to invite Olivier to come for a visit. He and I are hoping to find a way to help the ghosts communicate with each other."

"As Martin Luther King Jr. said: 'Darkness cannot drive out darkness; only light can do that. Hate cannot drive out hate; only love can do that,'" Ellis intoned with the little determined nod he gave when he'd made up his mind.

Alicia noticed it, too, and moved on to the next subject on their agenda.

I excused myself and slipped out.

Upstairs, Graham was in the parlor, Luz by his side.

"How did it go?" asked Luz.

"Ellis agreed to complete the renovation and let me seal up the tower. We'll make it look good."

"And that's it? He's okay with having ghosts at his retreat center?"

"He seems to be fine with it. He was quoting Martin Luther King Jr. I'm not sure how it applied to this situation, but it was a beautiful sentiment, and it seemed to settle things in his mind."

"Knowing Elrich, he'll make the ghosts a feature of Wakefield," said Graham, moving slowly. "It will be part of his message to live life to the fullest, embrace the moment, and all that motivational crap."

"I think you're right," I said. "*Nós ossos que . . .* What was that phrase in Portuguese?"

"I have no idea. I think you're just trying to get me to speak Portuguese 'cause you think it's sexy," said Graham, holding my gaze for a beat.

"Stick with Spanish," said Luz. "And that reminds me, I bought the ghosts a present."

"Seriously?"

She refused to meet my eyes, but she held out a Spanish-Gaelic dictionary.

"Where in the world did you find this?"

"Internet."

"And this is for . . . ?"

"You said the warrior guy couldn't understand the

woman in red. So maybe he can look up a few words. I don't know. Does it work like that?"

"I'm not sure." In fact, I didn't even know whether Donnchadh could read, but it was worth a shot. Poor guy had plenty of time on his hands to study.

"That's great, Luz. Thank you."

"So what now?" Luz asked, changing the subject.

I wanted to ask her about her reaction to the ghost recordings and my suspicions that there was something in her past she hadn't told me about. But that could wait.

"Well, there's lots of work to be done, obviously," I said. "This place isn't going to build itself, you know. And Elrich still wants to have that grand opening by the end of summer."

"The pace should pick up now that you know you need to keep the men out of the tower room," pointed out Graham. "You could stand to take an afternoon off."

"I should say so," said Luz. "You just solved a murder and put ghosts to rest, *chica*. As your own personal mental health professional, I suggest you take a wellness afternoon."

I laughed. "What would you suggest?"

"Hmm, well," she said, raising one eyebrow and gazing out the French doors at the spectacular view. "There's this gorgeous swimming pool that no one uses. . . ."

Read on for a preview of Juliet Blackwell's next
Witchcraft Mystery,

Spellcasting in Silk

Available from Obsidian in July 2015.

"Lily," Inspector Carlos Romero said with a nod, "a
moment in private?" His tone was curt, businesslike.

"Sure."

I gestured to Bronwyn and Maya that I was taking a
break and led Carlos through a deep red brocade curtain, which separated Aunt Cora's Closet's shop floor
from the work area. Here, a jumbo washer and dryer for
laundering inventory sat to one side, while a galley
kitchen with a dorm-sized fridge, a microwave, and an
electric teakettle lined the opposite wall. A pile of black
Hefty bags and a couple of blue plastic storage boxes
held clothing to be sorted, repaired, and cleaned. In the
center of the room was a 1960s dinette set, the table
topped with jade green Formica. The set was a replica of
the one in my childhood home in the little town of Jarod,
West Texas.

Carlos took his usual seat at the table.

"May I get you anything?" I asked, mostly out of
habit because Carlos never accepted my offers of refreshments. "How about a cup of tea? Bronwyn has a

new blend of carob, orange peel, and rose hips, which, I guarantee you, tastes a dang sight better than it sounds. It's all the rage."

"No, thanks," he said with a quick shake of his head.

I sat in the chair opposite him and waited. He said nothing.

"*One* day," I said.

"Beg pardon?"

"I would like one day. Just *one*. When I wasn't thinking about a suspicious death."

Carlos gazed at me for another long moment. He wasn't much of a talker under the best of circumstances, and in his line of work, the long pauses surely served a purpose. More than a few cagey suspects and reluctant witnesses had no doubt blurted out something incriminating simply to break the oppressive silence. But this time was different: Carlos appeared to be choosing his words with care. And that probably meant he was here because he had come across something he couldn't explain, something that fell far outside the purview of a routine police investigation.

That was where I came in: Lily Ivory, unofficial witchy consultant to the SFPD.

"Today's not that day," he finally replied.

"Yeah, that was my point. I was feeling so happy right before you came in."

One corner of his mouth kicked up in a reluctant smile. "That's me, all right. The bringer of bad tidings. So I ruined your day, huh?"

"Not yet you haven't. But something tells me you're about to . . ."

"I need to talk to you about a *curandera*'s shop gone haywire, a suspicious suicide, and a missing kid."

". . . aaaand there it is."

"I'll start at the beginning; shall I?"

I sat back in my chair. "Fire away."

"Last week a thirty-seven-year-old woman named Nicky Utley jumped off the Golden Gate Bridge."

"That's terrible. But . . . where does a witch come in?"

"She was into a bunch of weird stuff."

"Could you be more specific?"

"Her husband showed us talismans and pentacles, books on everything from Catholic saints to candle magic, medicinal herbs, and such. Things more . . . overtly religious than your stuff."

"But how is any of that related to her death?"

"That's what I'm trying to figure out. According to her family and friends, the woman had been consulting with a *curandera* named Ursula Moreno, who owns a shop called El Pajarito on Mission. What can you tell me about her?"

"Nothing. I've never heard of her."

Carlos looked surprised. "I assumed all of your ilk knew one another."

"My *ilk*?"

"You know what I mean."

"I do. But I'm still fairly new in town, remember?" And though I wasn't going to volunteer this to a member of the SFPD—friend or no—I kept my distance from *curanderas*. They were about as mixed a bag as the one I wore at my waist. Some were talented folk healers, others wise elders; a rare few were natural-born witches like me. Still others—the vast majority—dabbled in herbs and prayers and rituals, and enjoyed importing and creating talismans and amulets and good-luck charms.

And a few were out-and-out charlatans.

In the course of my life, I have learned a lot of things, not the least of which is that—witchy intuition aside—I am a wretched judge of character. So I tried to steer clear of such shops and their proprietors. Besides, it was cheaper by far to purchase my supplies at small apothecaries in Chinatown or local farmers' markets . . . or even the ethnic-food aisle of a large grocery store. For the more esoteric witchy items, Maya had introduced me to the wonder of the Internet. A few clicks of a mouse and a package of freeze-dried bats would appear on my doorstep in just a few days. As if by magic.

"Anyway," Carlos continued, "it looks like the herbs and instructions and whatnot she got from the *curandera* may have aggravated an underlying condition, which led to her suicide."

My stomach clenched. One of my biggest fears was that those who neither understood magical systems, nor gave them the proper respect, would end up hurting themselves or others. Amateurs experimenting with magic were like toddlers playing with matches—initially they may cause no harm, but sooner or later someone got hurt.

"I'm sorry to hear that. As I'm sure you know, *curandera* means 'curer' or 'healer.' The herbs and 'whatnot,' as you call it, are meant to help. But you have to know what you're doing."

Carlos nodded.

"So what happened?" I asked.

"That's what I'm trying to find out. We have a couple of witnesses to the jump, but . . ."

"But you think there's more to it."

He shrugged. "Possibly. And the mayor's been on a tear lately, going after folks bilking the public with phony love spells, palm readings, fraudulent psychics, that sort of thing. This fits right in with his cleanup campaign."

"I thought fortune-telling was covered by free speech?

ter all, who's to say they *aren't* seeing the future, or
orking magic for a fee?"

Carlos's lips pressed together. "I'm not interested in
scussing the ins and outs of the possible. But there's a
e line between spewing predictions and conning peo-
e. Most of the time we're looking at charges of grand
ceny and fraud, but in the case of Nicky Utley . . . well,
r husband's pushing hard to make something stick.
e DA is considering filing charges of gross negligence
d practicing medicine without a license, in addition to
ud."

"What was the *curandera*'s name, again?"

"Ursula Moreno. Her *botanica*'s called El Pajarito.
u sure you don't know it?"

I shook my head again. From the other side of the bro-
de curtain, sounds drifted in: the cheerful buzz of cus-
ners trying on different personas as they tried on a new
le of dress or hat. The chiming of the old-fashioned
ass cash register. A young woman cooing over Oscar,
o I imagined was preening, batting his sleepy eyes up
her as he stretched lazily on his bed. The bell on the
nt door ringing as another shopper arrived, and some-
e laughing in high, melodic tones.

They were comforting sounds, and I felt a fierce desire
tune out what Carlos was telling me. But I did not
ve that luxury. There aren't a lot of folks who know
ough, or have the requisite skills, to assist the police in
pernatural crimes. Carlos was here because he needed
special brand of help. Such, it seemed, was my fate.

"There's more," said Carlos.

"Oh, goodie."

"Something's happened, something odd." His finger
ced an invisible pattern on the green Formica tabletop.

"Odder than occult-inspired suicide?"

"Moreno's store. It's . . . acting up."

"I'm sorry?"

"After Moreno was arrested yesterday, the foren
team went to her shop to gather evidence."

I waited, but he said nothing.

"And?" I prompted.

"The place went haywire. According to the chief
rensics tech, stuff was flying off the shelves, the lig
kept flickering on and off, a statue tossed a lit cigare
at one of the guys, and a bird skeleton seemed to cc
alive. It started . . . flying."

"Flying? That's unusual behavior for a skeleton. *
you sure someone's not pulling your leg?"

"I know these guys well, Lily. They're pros who deal v
serious crime scenes every day. Chief forensic tech's b
on the job for years—it takes a lot to throw him off
game. But this time, he and his crew beat it out of the sl
in a hurry and are refusing to go back. This is . . . unusu

Indeed. "And you'd like me to take a look."

Carlos nodded. "Shouldn't take too long. See w
you see, feel what you feel. Try to figure out what's go
on there, and if it's connected in any way to what h
pened to Nicky Utley."

"All righty."

Carlos gave me a suspicious look, and cocked
head in question. "That's it? You're not going to try
get out of it?"

I shrugged. "You've worn me down, Inspector. Gu
I'm the SFPD's go-to witch. Right?"

He smiled, and I couldn't help but smile in return.
thing about Carlos was that every smile felt hard-w
and therefore more worth earning.

"Besides," I continued, "this sounds like a job for

ert. If something 'untoward' really is happening at
shop, somebody's bound to get hurt."

Carlos nodded and started to rise.

"I do have one question, though," I said, and Carlos
back down. "You're one of homicide's star investiga-
s, aren't you?"

Carlos shrugged and nodded.

"So why is the department asking its big gun to work
a case of possible fortune-teller fraud?"

"I requested it."

"May I ask why?"

"First, because of the strange behavior at the store. I
ieve I've told you, I've become the station's woo-woo
. But, in the interest of full disclosure, it's also true
t I knew the deceased, Nicky Utley, and her husband,
ry, though not well."

"Friends of yours?"

"Acquaintances more than friends. They went to my
rch, St. Olaf's."

"This would be a . . . Catholic church?" I had met
ny Catholics in my life—including Carlos—and had
covered they were good people who lived according
a creed of kindness and respect. Still, organized reli-
ns made me nervous, what with the witch hunts and
pogroms and the Inquisition and all.

He nodded.

"If Nicky Utley was a practicing Catholic," I said,
hy would she turn to a *curandera* for help?"

"You tell me."

"Well, of course the two don't preclude each other . . ."
aid, thinking aloud. "Where I'm from, it isn't unusual
churchgoers to turn to my grandmother for herbs
d charms. I just haven't run into this sort of overlap
e in San Francisco."

Carlos stood. "People are people, Lily. They're not that different, no matter where they live. Listen, I hav quick errand to run. Why don't I pick you up in, say, h an hour?"

"I could meet you at the shop, if that's easier."

"That would be better. Thanks. El Pajarito on Missi near Twenty-second." He checked his wristwatch sporty model with lots of knobs. "Let's make it an ho to be on the safe side. And, Lily, if you get there fi don't go in without me."

I nodded.

"I'm serious."

"I can tell. I won't go in without you."

He gave me another suspicious look.

"What?" I asked.

"All this easy cooperation is making me nervous. T me you're not blowin' smoke up my caboose."

"I'm not even sure how to do such a thing," I laugh "I told you: I'm resigned to my fate. But I do have c last question. . . ."

"What's that?"

"Since I'm the SFPD's official paranormal consulta do I get dental coverage?"

Carlos flashed me a bright white smile. "You're o cial only in my book. If the department knew I v bringing in a witch to consult on this case . . . well, l just say I put up with enough ribbing from my colleag as it is."

Carlos drew aside the curtain. Folks were milling ab crowding the aisles, inspecting long peasant skirts, fa bell-bottoms, and fringed leather vests.

"Looks like quite the hippie convention out here."

"We've been as busy as Grandpa's Sunday tie, as t say."

Carlos looked amused. "*Who* says that?"

I laughed. "I guess we say that back in Texas. Anyway, the Haight Street Summer of Love Festival is this weekend."

The Summer of Love Festival was held annually to commemorate one of the neighborhood's most famous eras. It had been nearly fifty years since hippies sent out the call for "gentle people" to put some flowers in their hair and meet in the Haight-Ashbury to build a new world order of peace, music, and harmony. They hadn't quite achieved their goals, but the neighborhood had retained its willingness to accept iconoclasts and freethinkers of all stripes.

Ambitious festivalgoers had been flocking to Aunt Cora's Closet in search of "authentic" hippie clothes for weeks now. Vintage tie-dye and flouncy peasant dresses were flying off the racks; love beads and headbands were in short supply. Bell-bottomed jeans, pants in wild colors, and embroidered Mexican blouses—most of which I had picked up for a song at flea markets and yard sales—were in great demand.

"Sure, the Summer of Love Festival." He nodded. "I know it well."

"It's my first time; I'm pretty excited. So, do you have a costume?"

"I'm wearing it." Carlos passed a hand over his khaki chinos and black leather jacket.

"Think you look like a hippie, do you?"

"Even better. I'm a narc."

I smiled. "You should at least wear a few love beads around your neck."

"Maybe I'll dig through your treasure chest before I leave."

Recently I had started tossing cheap costume jewelry and plastic items—except for the valuable Bakelite, of

course—in an old wooden chest that had supposedl
come to San Francisco with the pioneers. Now cleanse
of cobwebs and its sordid past, it had become my "trea
sure chest": Everything in it went for under five dollar
and many items were just a quarter. Customers spent
lot of time digging through it with childlike abandon.

Which reminded me . . .

"Carlos, hold on. Didn't you say something about
missing child?"

"Fourteen-year-old Selena Moreno. We're not posi
tive she's missing . . . Weird thing is, we can't get a wor
out of Ursula. But according to the neighbors, Selen
used to live with her grandmother. Hasn't shown up t
school, but it looks like her attendance has always bee
spotty, so it's hard to say what's going on there. Mos
likely she's staying with relatives, but I'd feel bette
knowing for sure."

"Do you think something in the shop might point m
in her direction?"

"You know me, Lily. I don't think anything in partic
ular."

"But you're suspicious of everything."

He gave me a wink and a smile.

About the Author

Juliet Blackwell is the pseudonym for a mystery author who also writes the Witchcraft Mystery series and, together with her sister, wrote the Art Lover's Mystery series. The first in that series, *Feint of Art*, was nominated for an Agatha Award for Best First Novel. Juliet's lifelong interest in the paranormal world was triggered when her favorite aunt visited and read her fortune—with startling results. As an anthropologist, the author studied systems of spirituality, magic, and health across cultures and throughout history. She currently resides in a happily haunted house in Oakland, California.

CONNECT ONLINE

julietblackwell.net
facebook.com/julietblackwellauthor
twitter.com/julietblackwell